The *Loyal* WIFE

B. LOVE

BLACK ODYSSEY MEDIA

WWW.BLACKODYSSEY.NET

Published by
BLACK ODYSSEY MEDIA

www.blackodyssey.net
Email: info@blackodyssey.net

Library of Congress Control Number: 2023919170

First Trade Paperback Printing: March 2024
ISBN: 978-1-957950-10-5
ISBN: 978-1-957950-11-2 (e-book)

Cover Design by Ashlee Nassar of Designs With Sass
To the extent that the image or images on the cover of this book depict a person or persons, such person or persons are merely models and are not intended to portray any character in the book.

10 9 8 7 6 5 4 3 2 1

Manufactured in the United States of America

Distributed by Kensington Publishing Corp.

Dear Reader,

I want to thank you immensely for supporting Black Odyssey Media authors, and our ongoing efforts to spotlight more minority storytellers. The scariest and most challenging task for many writers is getting the story, or characters, out of our heads and onto the page. Having admitted that, with every manuscript that Kreceda and I acquire, we believe that it took talent, discipline, and remarkable courage to construct that story, flesh out those characters, and prepare it for the world. Debut or seasoned, our authors are the real heroes and heroines in *OUR* story. And for them, we are eternally grateful.

Whether you are new to B. Love or Black Odyssey Media, we hope that you are here to stay. We also welcome your feedback and kindly ask that you leave a review. For upcoming releases, announcements, submission guidelines, etc., please be sure to visit our website at www.blackodyssey.net or scan the QR code below. We can also be found on social media using @iamblackodyssey. Until next time, take care and enjoy the journey!

Joyfully,

Shawanda Williams

Shawanda "N'Tyse" Williams
Founder/Publisher

DANTE

THEY WERE FUCKING screwed—there was no doubt about that. They were all going to prison, and at that point, Dante could do nothing about it.

Worse, from the looks of it, someone was setting Dante up to take the fall.

Since he was the one who handled the taxes for their company, it was Dante's responsibility to make sure every dime they brought in and paid out was accounted for. His heart raced and thumped harder against his rib cage as he swiped from one page to another.

None of it made any sense.

There were incorrect amounts on payroll invoices and financial statements, imaginary customers who hadn't received services were billed, and many customers appeared to have been charged two or three times the amount they should have been. Tossing the papers onto his desk, Dante sat deeper in his seat and released a slow, tired breath.

When he opened his credit repair, loans, taxes, and investment business five years ago, it was with the belief that his partners all had the same intentions as him. His wife and their best friends, Eric and Jessica, were the closest people to Dante. If there was anyone he trusted with his life and business, it was them. Now, Dante had to figure out who was stealing from him and their customers... and quickly.

Their accountant was expecting their financial documents in seventy-two hours to start preparing their taxes for the previous quarter. How in the hell would he explain this mess that someone had created? Dante couldn't focus on that. Right now, he needed to call an emergency meeting to figure out who was stealing from their company and why.

But would they actually tell me?

Dante's head shook as he sat up in his seat. Looking around at the papers sprawled against his dark brown desk, he gritted his teeth as he thought over his next move. There was no doubt someone was stealing, but they probably wouldn't just come outright and say it. Whoever it was would need to be confronted with irrefutable evidence. As he scratched the back of his head, Dante decided to call one of his tech friends to have some software downloaded on everyone's computers in the office. Then he'd have cameras installed. If that didn't help him catch whoever it was in the act, he'd inform his wife and seek her help.

Grabbing his phone, Dante decided to go and search everyone's offices. Their office was on the ninth floor of a twelve-floor building. When guests first entered, they stopped at the light-colored reception area before being guided to Dante or someone else for help. His wife's office was right next to his, but he decided to save hers for last. She was his life partner; Dante was confident she had nothing to do with this.

Starting with Eric, Dante went into his best friend's office. They had been friends for over fifteen years. He prayed he wouldn't find anything proving Eric stole from their company and customers. Though Eric had always been ambitious, it was never to the point where he'd take what didn't belong to him and risk going to prison. Dante entered the dark office, heading first to Eric's iMac. If he were falsifying statements, they would have to be done on his computer, right?

"Of course not. Eric isn't stupid enough to do this on his office computer," Dante grumbled, sitting down. "But I have to check at least," he decided, typing Eric's password into the computer.

Once he was logged in, Dante went through Eric's 2023 files, coming up empty. Everything seemed to be correct, which didn't surprise him. If anyone was up to something corrupt, it had to be Jessica. She was Eric's wife and the person Dante trusted the least. He made his way to her office, coming up empty there too. Jessica printed all her clients' files, making it easy for him to scan each one.

Dante was about to leave, but when he passed his wife's office, he felt the urge to go inside. Before going to her desk, he looked around, trying to convince himself it would be a waste of time. Her office was immaculate, as always. The green and silver décor matched her home office. He walked over to her customized silver desk, running his fingers across it. Releasing a low breath, Dante glanced at the pictures of them behind her desk before sitting down.

Her iMac desktop and laptop were on her desk. He started with her laptop, surprised when he realized she'd changed the password. Dante released a low hum and briefly tapped his fingers on top of the desk.

"What are you hiding?" he mumbled, going to her desktop when none of the passwords he tried on the laptop worked. That password was still the same, causing Dante to sigh in relief. Instead of going through the files on her desktop, he accessed her iCloud, where he found fictitious statements and invoices mirroring the ones in his office.

Refusing to believe his wife was the one committing fraud, Dante immediately logged out of her computer and returned to his office. He just sat there for a while, staring out into the darkness. It was a little after midnight, and the downtown streets of Memphis were eerily quiet. Standing, Dante made his way to the large window on the side of his office. Hands stuffed in his gray slacks, Dante cursed under his breath.

If she's stealing from the company, there must be a reason.

If she's stealing from the company, what else is she doing behind my back?

He tried to think of anything over the past few months that may have hinted at his wife's greed, but Dante was coming up empty. Nothing was out of the ordinary—no big, unexplained purchases or unaccounted-for money deposits. His mind played scenario after scenario of what his wife could have been into.

Well, if he was honest with himself, there didn't have to be any unusual extravagant purchases because his wife was extravagant herself. If anything, her *not* spending a lot of money would have been more surprising than seeing that she was.

"No," he whispered, leaving his office to return to hers. "There has to be a reason. Maybe someone is setting her up to take the fall, just like they set me up to find these statements." Nibbling his bottom lip, Dante paused in the hallway. "Who has the most to gain by getting my wife and me out of the business?"

He scratched his brow as his eyes shifted from Eric's door to Jessica's. Or was it one of their executive assistants? All four of them had access to their clients and files. Dante hadn't considered them before, but he was willing to consider just about anything or anyone to prove his wife's innocence.

As his hand covered her doorknob, Dante's phone vibrated in his pocket. He pulled it out, surprised to see his cousin's name and picture so late at night. Chelsea worked for the Memphis Branch of the FBI; if she was calling, it couldn't be for anything good. Either something had happened to a family member, or the FBI knew what someone at the office had been up to.

"Hey, Chels," Dante answered, leaning against the wall. "Are you okay?"

"I could lose my job for this, but I must tell you."

"Tell me what?"

Chelsea sighed into the receiver. "A few agents are on their way to your office. You're about to be arrested."

"Arrested?" he repeated, speed walking down the hall toward the elevator.

"Yes."

"For what, Chelsea?" he asked, hoping his voice sounded calm while his insides were heating from anger and bubbling up with confusion.

"Fraud, corruption, and money laundering. There's also a civil case against you. Apparently, several of your old clients went to MPD to file reports because they were being overly charged, but the police told them to go directly to you or hire an attorney and file a civil case against you. One lawyer is heading the case and involved the FBI."

"Okay, but why me?" Dante asked, repeatedly pressing the *L* in the elevator to get to the lobby. Dante didn't know how much time he had, but he wouldn't spend it waiting around to be arrested. He knew he was innocent, but the FBI wouldn't care about what he had to say. He needed time to figure out who was setting him up, and he wouldn't be able to do that if he were in federal prison.

"I can't go into detail about that, especially over the phone. I'm sure they have your line tapped, and I'm probably facing suspension or termination for even calling you."

"And I really appreciate that," Dante replied quickly, calmly. "But I need more than this, cuz. If you know who's trying to set me up, I need you to tell me."

The elevator dinged, providing noise that filled the space of Chelsea silently holding the phone.

Seconds passed, and when she remained silent, Dante asked, "Chelsea, who is setting me up?"

"Where are you?"

"I'm leaving the office now."

"How do you think I know you're at the office, Dante? Think. Who knows you're at the office and could be working with the FBI to send you to federal fucking prison?"

As the elevator lowered, Dante considered his cousin's question.

"No." His head shook as revelation set in. "My wife wouldn't tell them I was here, and even if she did, it would be because she's scared. Not because she's trying to set me up."

Chelsea huffed. "I know that's your wife, but she is not to be trusted. Do you hear me?"

"She's loyal. She wouldn't—"

"You need to go downstairs and wait for them in the lobby. Do not speak without your attorney present. I'm going to help you in any way that I can, but if it comes down to you or her, which I know it will, you need to accept that your wife is behind this, and she's setting you up to take the fall."

Absently, Dante disconnected the call and made his way to the parking garage. His eyes went from his black Camaro to Tarik's white Toyota. If the FBI or police were after him, they'd be looking for his car. Still, Dante had too much integrity to steal someone else's.

"Fuck it," he grumbled, jogging to his car and hopping inside.

Dante's eyes stayed trained on the rearview mirror at the sound of sirens as he swerved out of the parking garage. He'd just made it out in time to avoid all the cars and trucks pulling into the parking lot and garage for his arrest. He made a sharp left, trying to decide his next move.

Grabbing his phone, Dante called the only person he believed could help him—someone who wasn't tied to his business or day-to-day life, for that matter. As the call connected, the sound of a truck approaching behind him gained his attention. It was speeding down a residential street faster than Dante believed it should have been, but he had more pressing things to worry about.

"Dante?" the woman answered, sleep thick in her voice.

"Hey, I know it's late, but I need to leave Memphis. Can I crash at your spot until I figure out my next move?"

She cleared her throat. "Um... sure. Is everything okay?"

"No, but I'll talk to you about it when I arrive. I'm heading your way now. Should be there in about an hou—What the *fuck*?"

"Dante?" she called, but he didn't reply as he ended the call.

He was too distracted by the bright lights of the truck coming straight toward him. Dante sped up, and the truck did too.

"What are you doing?" he asked, knowing they couldn't hear or respond. "*Shit!*" he roared, gripping the steering wheel and trying to prepare for impact with the truck. But nothing could have prepared him for that. As soon as the wide truck hit the back of his car, Dante crashed into a light pole. His seat belt kept him from being ejected from the vehicle, but it didn't stop him from being thrown against the front of the car while feeling like his body was being ripped in half.

"Argh!"

Dante grunted, trying to guard his head from the windshield. He flung back, eyes squeezing shut immediately as the airbag opened and pushed into his face and chest. With ringing ears, he tried to stay awake, but that was proving to be more and more difficult. As his eyes fluttered, he noticed an arm reaching into his car through the broken glass. He thought they were trying to help him... but he realized that wasn't the case when their hand went into his pocket to grab his wallet.

"St-sto—"

Dante blacked out before he could tell them to leave his phone and wallet.

SADE

No HOSPITAL IN Memphis initially gave her any details, so Sade extended her search. After checking both hospitals in the small town of Vanzette, Tennessee, and surrounding minor medical centers, Sade started her search in Memphis again. It wasn't like Dante not to answer his phone or immediately go home after work, and she'd been worried sick about him. None of the hospitals had a patient named Dante Williams, but Sade was convinced something had happened to him. If he had been arrested for some reason, it would take hours for him to be processed and show up in the inmate lookup, and Sade didn't have that type of time.

She feared the worst—he was somewhere dead or severely hurt.

"Do you have anyone here that doesn't have an ID?" Sade asked, her leg bouncing as she leaned against the desk.

"We do, but I can't give you any information on those patients, ma'am."

Rolling her tongue across her cheek, Sade smiled bitterly as her foot tapped the floor. "If he's here and you've kept me away from him, I'm going to sue the hell out of this hospital."

"Ma'am—"

"All I'm asking for is to see anyone, dead or alive, that came in without identification. Something is wrong with him, and you're wasting my time!"

With a huff, the nurse stood. "Are you related to him?"

Relief washed over Sade as her body weakened against the desk. "I am."

"Are you his wife? Because that's the only way I can—"

"Yes," Sade cut her off to say, "Now, *please*, show me anyone brought in tonight without an ID."

Nodding, the nurse flagged down another nurse who was standing nearby. After explaining the situation, she told Sade to follow Nurse Richardson. She did, and the entire time they went down one hall to the next, Sade's body heated, and her heart palpitated. Only one person was alive and had been brought in without identification, but three were in the morgue. Richardson took her to room 1312.

"If this is your husband, I'll get the attending doctor so he can get you up to speed on John Doe's condition."

All Sade could do was bob her head. Her mouth had dried out from nervousness. The nurse opened the door, and as soon as Sade stepped inside, she covered her mouth and sobbed. She knew it was him, even with Dante's head wrapped in white bandages.

"Oh my God," she cried, running over to him and taking his hand. "What happened to him?"

"He was in an accident. That's all I know. I'll go and get his doctor."

"Okay," Sade replied, wiping her face with her free hand. Sniffling, she stroked Dante's hand with her thumb. "Please, God, let him be okay." She asked Dante what happened as if he could respond. It didn't matter how much Sade called his name or gently shook him. Dante didn't wake up. Finally accepting defeat, Sade paced as she waited for the nurse to return with his doctor.

It took what felt like forever, but eventually, a light-skinned, heavyset man returned wearing a white coat and weary smile.

"Apologies for the delay," he stated, lifting his clipboard to his face.

"What's wrong with him? Why isn't he waking up?"

"He's in a coma. There was a car accident, and it was pretty bad. Thankfully, he was wearing his seat belt, so he wasn't ejected from the car, but the impact caused some damage to his head and chest, and he has a few broken ribs. He also fractured both wrists. I'm assuming he tried to use his hands to shield his head and face when he was about to collide with the windshield. He sprained a few bones in his knees because he was in a low-sitting car, according to the police. The injury I'm most concerned about is to his head. There is excessive bleeding, so we can't get in there to see how much damage has been done. I have him on blood thinners. Once we get the bleeding and swelling down, our neurologist will have a look to determine our next steps."

It was all too much at once. Sade could not process anything he'd said. All she could ask was, "But he's going to be okay?"

"I don't want to give you false hope. Once the neurologist can get some scans done, we can confirm the severity of the damage. Aside from a few broken ribs and the head injury, I can tell you that the rest of his injuries are minor and nothing to be overly concerned about. That's about all I can give you at the moment."

Nodding, Sade crossed her arms over her chest. "Okay." Her eyes shifted to Dante as she asked, "Can I stay with him?"

"Absolutely. Nurse Richardson will linger back to get some information on your husband. Then she'll leave you alone with him. If you need anything, you can press the call button on the right side of his bed or visit the nearest nurses' station."

"Thank you," she almost whispered, unable to keep her eyes off Dante. Sade was grateful he was alive and praying his head injury wouldn't cause permanent damage. They had a lot to talk about, and the sooner he woke up... the better.

DANTE

DANTE LOOKED FROM the woman staring down at him with a goofy smile to the doctor holding a pen up in front of him. He didn't know how he'd gotten to the hospital or how long he'd been there, for that matter. The woman rushed out after he woke up in pain, yelling for the doctor.

"Do you know what this is?" the doctor asked, waving the pen.

Dante tried to tilt his head and regretted it immediately when a dull pain shot through it. "It's a pen." Closing his eyes, he tried to lift his hand and groaned in pain. "Can someone cut the lights out? My head is killing me."

"I just need you to answer a few questions. Then I can get you some pain medicine. Do you know what year it is, Mr. Williams?"

"It's 2024, right? How long have I been here? And why am I here?"

"You were in a car accident. You've been here for three days," the woman answered. "Do you... remember who I am?"

When he chuckled slightly, Dante regretted it immediately. It felt like every piece of his ribs was crushed and barely holding together. As painful as it was to speak or breathe, it was even more painful to laugh.

"Not at all." He opened his eyes, unable to deny the sadness in hers.

The doctor cleared his throat and spoke up. "Selective or retrograde amnesia is common after head trauma. Try not to take it personally."

"How long before he gets his memory back?"

"It's hard to say. It could be minutes, days, months, or years. Maybe never. I would need to consult with the neurologist. Once we get him a new dose of pain medicine, we can check the bleeding on his brain. If it's cleared enough for us to run some tests, we can have more answers for you both in a few hours."

She nodded and thanked him softly, waiting until the doctor left before she shifted her attention back to Dante.

"Is there anything I can do to make you more comfortable?"

"Who are you?" Dante asked before taking in choppy breaths.

She smiled softly, taking small steps toward his bed. "My name is Sade. I'm your wife. Do you remember anything about me or yourself at all?"

"I remember me. I just don't remember you. My name is Dante, right?"

Sade's body relaxed as she smiled warmly, clutching her chest.

"It is," she replied, closing the space between them. "Do you remember your birthday and how old you are?"

"January tenth. I'm thirty-two, right?"

"Yes. Well, you're thirty-three now. Your birthday was two days ago."

"Damn." Dante's head shook as he processed her words. "So I was in a car accident?"

"Yes, that's correct."

"Do we have kids? Why can I remember the facts about me but not you?"

Sade shrugged. "I don't know. I guess the doctor will be able to answer that soon enough. And, no. We don't. Not yet, at least. Would you like to see some pictures of us or rest?"

Dante may not have remembered her, but he knew himself. His character. He knew he wouldn't say or do anything intentionally to hurt someone, especially his wife. So, as much as he wanted to tell her to get out and leave him alone, he decided to take a softer approach instead. It wasn't Sade's fault that his memories of her had been completely wiped. But the last thing he wanted to do was be around a woman who reminded him of a past life he had no recollection of, especially while he was in so much pain.

"I really just want to try to sleep. You can leave. Do you have a job or something to go to?"

Sade's head shook as she took his hand into hers. "Don't worry about that. Even if there were a job or some pressing matter needing my attention, I'd put it off to be here with you. I understand this is a lot to take in, though, so if you need space, I can make myself scarce for a while. I've been here for the past three days, so I can go home, put on some fresh clothes, and eat something besides hospital food."

"Yeah, do that. Get you some rest too. I should have your number in my phone to call you once I know more about what's happening."

"Someone took your phone and wallet, but I can write my number down for you."

"How did you know where I was then?"

Her head lowered briefly. "I called all the hospitals and police stations between Memphis and Vanzette. I had to physically come to Memphis because they were being assholes on the phone, and this is where I found you. You were here under John Doe, but I made them show me you. I've given them all your information, so you're good."

Wow.

She must have been worried about him. She must care about him. She must love him. Of course, she loves him. She's his fucking *wife*. Gritting his teeth, Dante sighed and casually pulled his hand from under hers. It made him feel worse not having a connection to a woman who had done so much for him.

"Thank you for that. Why don't you go home and get some rest? I'll reach out later."

"Okay, D. I love you and don't feel obligated to say it back. You don't even know who I am, so I don't expect you to feel anything toward me."

As she turned to leave, he asked, "Is that going to be a problem for you?" Sade turned to face him, but her feet stayed planted where they were. "I don't know how long this is going to last. Will me not remembering you and our history hurt you?"

Sade shrugged. "I'm sure it will, but I'll have to learn not to take it personally. Besides, this will allow us to fall in love all over again. I'm looking forward to that."

She winked, and Dante couldn't help but smile. Sade was beautiful—that he wouldn't deny. Her slim frame was covered in honey-brown skin, and she had the prettiest under-turned dark eyes with a beautiful, bright smile.

"You're beautiful," he couldn't help but say before a stabbing pain shot through his head. The guttural groan he released caused her to gasp. There seemed to be no escape from the pain. He couldn't move his arms or the top half of his body for relief.

"Here..." Sade jogged back over to him and lifted the small cup of ice that was next to the tray of food she'd barely touched. After wetting a thick paper towel, she wrapped it around the ice and asked, "Where does it hurt the most?" Biting down on his bottom lip, Dante tried to lift his hand to show her, forgetting about his wrists. "Just tell me, D."

"Behind my right eye and ear."

Sade lifted the ice and placed it near his right eye. The pain didn't dissolve completely, but Dante did experience relief.

"How's that?" she asked softly, sitting beside him on the bed.

"Better. Thanks."

"Maybe I should just stay, Dante. We don't have to talk."

Sighing, Dante turned slightly. "I appreciate that, but I really just want to be alone."

"Okay. Well... I will put the call button thingy by your right hand in case you need it. I hope you feel better soon. And please call me as soon as you hear something, okay?"

Dante bobbed his head, not wanting to speak or move much, for that matter. He was finally feeling enough relief to try to get back to sleep.

"I'm going to slightly shift you so you can lay your head directly on the ice."

"Sade, you don—"

Before he could decline, she'd moved his head enough to where it was holding the ice up instead of her hand. "Thanks," he grumbled. "I'm sure you're used to me not liking to feel dependent."

Sade laughed softly. "Yes, I am, and that's the only reason I'm leaving, even though I really, really want to stay." She placed a soft, featherlight kiss on the center of his forehead. "I'll be back later."

"All right," he replied, trying not to yawn, fearing it would make his head and chest hurt worse.

Dante kept his eyes closed, and at the sound of the door shutting, he finally relaxed into the frustration and sadness he was feeling. A million curses and questions wanted to erupt, with the biggest one being... *why him?* But in that moment, Dante was just grateful to have his life... even if he couldn't remember all of it.

SADE

"It just doesn't make sense," Dante said for what had to be the millionth time.

It was the following day, and when Sade arrived to bring him breakfast, the neurologist was preparing to give him the results of his tests. Some slight damage was done to his hippocampus, which explained why Dante's memories were fuzzy. While he remembered basic things about himself and survival facts, he didn't remember anything about Sade, their life together, or events that happened right before the accident.

Dante's doctor assured him that his memories could return on their own at any point, which was the only thing that gave them slight relief. Still, that didn't stop Dante from randomly expressing his disbelief all morning.

"Would you rather not be able to remember anything at all?" Sade teased, throwing the Waffle House container into the trash can.

"Honestly, yeah. I feel like I don't know the things I should know. About you. About us. I'm grateful to know how to survive and care for myself, but I just wish I remembered you."

"Don't worry about that, baby. There's no point in getting frustrated over something we can easily fix. Whatever you want to know about me, I can tell you, and when you get out of here, we can create new experiences and memories. How does that sound?"

While Sade hoped that would make him feel better, a part of her also hoped he wouldn't want to know too much about his past. Dante would probably ask questions if she had to explain why they were living in a small town outside of Memphis with no contact with their family and old friends—questions she didn't want to be responsible for giving him the answers to.

"I guess I don't have much of a choice, do I?"

Sitting beside him, Sade reached for the remote to cut the TV up louder. *Family Feud* was playing, which was one of their favorite games to play.

"Does this bring up any memories?" Sade checked, looking down at him. The white bandage had been removed, exposing more of his handsome face. There were a few scratches on his arms, neck, and face, but Dante Williams was still one of the most handsome men Sade had ever encountered.

"No. Is it supposed to?"

"Well, we have the Family Feud game at home and play it all the time. Also, you dressed up like Steve Harvey for Halloween last year. So there's that."

Dante laughed softly, wrapping his arm around himself as he grimaced. He'd lifted his entire arm instead of trying to raise his hand at his wrist, which gave him some relief, but it was apparent he was still sore.

"Are you serious?" The smile that lingered on his face warmed her heart.

"Dead. And it was so funny because we went to a party and three other people dressed like him, one of whom was a woman. Y'all spent the evening doing Steve Harvey impressions and break dancing, fake bald heads shining with sweat and all."

He laughed harder through the pain, and Sade couldn't help but join in as she pulled her phone out to show him a picture, but she pulled it away when he laughed so hard he started coughing.

"Okay, let's take a break from talking. I don't want you to be in too much pain knowing they won't give you any more medicine for a few hours."

"I don't have to talk, but I want you to tell me more about you."

"Okay. Hmm..." Sade's mouth twisted to the side as she considered his request.

There were things about herself that she wished she could change, and that felt like the perfect time to do so. To reinvent herself. However, there was the chance that Dante's memory would return, and he'd be upset about the lies she told. Sure he'd understand her desire for a fresh start, Sade presented herself with the version of her life and childhood that she *wished* was authentic instead of the facts.

"I'm thirty-two, but I'll be thirty-three next month on the tenth. I'm an only child. Both of my parents are dead. My family is originally from Chicago, so I don't stay by any of them. I've always been a loner, though, so it's fine. You and I moved from Memphis to Vanzette after college, and we love it there. I stayed in Memphis with my grandparents, and you and I met in school. We were best friends in high school but started dating in college."

"How did we take things to the next level?"

"It sounds silly now," Sade admitted, smiling softly. "It was sophomore year, and we were at a party. We were all a little tipsy and, for some reason, started playing Truth or Dare. One of my truths was who I would hook up with in the room if there were no consequences, and I chose you. When you took me home, you asked if I was being serious, and I told you I was. You came in, we had sex, and the rest, as they say, is history."

"I'm glad to hear we were friends first. Do we... have a good marriage? How long have we been married?"

"We have a great marriage," Sade assured him. "We got married right out of college."

"And we don't have kids? Is it because you don't want them? Because I feel like I always have."

"You do, and I do too. We said we would wait until we were thirty to start our family, and it just hasn't happened yet."

His brows wrinkled as he nodded and looked away from her. "Let me know if I ask too many questions."

"It's fine. I know there's a lot about me you'll want to know. Especially when you're able to come home."

"That's... actually what I want to talk to you about. Because of the fractures on my wrists, I will stay at the rehab physical therapy clinic Dr. Smith recommended while I heal. It's bad enough that I have to get to know you all over again; I don't want to be reliant upon you too. It would be fine if it were just one of my legs, but being unable to use my arms or legs the way I want will drive me crazy. I don't want to take that out on you."

Sade blinked rapidly, trying to process his words.

"I get that, but I really don't mind helping at all. Are you sure you want to go from one strange place to another? If you came home, the physical therapist could work with you there, and you'd have your own personal space. And maybe something there will trigger your memories."

Swallowing hard, Dante considered her suggestion quietly.

"I also don't want you to put your life on hold for me, Sade. If you want a divorce..."

Sade chuckled and waved him off dismissively. "Dante, stop. We made vows—for better or worse, in sickness and health. You might not remember me now, but I believe you'll get your memory back soon. For once, stop worrying about me and focus on yourself. I'll be by your side every step of the way, but I'm a big girl, and I can handle when you need space."

"Only if you're sure," Dante agreed.

"I've never been surer of anything except wanting to spend the rest of my life with you. I got you, Dante. I promise."

Her eyes lowered to his hand. It shook as he opened it and turned his palm up so she could put her hand inside his. Sade did, her eyes watering in the process. It felt like she was finally making her way back into his heart. As fast as she wanted to take things, Sade reminded herself to take it one slow step at a time.

This was a lot for any one person to handle. Though they expected him to recover fully, the road ahead would be long, frustrating, and painful. On top of that, he was missing a massive chunk of his memory. Sade wanted to do anything she could to make this easier for him. Anything except leave him—that was something she'd *never* do.

DANTE

A LITTLE OVER A week later, Dante was released from the hospital. Though he knew Sade wanted him to go straight home and do his physical therapy there, Dante wasn't comfortable with that. It was one thing to be battling amnesia on its own, but being unable to fend for himself and move around freely had already been driving him crazy. Doctor Smith warned him that peace and quiet were best for his nerves, but he could also experience frustration when he couldn't remember things. There was still no guarantee of when his memory would return, and Dante wanted to focus on one big issue at a time.

Sade wanted to see him before he left for the clinic, and Dante granted that. They were having great conversations, and he did feel more comfortable around her, but more than anything, he wanted space and the time and opportunity to try to will his memory back. Though Dante knew getting his full memory back wouldn't be easy, he was determined to try.

After three light taps on the door, Sade stepped inside. She looked beautiful as always, even dressed down in a burgundy sweat suit with matching Nikes. Her hair came down to her armpits, and it was in big, loose curls that reminded him of a '70s roller set. Sade's bow tie-shaped lips were covered in a clear gloss that he wanted to kiss at the sight of the balloons and cake in her arms.

"What's all this?" he asked, sitting up as carefully as possible.

21

The broken ribs had him resting high on pillows, but he'd leaned back some while he slept.

"I didn't want you to go without celebrating your birthday."

Dante smiled as his heart squeezed. His head shook as he searched for the right words. "Wow. That's... very thoughtful of you, Sade. Thank you."

"You can't remember this, but I'm a horrible singer. Usually, when I sing you Happy Birthday, it's to make you laugh, but we'll skip that today because of your ribs."

Dante chuckled as she placed the cake on his food tray and rolled it across to him.

"Though I would love to hear that, I'm glad. I haven't been in as much pain today and want to keep it that way."

"Good. I hate you can't walk around as much because of your knees. I know they said that would help your ribs."

"Yeah, but I've been able to move my shoulders and arms more, which gives me some slight relief in my chest."

"Any more mucus buildup?"

"Nah, thankfully."

"Good." Sade made her way over to the right side of the bed after setting the balloons down. "Happy belated birthday, baby. I'm so happy you're still here with me."

"I need you closer," Dante confessed, fighting back his emotion. All this time, he'd been pressed over not remembering her when he should have thanked God for her. She could have left him without a memory in the hospital with no one to claim him. Instead, she'd been by his side every step of the way... just like she'd promised to do.

Sade sat next to him on the bed. "You okay?" she checked sweetly, wrapping her arm around his neck.

"Thank you for this. For everything. I really appreciate you, Sade. I know this isn't how you saw us bringing in the New Year. I'm just... very grateful to have you."

"You're my husband. That's what I'm here for. If you want to come home early, call me, and I'll come get you, okay?"

His head bobbed once, and his eyes lowered to her lips as he licked his. Leaning more in her direction, Dante covered his lips with hers for a brief kiss. It didn't feel like the kind of kiss he usually gave her, but it felt fitting. When he pulled away, Sade blushed so hard, and her cheeks were so high her eyes had almost sealed shut.

"Thank you for being patient with me."

"Always. Now, let's cut this cake before the van arrives to pick you up."

Though Dante agreed, he couldn't take his eyes off her. When he left therapy, Dante hoped he was in good enough condition to show her how much he appreciated her.

SADE

Six Weeks Later

SADE NERVOUSLY TWIDDLED her thumbs as she looked straight ahead. She had been counting down the days waiting for Dante to call her from the rehab facility. As excited as she was for him to be with her, a part of Sade feared it wouldn't be easy for Dante to open up to her. He'd always been an independent man. Now, he was facing a double battle with amnesia and limited mobility.

His time at rehab and physical therapy had done wonders for his ribs and wrists, but his knees were still his most significant issue. His casts were removable, so he wore them for a few hours of the day and used a wheelchair for others. Regardless, Sade was just glad he was alive and able to move around a bit more freely.

"Are you ready to go inside?" Sade checked, killing the engine of her black Nissan Maxima. Of her three cars, it was the one she drove consistently. The white Infinity she usually brought out on weekends and saved her red BMW for special occasions.

"Yeah, I guess."

Sade turned slightly to open the door, gasping in surprise when Dante gently gripped her wrist. "What are you doing?" he asked.

"About to open the door," she said with a soft smile.

"I don't think that's something I would let you do."

Her smile widened. "It isn't, but you don't need to come all the way over here just to open my door, Dante. I need to get your casts and walker or wheelchair, anyway."

Dante sucked his teeth, giving her a dismissive wave of his hand. "I don't need any of that. I'm just gonna take my time. I'll be fine."

Not wanting to nag him, Sade only nodded silently in agreement. Before the physical therapists signed off on his discharge, they put him through a series of tests and did X-rays on his wrists and knees. He was in good enough condition to go home and do small things here and there for himself, but he would still have a physical therapist coming weekly to help him rebuild his muscular strength and movement for the next few weeks.

As much as she didn't want to, Sade waited for Dante to make his way to her side of the car, shaking her head as he wobbled slowly and grimaced from discomfort. After he opened the door for her, she said, "You are so stubborn."

Dante chuckled as he used his hip to close her door. When they made it to the entryway, he paused.

"Do you need the wheelchair?"

"Nah." His head shook as he looked around. "I don't remember where anything is, though."

"For now, I'll just show you around the first level. I put some things in this first guest room for you to make sure you can move around easily, and I also figured that would be best until you got more comfortable with me."

She saw the relief as it washed over Dante's face. "I appreciate that."

Sade led him into the guest room, mentioning the bathroom having a walk-in shower, which was also convenient.

As they slowly walked through the den and living room, Dante said, "This doesn't look like my style," referring to the modern silver, black, and gold color scheme. "It's dope... just doesn't look like me."

"Well, that's because you didn't want anything to do with the design process. You told me I could pretty much do whatever I wanted as long as it wasn't feminine."

"*That* sounds like me." Sade chuckled as they sat on the black sofa in the living room. "Thank you for easing us into this and not expecting me to be in the master bedroom with you."

"Of course. I'd love to have you in there, but I can't imagine how you feel about this. There's no rush. We have the rest of our lives."

"If this ever gets too much, I want you to know you can leave. We can get a divorce, Sade. I'll be at peace with that."

"Is that what you want?"

With a sigh, Dante's head tilted and avoided her eyes. "I don't want a divorce, but I am struggling with the idea of being married to a woman I don't have a memorable connection with. I saw the pictures, and I know we have a history. It's just frustrating not to be able to remember it."

Sade scratched her neck and breathed deeply. They'd briefly discussed this before he left, and Sade hoped he would be over it by now. It would have been selfish of her to hold on to their relationship, but no part of her wanted to tell him divorce would be okay.

"I don't want the responsibility of ending our marriage because I won't. If that will make this easier for you, you can leave."

When Sade stood, she held her breath, hoping that would keep her eyes from getting watery. What felt like a second chance at love was ending already. It was more difficult than she expected to keep her eyes from watering. Wiping a quick tear, Sade released a shaky breath. As excited as she was for Dante to get there, she hadn't prepared for this to be how his first day back ended.

"Sade," he called softly.

Her feet stopped, but Sade couldn't turn to face him. Instead, she closed her eyes and took a deep breath. She heard his feet shuffling, creating a melody that made her heart drum against her ribs. His fingers wrapped around her elbow softly, turning her like revolving doors. Avoiding his eyes, Sade wiped a tear from her eye before it could fall down her cheek.

"Look at me," he requested, but she couldn't.

She couldn't look into his eyes while he ripped her heart to shreds. "Dante, I—"

"What did you hear me say?"

Her brows wrinkled as she looked at him. Even with the hair on his head and face longer, Dante was still just as handsome as ever.

"That you want a divorce."

He smiled softly, shaking his head once. "I didn't say that, Sade."

"Then what did you say?"

"I said I don't want a divorce, but I am struggling with the idea of being married to a woman I don't have a memorable connection with."

Her bottom lip poked out, and her eyes blinked as she broke down each of his words. Dante chuckled, tilting her head slightly and caressing it with his thumb. "I don't want you to think I don't want you, Sade, but I must be honest with you."

"Yeah, I guess I just got really defensive. I don't want you to be with me if you don't want to, but you're saying it's uncomfortable, yet you're willing to try?"

"Yes, that's what I'm saying."

Her chest caved as she released a relaxed breath. "Okay, good. That makes me happy."

Dante chuckled before licking his lips. "Good. I'm glad we got that cleared up."

Before she could say anything else, Dante was heading out of the living room toward the guest room.

"Are you hungry?" she asked quickly, stepping forward. "Can I get you anything?"

"I'm good, Day. Rest your mind."

Her heart skipped a beat as she watched his back retreat.

Rest your mind.

He said that to her over the years whenever she was worked up about something. Dante might not have remembered their past, but small things like that gave her hope that they still had a future.

DANTE

"YOU ACT LIKE you've never seen my body before," Dante teased, drying his chest with one towel while another remained wrapped around his waist.

He'd showered after teasing Sade about giving him a sponge bath. For her to have been his wife, she bashfully turned red and grew so nervous it was cute.

"It's not that." Her eyes rolled playfully. "It's just been a while since I've seen you naked or even touched your bare skin, for that matter, and it caught me off guard."

"Mmm," Dante hummed, eyeing her frame. He couldn't imagine letting too many days go by without making love to her, so he hoped she was nervous because of the time apart from the accident... unless their marriage had gotten stale. Figuring that was as good of a time as any to ask, Dante wondered, "How's our love life? Do we still date? Have sex?"

Sade rubbed her hands together, avoiding his eyes. "Dante," she cooed. "I don't want to talk to you about that."

Laughter erupted from the pit of his stomach, reminding him of his still-healing ribs. "How do you not want to discuss our love life, Sade? Was it *that* bad?"

"No, not at all." Her head shook adamantly. "I'm just shy, that's all."

"So, how was it when we had sex?" Dante couldn't deny how good it felt to unnerve her. To watch her shrink in front of him. "Come here, Sade." She slowly walked over to him, still avoiding his eyes. Gripping her chin, Dante lifted her head and forced her to look into his eyes. "Did I talk dirty to you? Was it nasty? Did I handle you gently?"

Her eyes fluttered as she gripped his wrist. "Dante," she whispered firmly, chest heaving.

"Tell me how it was."

"I-it was... all of those things." She took a deep breath. "Sometimes, we made love, and sometimes, we fucked. Sometimes, you were gentle, and sometimes, we got rough. Sometimes, you talked dirty, and sometimes, it was so good you could barely moan."

Effortlessly, she'd turned the tables on him. Licking his lips, Dante swallowed hard as his nostrils flared.

"And the dating?"

"Once a week outside of the house, but we hung out a lot here too."

"Do we have a lot of friends? I feel like friendship and family are important to me."

She exhaled a long breath, putting a bit of space between them. "Should you be standing so long? Why don't you sit down?"

"I'm fine, and why do you always avoid questions about family and friends when asked about both?"

Massaging her temple, Sade stepped further away from the bed and paced.

"The neurologist said to avoid anything that might cause stress or anger. We don't know what's going on in that head of yours until your next appointment. I don't want to say anything that will upset you and cause you to have any symptoms from the accident. It's bad enough stressing over you having a blood clot, and we do not know it until you go for your checkup. I just want to be careful, Dante."

Dante considered her words carefully, walking over to the small black futon on the left side of the room. He didn't care as much about his health as she did at that moment. Right now, his biggest concern was, "Are you saying knowing the truth about my family and friends will stress or anger me?"

She nodded, nibbling her cheek. "Yes," she almost whispered. "After your appointment, if the doctor confirms you're good, I'll tell you everything you want to know. Until then, I'm uncomfortable telling you anything that might upset you. I hope that doesn't upset you."

As much as Dante didn't want to, he found her care and concern cute. They were causing him to develop feelings for her with each passing encounter they had. He was quickly learning why he would have chosen Sade to be his wife.

"I appreciate you caring about me."

"I'm glad," she replied softly, slowly approaching the futon and sitting next to him.

"I guess it's just me and you for now, huh?"

"Would that be such a bad thing?"

"Nah." Dante shook his head as he took her hand into his and kissed it. "So what do we do when we're chilling at home?"

"Well, do you remember your hobbies and interests?"

"I do. I have an Xbox, right?"

"Right. You play that shit for hours. Are you okay to play that now, though, with your ribs?"

"I'll be careful," Dante replied, standing with a grin. "Did you ever play with me?"

"No. I tried when I first bought you a new one for Christmas one year, but you didn't have the patience to teach me, and you got mad because I kept dying."

Dante laughed as she stood. "Besides that, I like clubbing, poker, and sports."

"Right. And I love to draw and paint."

"That's dope, Day."

"Thank you." As she blushed, she pulled hair behind her ears. "Together, we do whatever we're in the mood to do. Cook or bake, watch TV, read, listen to music, and dance. We dance together a lot."

"And sing? You said you're bad at that, though, right?"

Her smile was wide as she nodded. "Right, but I do it a lot. We have a karaoke machine upstairs in the entertainment room. That's where your gaming systems are. We have a lot of board games up there too. And a pool table. So we have a lot of fun here, but we go out regularly too."

Pleased with the sound of that, Dante exited the guest room he was occupying. He knew she'd be concerned about him going upstairs with his knees in their condition. More than anything, they were tight and sore. Dante was grateful he'd started physical therapy as soon as he did because that kept his muscles from atrophying. His daily workouts kept him from stiffening up too much, but if he stayed immobile for too long, the pain would start up.

"I can... bring the games down here if you'd like," Sade offered. "So you won't have to go up and down the stairs."

Scratching just above his top lip, Dante looked from Sade to the stairs.

"I'll be all right, Sade, but thank you."

"Okay," she agreed, retreating and allowing him to slowly go up the stairs. Dante may not have been able to control many things in his life, but he could control his movements, and he'd take full advantage because it felt like that was all he had. He didn't want to admit it, but Sade's wanting to keep his family and friends a secret didn't sit well with him. She hadn't done anything to make him not trust her, so Dante would follow her lead... but if she didn't give him the answers he was looking for soon, he would find them himself.

SADE

Two Days Later

So FAR, THINGS have been going well. Dante was still considered a missing person in Memphis, and no one in Vanzette knew he was with Sade. There were moments she feared he'd regain his memory and realize they weren't married, and there were also moments things didn't feel right or make sense to him, and she hoped it wouldn't lead to him becoming suspicious of her.

When Sade opened the door and saw Patrice standing on the other side, she was sure all of her hard work would be for nothing if she didn't think of a lie quickly.

"Sade?" Patrice called, eyeing her frame before chuckling. She crossed her arms over her clipboard and ran her tongue over her cheek. "You live here?"

Nodding, Sade gave Patrice a once-over. When they were in high school, Patrice was among the beautiful, popular girls who hardly paid Sade any attention unless it was to tease and bully her. Sade was surprised when she moved to Vanzette, and Patrice made friendly banter with her when they were in the same place. She wouldn't say the two were friends by any means, but they spoke occasionally.

"Yes, I do. What can I help you with?"

"I'm a physical therapist assistant. I came to do a quick checkup on my boss's patient before he came to start his therapy." Patrice looked down at her clipboard. Her head tilted and brows bunched. "Dante Williams? The one that went to high school with us?"

Sade scratched her neck and shook her head. "Not at all." She chuckled nervously. "Actually…" Sade stepped closer, looking around her empty street both ways before speaking. Patrice's curiosity had her leaning forward. "That's not his real name." Sade tsked. "It's a friend of mine who didn't want his wife to know he was driving drunk. When I arrived at the hospital, I told them the first name that came to mind."

"What?! Sade—"

"I know; it probably wasn't the wisest choice to make, but he begged me to lie so his wife wouldn't find out."

Patrice eyed her skeptically, and the seconds felt like eternities while Sade waited for her to speak. "Well, okay. I need his real name, though. I'm not calling him Dante." When Patrice tried to walk past Sade to go into her home, Sade grabbed her arm a bit more forcefully than she wanted to. "What are you doing?"

"You can't go in there."

"Why not?"

"He isn't here."

Patrice chuckled. "Where is he?"

"Back at home with his wife."

"Is he rejecting treatment? If so, I need to let my boss know."

"Um… I don't know, Patrice. Let me call him and see, then I'll call and let you all know."

Patrice sighed with a roll of her eyes. Her head shook as she pulled her arm from Sade's grip.

"Fine. Make sure you call before his next scheduled appointment. I'll need to see him before my boss does."

"I will; I promise."

Patrice's movements were slow as she backed away. Sade waited until she was in her car and driving off to breathe. Stepping into her home quickly, she leaned against the door and took another deep breath as her body relaxed. Massaging her temples, she shook her head and grumbled, "What the hell was I thinking? I can't just... keep this man here. Even if I did keep people away, if Dante regains his memory, he will fucking *kill* me."

Though they had never been a couple, they had always been friends. Best friends. That was why Sade had pictures and stories for days. It didn't matter how loyal they were to each other throughout the years; Dante never took things to a romantic level, and Sade's heart ached because of that. She'd dated men and even fallen in love with a few, but none of them had left the imprint Dante's love and friendship did.

"Day!" Dante called from the kitchen, causing Sade to jump before scurrying toward the sound of his voice.

"Yeah, baby?"

"Who was that at the door?" Dante asked, turning to face her.

"Oh, it was the physical therapist's assistant."

"She's not coming in?"

Sade's head shook. "No, she stopped by to let us know she couldn't do your session today. I'm gonna call and see if we can get a different person for tomorrow."

"Cool," Dante agreed, lifting his cup of juice and taking a large gulp.

She was so infatuated with him that even the sight of his Adam's apple bobbing as he drank turned her on. He was dressed and prepared for his session in basketball shorts and a wife beater. Yesterday, he mentioned wanting to go to the barbershop, but Sade liked this unkempt version of him. Besides, if she let him go, she'd expect him to wonder why none of the barbershops in Vanzette felt familiar to him. She couldn't let him go to his barber in Memphis, or they'd call his wife since he was missing. Sade settled on telling him he cut his own hair, which was true because he was capable. That half-truth bought her a little time since he decided to wait until the weekend to do it himself.

"What do you want to do today?" Dante asked. "When are you returning to work? What do you do?"

Sade poured herself a glass of orange juice and sat on the brown bar stool beside him behind the island.

"I work from home, so that's why I could take off when you had the accident." She paused, trying to find a way to be as honest with him as she possibly could. If she told him she had wealth saved from the death of her parents, that would probably lead to more questions about her family and eventually his. Sade didn't have to work a day in her life if she didn't want to, but she loved kids and creating art for them, so she designed coloring and picture books along with canvas art that parents crashed her site to purchase when she made them available. "I make wall art, coloring books, and picture books for kids."

"That's amazing, Sade. I'd love to see some of your work."

"Sure. The bonus room upstairs is my home studio. You can go up there any time."

"Cool, and I'm in finance, right? I have a finance company." His head tilted as he processed his thoughts. "With several people. I can't picture them, but I feel like we're close."

Sade cleared her throat, mind racing for a lie. "You did have a financial firm, but you quit to go into business for yourself. There were some issues with the people you were in business with, and you decided you'd be better off by yourself."

Dante cupped his hands on top of the island. Sade's hand shook as she lifted her juice and took a small sip. There was a chance certain words, places, or conversations could spark a memory for Dante, and Sade hoped that wouldn't happen now.

If he remembered too much about his business, there was a huge chance he'd remember running it with his wife.

A wife who wasn't her.

"Am I right to assume you won't tell me what those issues were to avoid stressing me out?"

She chuckled. "You would assume correctly, sir."

He huffed in a way that made her laugh. "Then what was I doing for work because I know I wasn't letting you pay the bills?"

"Well, we have seven figures in the bank thanks to my parents, so money isn't an issue."

"Damn. So you're rich, and we live here?" Her bark of laughter made his expression soften. "I don't mean the house. The house is spacious and beautiful. I mean, in this small town. If you were a millionaire, I'd think you'd have more expensive taste and live in New York or Cali or even a different country."

That was true—Sade's home was spacious. It was custom-built on three acres of land, along with a man-made body of water that Sade couldn't live without. It had five bedrooms, a bonus room, a living room, a dining room, a sitting room, and a large kitchen. Each bedroom had its own bathroom and fireplace, and a guest bedroom was upstairs and downstairs.

She'd converted the bonus room into her office and two of the bedrooms into entertainment spaces, though she rarely had a lot of people over. The other two were guest bedrooms, along with her master bedroom. Her home was her pride and joy, and she loved the fact that her neighbors were a ways away. It came in handy now that she was, in essence, hiding out with Dante.

The house and her land were the only things she'd splurged on with the money her parents left her. Even her cars, though plentiful, were inexpensive. Sade had big plans for that money, all of which revolved around endless travel and spoiling her family whenever she got married and had kids. For now, Sade enjoyed her small town, simplistic living. Money hadn't changed her grandparents and how they raised and treated her, and it hadn't changed her either.

"I'm a simple woman, Dante. Money is just a resource to me. It allows me to get what I want and need, and I have all I want and need here."

"I can respect that, but still. It doesn't seem like I would be okay with not working, even if I did plan to start my own business. You weren't paying for that, right?"

"You wouldn't let me. Everything kind of happened really fast. Maybe you don't remember because it happened right before the accident. You hadn't started making any plans yet. And you have money saved, so you weren't in a rush to find work. Your own separate money, though we had the understanding that we shared and split everything down the middle."

"That sounds more like me," Dante admitted. "Me waiting until I had money saved before leaving." His head nodded. "Okay, I can accept that, but I'm definitely going to start back up with work soon. I've been relaxing, but I can't get too comfortable not doing anything. I'll get bored, and it'll drive me crazy." He stood and walked his now-empty breakfast plate over to the sink. "Hopefully, my wrists will completely heal in the next week or two, and I can start looking for work. Until I open a new firm, I will work for someone else. I feel a little unstable without my memory, so it's probably not wise to take on such a large responsibility immediately."

Sade nodded, unsure of what to say. She knew she couldn't keep him locked away forever, but she didn't expect him to want to start moving around so quickly. As long as she could keep him restricted to Vanzette, he was less likely to be recognized. Very rarely did Memphis news make it to Vanzette. If they reported a missing man, it would be on news websites instead of TV.

The FBI and Memphis Police Department were still looking for Dante, but they hadn't come to Vanzette in search of him. His family and friends insisted Dante wasn't the type to go on the run and not face the consequences of his actions, so the search was more so for a missing and presumed harmed or dead man. That worked in her favor because if his parents believed there was a chance Dante was alive, healthy, and in his right mind... there was a chance she would cross theirs, and they would be reaching out to her to see if she'd heard from him.

One day, she'd accept how toxic her love for him was, but that day wouldn't come anytime soon. Sade risked their friendship holding him here, but she was convinced this was her only chance to have a romantic relationship with the man she'd always loved. If that was the case, Sade planned to take full advantage of Dante not having his memory, and she would let the chips fall where they may in consequence.

SADE

High School Prom

SADE'S HEAD HUNG, *keeping her gaze on her ballerina flats. Her grandmother, Ava, told her to pack them in case her feet got sore from dancing the night away. Sade agreed though she knew the chances of that happening were slim to none. Outside of her preoccupied date, there were a few people there that she talked to, but only one she considered a true friend, and that friend had been spending the evening dancing with his date, who had made it her mission to keep Dante from interacting with Sade or anyone else.*

If Sade called for a ride early, she'd have to hear Ava complain about how high school was supposed to be the best, most carefree, and fun time of her life: no work, no bills, no responsibilities. However, high school had been the most draining, confusing time of her life. There was one highlight of the last four years for Sade, though, and that was Dante. He was all she'd ever needed. He was indeed her best friend.

Slipping her heels back on, Sade decided to go to the punch bowl where Lindsey and Nya stood. Sade wouldn't consider them friends, but they talked during their classes and lunch. Before she reached them across the gym, Dante was making his way in front of her. He looked so handsome in his brown and gold that Sade couldn't help but blush and look away.

"Where you going?" he checked, pushing a few loose curls out of Sade's face.

"*To get some punch.*"

"*Save me a dance?*"

Sade's eyes rolled as she looked down at her nails. "*I don't think your girl would like that.*"

Dante sucked his teeth and wrapped his arm around her shoulders. "*You're my best friend. I don't care what she thinks.*"

Sade smiled as he led her over to the punch bowl. "*Are you having a good time?*"

"*It's cool, but I'd rather be at home playing a few games with you.*" *He winked at her, and Sade blushed as she shook her head.*

"*If you don't stop. You know Imani would have a fit if you weren't here to be her arm candy. She will probably come over here any minute to take you back.*"

"*She'll be a'ight. I've been with her all night.*" *Dante grabbed them both a cup of punch as Sade waved at Lindsey and Nya.* "*I want to spend some time with you.*"

Dante stared at her as he sipped his punch, and Sade tried to think of something—anything—to say. She cleared her throat and squeezed her neck, looking back at the dance floor.

"*Um... Have you heard from TSU yet?*"

"*Yeah, they accepted me. So I got in at all three schools.*"

"*That's great, Dante! Which one are you going to go to?*"

He shrugged as he tossed his now-empty cup into the trash can. "*UOM is giving me a full ride. Plus... if I go there... I'll be with you.*"

Sade smiled. "*Actually, I was thinking about going to UT Chatt. It's probably the calmest of the schools. I don't think I'd have much fun at TSU since I don't party, and I want to get out of Memphis.*"

"*I feel you. TSU would definitely be live. You should come, though. We can do more than party.*"

"*I'll think about it,*" *Sade replied, knowing she'd go just about anywhere with Dante.*

When the song changed, he took her cup, set it on the table, and then led her to the dance floor.

"Dante, you know I don't like to dance."

"It'll be fun. Here..." He wrapped her arms around his neck and pulled her close.

So close she smelled the peppermint and fruit punch on his breath. Sade looked into his eyes, grateful she'd put her heels back on because they made them the same height. His arms wrapped around her waist, and Sade's breathing hitched. He'd hugged her a million times, but this was different.

As they swayed from one side to the other, Sade felt herself relaxing against him more and more.

"See, it's not so bad, huh?" he teased.

"No," she giggled softly. "Nothing's ever really bad with you."

Dante gave her a comfortable smile before licking his lips. "Good."

"So... What are you doing after this? Are you and Imani going to a hotel or something?"

He shrugged. "She wants to. TJ is having a party. I prefer to go to that. You wanna come?"

"Nah, I'll probably just head home."

"What about Lucky? Aren't you here with him?"

Sade scoffed. "He asked me to be his date, but he's spent most of his time huddled up with his friends. We've probably danced to two songs this whole time." Dante chuckled, gripping her tighter and pulling her closer.

"He's such a fucking loser. If you'd come here with me, I never would've let you out of my sight."

If anyone else would have said that, Sade would have been convinced they were flirting. But this was Dante. This was her best friend. He was simply being nice.

Their eyes were locked, but Dante's lifted above her and widened. His mouth opened, and he tried to pull Sade behind him, but before he could, the entire bowl of punch was thrown onto her head. Since she was midsway, Sade had no time to prepare for the impact, especially with the bowl being dropped onto her head. Before she could fall, Dante grabbed her arms as she tried to maintain her balance.

Gasps erupted before laughter as Sade's eyes landed on Imani's mischievous smirk.

"What the fuck are you doing, man?" Dante yelled, reaching for Imani.

Sade growled and tackled Imani, allowing her fist to connect with her face. She'd hit her three times before Dante pulled her off. That didn't stop Sade from kicking Imani twice as Dante carried her away.

"I hate that bitch!" Sade yelled. "I wish she was fucking dead!"

"It's all right," Dante said against her ear. "I got you."

He carried her outside, not putting her on her feet until they were in front of the gymnasium. As Dante tried to wipe the punch from her face and hair, Sade pushed his hands away.

"You need to go back in there because if she comes out here looking for you, you won't be able to pull me off her."

"Sade," he called softly, reaching for her hand, but Sade pulled it away.

"Don't touch me! You're the reason she acts like this. She hates me because of you. Just... Get away from me, Dante."

"I'm not leaving you out here. At least let me take you home."

"No." Sade adamantly shook her head as she took steps backward. "Leave me alone, Dante."

When she felt her tears about to erupt, Sade turned away from him. She should have known Imani would do something when she saw them talking and dancing, but she wasn't expecting this. Dante had been Sade's best friend long before Imani had even come to their school, but Imani was so possessive of him she didn't want Sade to have anything to do with him. Their arguments had turned into fights over the years, but never anything this humiliating. Never around this many people—never anything this infuriating.

"This... This was my mother's dress," Sade sobbed, looking down at the pale yellow silk material. "She ruined my mother's dress."

"Day…" Dante gently tugged her close and pulled her into his chest as she cried. "Let me take you home. Please."

Sade sniffled and wrapped her arms around him. "I don't want to mess up your seat."

"I don't care about my seats." Dante cupped her cheeks, forcing her to look into his eyes. "Let's just go, Day. I'll take you home so you can get changed, and we can just… chill. Just you and me."

Sade considered his request as he tried to wipe her face again. This time, she allowed him. Her breathing came out shaky before she agreed with, "Okay. That's fine."

Dante walked her over to his car and helped her inside. She wiped the last of her tears and looked toward the gym entrance. At the sight of Imani watching them with her arms crossed over her chest as she frowned, Sade couldn't help but smile.

SADE

Back to the Present
Five Days Later

"No, NO, NO, no, no," Sade whispered, going from one room to another.

Dante was gone.

She had no idea where he was, but he was gone.

She hadn't even bothered to put on any shoes before she went out to the garage. All of her cars were there, so he hadn't driven anywhere. After checking the backyard, Sade rushed back upstairs and grabbed her phone. Dante visited her often, because of their friendship, but not often enough to know anyone there. She grabbed her phone, unsure how she planned to find him, and relief quickly filled her when she noticed the notes section open.

Needed some fresh air. Booked an Uber on your phone since I don't have one. Be back soon.

Plopping down on the side of her bed, Sade cursed under her breath. Dante had his first therapy session at home, and it frustrated him to no end. So much so that he was snappy with her by the time it was over. He apologized, and Sade figured that was the end before she took a nap, but it was apparent Dante was still upset. Though she could understand his frustration, Sade hoped he didn't push himself too fast. He kept trying to do more than what the therapist recommended, which caused tension between the two.

At the sound of the front door opening and closing, Sade stood and hurried out of her bedroom. It would have been just her luck that someone from Memphis was there and had spotted him. She went downstairs, and seeing him holding her favorite flowers made her heart skip a beat.

White lilies.

"Those are my favorite," she whispered, pointing at them. "How did you know?"

Dante shrugged. "They looked like something you'd like."

She walked over to him, eyes watering. "I was worried about you."

"I apologize for that. I just needed some fresh air. And I'm sorry for taking my frustration out on you."

Sade waved him away and accepted the flowers. "It's fine."

"I need to talk to you. Were you doing anything important?"

"No. I just woke up and started looking for you. Is everything okay?"

Dante took her hand into his and led her into the sitting room. They sat on the sofa that was directly across from the window.

"My wallet and phone were taken after the accident, right? Was it a robbery gone bad, or did someone hit me and take advantage of it by stealing from me too?"

Sade rubbed her hands against her thighs. "I don't have a police report here, but an eyewitness said a truck ran you off the road. Once you crashed into the pole, they got out and took your wallet and phone. Your keys too."

"Is the witness's information on the police report?"

Sade's head shook. "No. Honestly, I don't know if they did one. That was before I got there and told them your name. By the time I'd arrived, the police had filled them in and left." Twiddling her thumbs, she asked, "What are you thinking?"

"Just trying to figure out who would want to come after me and why. Was I targeted for a robbery or something else? We don't appear to live a flashy lifestyle, and you said I'd quit my job, so it doesn't make sense for someone to want to rob me."

Sade had her suspicions, but she wouldn't voice them. Not right now, at least. They would only add to his confusion and make him want to search more.

"I don't think that matters now, babe. You're alive and safe, and that's all I care about."

Nodding, Dante released a hard breath and wiped his hand over his face.

"I don't know how long I'll be able to accept that, but I hear you. There's a lot I need to do. I can't just sit around the house all day. I need a new phone, new cards, and a new license. And I need to start looking for work."

Sade had to be careful. If she went against his wishes too much, it would raise suspicion.

"Why'd you Uber? The keys to the cars are by the garage door."

"I didn't know that, Sade, and I don't think I'm ready to drive just yet."

Good. That would keep him from straying too far alone.

"That's understandable. I can take you to run those errands whenever you'd like."

"There's no one else here that can help me with this stuff? I don't want to put it all on you."

Sade smiled and took his hand into hers. "Driving you to a couple of places is no burden at all, Dante."

"Still, I can't help but feel like I have family and friends that should be here too."

"I thought we agreed we would wait until after your next appointment before discussing that."

His head shook as he stood. "Just tell me if I have family I'm not on good terms with or if I don't have family at all."

She considered his question, wondering how deep she wanted to go with her lies. It stayed in the back of her mind that his memories would return one day, and all this would be over. Would he forgive her for the untruthful foundation she built?

Brushing her nose, Sade stood directly in front of him. She would need to satisfy his curiosity if she wanted his questions to cease. "You do have parents. You aren't close to them, like I'm not close to my family back in Chicago. That lack is why we got along so well in school. We made a family out of our friends. A chosen family with unconditional regard."

"Then where are they? Why haven't they come to check on me? On us? What could have happened that was so bad that I left the company I started with some of them?"

She licked the corner of her mouth and swallowed hard. "Life happened over the years. We lost touch with a lot of people. There were three that we remained in touch with, though. I stopped hanging with them so much when we moved here. You worked with them in Memphis." She paused. "They were doing some illegal things that you didn't approve of," Sade settled on, telling a half-truth.

When Dante called her the night of the accident, she knew what he wanted to discuss, but she'd been sworn to secrecy. She had decided not to give Dante any information unless he came to her for it, and that night, Sade was filled with peace because it was finally time. However, his abrupt ending of the phone call had her shooting up out of bed, fearing the worst, though nothing would have prepared her for what had happened and the reason for it.

How was she supposed to tell him that someone close to him bragged about setting him up with the FBI? That they planned for him to go to prison for their crimes? Did that mean they planned to have him killed on the off chance he got away too? Sleeping with that on her conscience had been futile since the moment she learned of it, but Sade was confident things would work out for his good. As soon as she found him, without his memory, Sade was sure that was God's way of protecting him.

No matter what it took, she'd keep him away from Memphis and the disloyal people waiting to bring him harm... even if it destroyed their friendship in the future.

"When you found out, you pulled your stock and made it clear you wanted nothing to do with them. They aren't going to come and see about you, Dante, because they don't care." Her eyes watered as she gritted her teeth. "Time and greed changed them all, but you remained pure. A man of integrity and—" She huffed, covering her face as her head shook. "I won't let them come here and pretend to care about you. So if I'm not enough, you'll just have to make new friends because none of them are stepping foot in our home."

Lifting her head by her chin, Dante cupped her cheeks. "You *are* enough," he muttered against her lips before kissing them sweetly. "But... I need more than just you. I hope that doesn't offend you. I'm trying to put my life back together in my mind, so I'll have questions, Day. If answering them makes you feel some type of way—"

"No, you're right. You have every right to ask questions. I just hate talking about them because of the way they talked to and treated you before the accident. We're very protective of each other. I wanted to spare you from that, but it's obvious I can't."

His smile was warm as he pulled her into his chest. "I'm a grown-ass man, Sade. If you want to protect my heart, treat me right. But you don't have to protect me from the actions of others, especially while I'm trying to piece things together. I can handle it. I appreciate you, though, all right?"

Nodding, Sade clung to him tightly. He may have thought he could handle what their friends had in store for him, but he couldn't, and that's why he was on his way to her that night. Dante may not have known or understood that now, but Sade was going to give him the safe haven he needed... no matter what.

DANTE

"ARE YOU SURE, Dante?"

Dante chuckled as he put the Maxima in reverse. After riding in the passenger seat for two stops, he couldn't take it anymore. Sade wasn't a bad driver, but she was a slow, careful driver, and he hated how she didn't like to reverse into parking spaces. Instead of taking the first spot, Sade had been driving around looking for what she considered to be the perfect spot.

"I'm positive," he replied, deciding now was as good of a time as any for him to start driving again. The last thing he wanted was to allow fear from the accident to keep him from wanting to get behind the wheel again. His head shook as they headed out of the parking lot. "It's crazy to me how I can remember things about myself but nothing else. I don't know where the hell we are or how to get to the bank from here."

"Well... The mind is truly an enigma. I'm just glad you remember who you are. You're my favorite person."

A slow smile lifted the corners of his mouth as he briefly looked over at her. Day by day, he was becoming more and more intrigued by her. There were things she said or avoided saying that stuck out to Dante, but he tried to let those things ride. One thing had always been a guiding light for him, and that was the fact that the truth would always come out when it needed to. If she was hiding something that he needed to know, Dante was confident that he'd find out when the time was right.

"That's a high honor."

She shot him her notorious wink, and Dante couldn't help but take her hand into his. So far, she hadn't asked him how he felt, and he appreciated that. There was still a hell of a lot of soreness, but it was nothing he couldn't handle. The more he moved around, the better, but Dante had the common sense not to overdo it.

After putting the address to the nearest Wells Fargo into his GPS, Dante gave Sade his new phone and allowed her to choose the music they'd be listening to. She played a random mix of TikTok songs that he'd never heard before in his life. They took the time to talk about their favorite music and shows, and Dante wanted to take her on a date and start getting to know her fully all over again. Until that point, he'd spent a lot of time obsessing over the fact that he didn't remember their past. Now, he felt like he was finally ready to start getting to know her in the present for their future, especially since it seemed like he didn't have anyone else.

By the time they made it to the bank, their conversation had shifted from one thing to another, and more than anything, Dante loved how their friendship was blossoming. He was attracted to her physically and sexually, but the most they'd done so far was kiss. While he was sure Sade would love to take it there, that wasn't his current priority. He really wanted to establish a connection with her before that happened. The last thing he wanted was to give her hope that their marriage would return to normal while he still had doubts.

It didn't take him long to withdraw some funds and place an order for new bank cards. When they left there, they grabbed lunch at the nearby pizza café. Dante noticed the woman who had been checking him out since they arrived, but he didn't bother mentioning it to Sade or making a big deal out of it. He figured she would have spoken if she knew them, so she was obviously attracted to him. That was confirmed when Sade went to the bathroom and the woman approached him.

She sat directly across from him in the booth, wearing a smile that made Dante chuckle and shake his head.

"Hey, handsome," she greeted, crossing her arms on top of the table.

"Wassup?"

"Are you single?"

Dante looked down at his left ring finger and the ring that occupied it. "No. The woman that just got up from the seat you're in is my wife."

Confusion covered the woman's face before she chuckled. "Sade is your wife? I thought maybe you were a family member who came here to visit her."

"Oh, so you know my wife?"

"Yeah, I do. I didn't know she was married, though." The woman shrugged as she stood. "We're not close enough for me to know that, I guess. We get our hair done at the same place."

Dante nodded, not feeling the need to respond. He did, however, find it weird that the woman didn't know Sade was married. He brushed it off, figuring his wife was reserved and to herself when getting her hair done. It wasn't until Sade came and sat back down that he noticed she wasn't wearing her ring. Head tilting, he looked from Sade to the woman, who sipped her drink and eyed them with no shame.

"Where's your wedding ring, Sade?"

"Hmm?" She looked down at her left hand before giggling. "Oh. Before the accident, you wanted to upgrade it for my birthday. I guess with everything that's been going on, I forgot to pick it up. It's at Erlin Jewelers."

"Your birthday. We didn't celebrate."

"Babe, how were we going to celebrate?"

"I should have made a way. You brought me the cake and stuff before I left the hospital. I should have had the same energy behind you."

Sade playfully rolled her eyes as she stood. "You barely wanted to be around me then, so I wasn't expecting you to do anything for my birthday."

"Still, I'm going to do something," Dante informed her as he stood. "You've been amazing these last couple of months, and I want to show you how much I appreciate you and what your loyalty means to me."

His arms wrapped around her, and he pulled her close. She allowed him to kiss her for as long as she could before her smile made it impossible.

"What's gotten into you?" she asked, grinning as she squeezed his arms.

"Just... want you to know that I'm yours. And that I appreciate you," he said, but he was also doing it for the woman's benefit. She may not have known he was Sade's husband before, but by the frown she wore, that was a truth she'd never forget.

Hand in hand, they headed out of the café. As they approached the exit, Dante said, "Did you want to speak to her?" He pointed in the woman's direction, gauging Sade's reaction to her.

"No, why? She tried to talk to you?"

Dante chuckled as the woman scoffed and headed toward the beverage station to refill her drink.

"She did. She said she didn't know we were married and that y'all got your hair done at the same place."

"I don't gossip like they do, so she doesn't know any of my personal business. It doesn't surprise me she waited until I left to try to talk to you, though. She obviously knew something was going on between us; otherwise, she would have spoken and tried to get me to introduce you to her."

"I agree," Dante said, holding the door open for her. "I don't know too many brothers and sisters or cousins who feed each other and wipe each other's mouths the way we do."

"Maybe she and her kissing cousins do."

Between her statement and Sade's serious expression, Dante couldn't help but laugh. He wrapped his arm around her, holding her close to his side.

"Look at you. You're not jealous, are you?"

"Hell no. Why would I be jealous of her when I have you?"

Unable to argue with that, Dante kissed her on the temple as they crossed the street. This town was small, so he was sure this wouldn't be the first time he ran into someone who knew Sade, but he couldn't help but hope one day he stumbled across someone who knew him too...

SADE

WHEN SADE ARRIVED at Michelle's Magical Hair Salon and saw Patrice, her eyes rolled. It didn't help that Trina, the woman who tried to talk to Dante at the pizza café, was there too. Sade went over to her stylist's chair to let her know she'd arrived, then returned to the waiting area. She made herself comfortable in the burnt orange seat and looked around briefly.

Michelle's shop was long and slim, with chairs and booths for her stylists on the left and shampoo bowls and dryers on the right. The burnt orange and gold décor were pleasant on the eyes, and she had a small snack and beverage area in the back of the salon. Sade hoped Patrice wouldn't notice her, but she did, and as soon as she did, Patrice sashayed over to Sade and took the seat next to her.

"Hey," Patrice greeted, looking at the side of Sade's face.

"Hey." Sade looked over at her briefly before pulling her phone out of her pocket and hoped her lack of interest in a conversation would make Patrice leave.

"So, I've been thinking," Patrice said, forcing Sade to set her phone in her lap and look at her again. "It's been bothering me...that little story you told me when I came over. It doesn't make sense."

"Good thing it doesn't have to."

Patrice chuckled. "It kind of does." Patrice leaned forward in her seat, resting her forearms on her thighs. "When I saw your face and then Dante's name on that file, I didn't get a good feeling about that at all. I tried to believe your story about you using his name for a friend's protection, but that didn't sound right, so I looked him up on social media. Do you know what I found?"

"I'm sure you're going to tell me."

"He's missing, Sade. You expect me to believe you using his name while he's missing is a coincidence? Is Dante the man at your house? And if so, why haven't you told his wife?"

Rolling her eyes, Sade sat back in her seat. "Do you really think I'd keep Dante in my house and not tell anyone about it? He's my best friend..."

"Exactly!" Patrice whispered firmly. "He's your best friend, and you said another friend used his name. I just don—"

"Look!" Sade yelled louder than she wanted to, turning in her seat so that she and Patrice were face-to-face. "I don't care what you believe, okay? I don't owe you an explanation, and even if I did, I told you the truth. My friend was in an accident that he didn't want his wife to know about because he was drinking, so I used Dante's name because we're close, and his name is the first that came to mind."

"But why wouldn't he want his wife to know, Sade?"

"Because he has a drinking problem, and she told him she would divorce him if he had another accident."

"And you're okay with covering that up?"

"I don't have anything to do with what happens in their marriage. Besides, once he can move around freely, he's going to rehab for his drinking. He doesn't want his wife to know until he's about to check in because he's told her he would go to rehab before and didn't see it through. This was a wake-up call for him, not that this has anything to do with you."

Patrice tilted her head, eyeing Sade's face intently. "And you promise it's not Dante?"

"Yes," Sade stressed, nodding her head.

"Fine," Patrice agreed, sitting back and crossing her arms over her chest.

"Why in the hell do you care, anyway? You haven't fucked with any of us since we graduated from high school."

"So? That man is missing, and his family is going crazy wondering where he is. If he's with you, they need to know."

"Well, like I said, he isn't."

"Mmm," was all Patrice said, and Sade was okay with that. If she started asking too many questions, Sade would have to shut her up permanently. No one was going to ruin her chance at a happily ever after with Dante.

No one.

"All right, Sade, I'm ready for you," Michelle called, and Sade was grateful.

She stood, not even bothering to look at or say anything else to Patrice, before heading to Michelle's chair. Michelle asked her what she wanted done to her hair, and it was hard for Sade to answer. Her attention was on Trina, who had stopped to talk to Patrice instead of heading out the door. Sade tried to convince herself that they weren't talking about her, but that theory went out the window when they looked her way at the same time.

"They looking at you like you stole *both* their men," Michelle teased, nudging Sade's shoulder softly before continuing to massage her scalp.

"Ain't they, though? I don't even know Trina well enough for her to be looking at me *any* kind of way."

"Now, you know I'm not one to gossip, but when you first walked in, she said she saw you out with your man, and she could have taken him if she wanted to. She said you were married. How come I didn't know that?"

Sade sucked her teeth before she chuckled as her nostrils flared. It was just like Trina to think Dante wanted her. Even in his right mind, Trina wouldn't have been his type.

"I don't like for people to know personal things about me, so keep that between us, please."

"Of course. I'm the same way. The less people know about you, the better. The less access they have to your life, the less of a chance they have to fuck that shit up. Keep your man away from women like her, Sade. Trina is not to be trusted."

Though Sade already knew that, she appreciated the warning.

Under normal circumstances, Sade was a peacemaker, but the thought of Patrice and Trina trying to figure out what was going on with her and Dante had her wanting to shut them both up—permanently.

She'd never had a lot of friends, so Sade clung closely to those she had. Not having friends also made it easy for her to be alone or not care about the thoughts and opinions of others. As long as they stayed in their place and minded their own business, Sade wouldn't bring any harm to Patrice and Trina. As much as she prayed they would let it go, her intuition told her she'd have a run-in with both of them soon.

SADE

SADE COULDN'T TAKE her eyes off Dante. His black V-neck shirt was covered with a black blazer. Black slacks with a brown belt and loafers, along with gold jewelry for the evening, completed his look.

He surprised her by asking her out on a date. She planned to be as patient with him as possible with dating and sex because she knew both would be worth it when it finally happened. They didn't have much in common regarding their hobbies, but they were always able to have a great time no matter what they were doing.

There were a lot of fun and unique things to do in Vanzette, so they decided to split the evening doing something he chose and something she chose. They started the date at a distillery, where they could craft their own cocktails. After that, they went to Sade's favorite soap shop, where they created the perfect liquid soap and body butter scent that fit them perfectly. It was spicy and sweet at the same time.

Their last stop was Lucas Steakhouse for dinner, and Sade was absolutely smitten with him. As often as the pair had hung out together, it had never been this intimate. And it wasn't supposed to be. They were friends. He was a married man. So much about this was wrong, but Sade couldn't stop now.

"What's wrong?" Dante asked before taking a sip of his wine.

"Nothing. Why do you think something is wrong?"

"You look distant."

"Sorry. I didn't realize it."

He nodded. "We can skip dessert and head home if you're tired."

"Not at all. I just..." She paused and licked her lips, deciding to be completely honest with him. "Being here with you is making me really happy. I'm trying to stay in the moment and not in my head, but I can't help it. I love you so much, Dante, and I—"

At the sound of a woman clearing her throat, Sade looked up. Her eyes rolled at the sight of Trina. She was dressed provocatively in a red dress that stopped midthigh with a low V-cut. Sade's eyes scanned her frame, stopping at her six-inch heels.

"Sade, it's good to see you and your... husband?" Trina confirmed, extending her hand for Dante to kiss. "It's funny because when Patrice and I were talking at the salon—"

Sade stood and stepped directly in front of Trina, silencing her instantly. "The first time you disrespected me, I let it slide. Trust me that won't happen again."

Trina chuckled as Dante stood and tried to step between the two, but Sade wouldn't allow him to.

"Disrespected you? That's not my intent at all. I was just trying to figure out—"

"Excuse me," Dante called. "My wife and I are on a date. If you could please return to your table and give us some privacy, I'd really appreciate that."

Trina's head bobbed once as she chuckled softly. "Sure. I didn't mean to interrupt." Her eyes returned to Sade as she said, "We'll talk soon."

Sade only smiled with one side of her mouth. "Sooner than you think." Then Sade returned to her seat, watching Trina as she walked away.

"Is something going on between the two of you?" Dante checked.

"No, she's just sticking her nose where it doesn't belong."

"Why?"

"Because she wants something she can't have."

"I'm sure I never cheated on you before, and I want you to know I won't cheat on you now. No matter who wants me, I will always be faithful to you, Sade."

While Sade appreciated his words, she was too trained on Trina walking into the bathroom to fully receive them.

"I'll be right back, okay?"

"Sade..." Dante called, voice low and irritated.

She gave him a quick kiss before heading toward the bathroom. Once she entered, she checked the other stalls before locking the door and leaning against it. As she waited for Trina to come out, Sade hummed quietly under her breath and looked over her nails. After her hair appointment, she stopped to get a gel pedicure and a dip powder manicure, both in white. Sade pushed herself off the door at the sound of the toilet flushing. Trina walked out, chuckling at the sight of Sade.

"The fuck do you want?" she asked, turning the water on in the sink.

Instead of answering, Sade walked over to her, wrapped her hand around her neck, and smashed her forehead into the mirror. The sound of Trina shrieking only made Sade do it again.

"I'm only going to say this once. Stay the *fuck* away from me and my husband, do you hear me?"

"Y-yes!" Trina cried, clawing at Sade's hand, but her grip was too tight.

"I don't know or care what Patrice told you, but if you had any sense, you'd avoid her when it comes down to me too. If you don't, I swear to God, I will kill you."

Sade bashed her head into the mirror again, this time knocking Trina out completely. She dragged her limp body into the bathroom stall and sat her on the toilet before locking the door and crawling out underneath it. Sade washed her hands and smoothed her dress, making sure not one hair was out of place before leaving the bathroom.

A part of her wanted to kill Trina and get it over with, but she couldn't do that in a public place. For now, she'd wait to see if Trina would heed her warning. If she didn't, Sade was fully prepared to finish what she'd started.

Back in school, it didn't matter how much Sade kept to herself. It was already difficult navigating the social structures of high school as an introvert, but she was also considered an ugly duckling. She was teased to no end and bullied so much her grandfather signed her up for boxing lessons. Even when she didn't want to fight, she had to, just to get people out of her face.

That was part of the reason she loved Dante as much as she did. No matter how many people called her names and teased her about her looks, Dante had always been kind to her. By the time she blossomed and became more aesthetically pleasing based on the world's standards, Dante was in love with someone else. He'd always been a good man, refusing to flirt or do anything to taint his character.

As she returned to the table, Sade pulled in a calming breath. She refused to let Trina ruin her very first date with Dante. Gasping, Sade covered her mouth at the sight of the slice of cake with a candle in it and a gift bag next to it. Dante stood, wrapping his right arm around her and placing a kiss on the top of her head.

"Happy belated birthday, baby."

"This is so sweet. Thank you, Dante." She wrapped her arms around his neck and kissed him before sitting down and blowing the candle out. "You know you didn't have to do this, right?"

"I wanted to. Now, open your gift."

Sade wiped a few tears away before biting down on her bottom lip and opening the gift bag. She pulled the long Erlin Jewelers box out and held her breath.

"Wow," she mumbled at the sight of the diamond necklace. "This is... beautiful. I-I love it."

Dante stood and walked over to her side of the table. After putting the necklace around her neck, he planted a kiss there, making her nipples harden as she shivered.

"I'm glad you approve."

"Let's go back home, and I'll show you just how much..."

SADE

SADE'S EYES FLUTTERED as Dante sent a trail of kisses down her neck. She gripped his biceps, tilting her head back to give him more room. There was a time she never thought they'd be able to experience this kind of intimacy. Now that they were, Sade wanted to make it last forever.

They undressed each other slowly before Dante carried her to bed. He made his way between her legs, feasting on her before making love to her tenderly until she begged for sweet release. As their bodies pulled apart, Dante made his way on her side and regulated his breathing.

"Wow," she mumbled, wiping her hair off her sweaty forehead. "That was amazing."

"Agreed. I hate I waited so long to reintroduce myself to your pussy now."

Sade chuckled. "That was…" Her head shook as she stared at the ceiling. "As perfect as I always dreamed it would be."

"What do you mean?"

She looked over at him, stumbling over her thoughts. Sade closed her eyes briefly and inhaled a deep breath. "I mean, I've been thinking about this moment since right after the accident. Dreaming about how it would be when we made love again. It was perfect."

Dante took her hand into his and kissed it. "Thank you for being patient with me. It's not that I haven't been attracted to you or wanting this because I have. I just knew sex would change things between us and bring us closer. Before that happened, I wanted to try to connect with you as deeply as possible in other ways."

"Well... How do you feel now?"

"Like I'm the luckiest man on this earth. I have a beautiful, supportive, caring, loving wife. No one is better for me than you."

Sade straddled him, wrapping her arms around his neck and connecting his lips with hers. His hardened shaft throbbed underneath her, causing her to moan. "Is that for me?"

"It is. Sit on it."

With no hesitation, Sade slid down on his shaft, back arching as she made room for him. As she bounced up and down at a medium pace, Dante connected his hands with hers and pulled them behind her back. His tongue slipped into her mouth as he moaned, vocally proving that he was enjoying her just as much as she enjoyed him, and Sade hoped he had the energy to last all night.

DANTE

"WHAT THE FUCK?"

"Dante?" she called, but he didn't reply as he ended the call.

He was too distracted by the bright lights of the truck coming straight toward him. Dante sped up, and the truck did too.

"What are you doing?" he asked, knowing they couldn't hear or respond. "Shit!" he roared, gripping the steering wheel and trying to prepare for impact with the truck. But nothing could have prepared him for that. As soon as the wide truck hit the back of his car, Dante crashed into a light pole. His seat belt kept him from being ejected from the vehicle, but it didn't stop him from being thrown against the front of the car while feeling like his body was being ripped in half.

"Argh!"

Dante grunted, trying to guard his head from the windshield. He flung back, eyes squeezing shut immediately as the airbag opened and pushed into his face and chest. With ringing ears, he tried to stay awake, but that was proving to be more and more difficult. As his eyes fluttered, he noticed an arm reaching into his car through the broken glass. He thought they were trying to help him... but he realized that wasn't the case when their hand went into his pocket to grab his wallet.

"St-sto—"

Before he could tell them to leave his phone and wallet, Dante blacked out.

Jumping up and out of his sleep, Dante struggled to breathe. Chest heaving, he looked around the darkened room, eyes lowering to Sade as she slept beside him. At first, he thought he was having a nightmare; now, he was sure he was having a flashback from the accident. Wiping the sweat from his forehead, Dante released a shaky breath.

He was about to reach down and wake Sade up to talk to her about the dream, but a sharp pain shot through his head. He groaned, squeezing his eyes shut as the pain grew worse. He tried to lower himself back down but felt paralyzed. Sade shifted and turned to his side. Her arm wrapped around him, and when she felt him sitting up, Sade leaned up on her elbow.

"What's wrong?" she asked with sleep thick in her voice.

"My head."

Sade sat up quickly. "Like when you first had the accident?"

He nodded. "I'll get something frozen to put on your head."

He couldn't respond as his head throbbed. Dante wasn't sure how much time had passed, but eventually, Sade returned with something out of the freezer that she was putting on his head where his hand was.

"Try to lie down, baby."

"I can't."

The cold wasn't working like it did in the hospital. The pain was actually getting worse. It was so bad he felt himself getting nauseated. Dante gently pushed Sade to the side and stumbled toward the bathroom, hovering over the toilet as he released the contents in his stomach. When he was sure nothing else would come out, he stood and walked over to the sink. He stood there for a few seconds before oil pulling, brushing his teeth, and doing a few rounds of mouthwash.

As Dante left the bathroom, Sade placed Gatorade and crackers on his side of the bed.

His side of the bed.

This was their first time sleeping together, and *this* was what happened?

What was he supposed to make of that?

Was the memory a good sign... or bad?

"How can I help?" Sade asked, waiting until he was back in bed to cut the light out.

Dante wasn't sure if he wanted to tell her about the memory now. If there was a chance he could piece together what happened to him, he didn't want her concerned and worried about him. One thing Dante could no longer deny was someone had intentionally run into him and left him for dead. Not only had they left him for dead, but they didn't want anyone to know who he was when they found him.

"I feel a little better now."

She stared at him, taking his hand into hers. "Those are symptoms of your injury. We need to get you scheduled for a follow-up appointment, babe."

Sighing, Dante rested his back on the headboard. He'd been avoiding going in for his checkup out of fear of bad news.

"I wanna ask you something, but I need you to promise me you won't make it about your fear for me."

Sade nodded, pulling in a deep breath. "Okay. I can do that."

"I really think someone was trying to kill me the night of the accident."

"I agree. Do you have any idea why?"

"No, not at all. Was I into something illegal?"

"You weren't." Sade pushed her hair out of her face and off her shoulders. "The neurologist did say your immediate memories right before the accident would be limited and possibly never come back at all. So I can't say for sure what you were doing or coming from or who you were talking to, but I can say you weren't doing anything bad or deserving of that."

Dante took a few seconds to process her words. "What about a fight? Was I into it with anyone? Can you think of anyone who would want me dead?"

Her brows bunched, and her nostrils flared. "If that were the case, we would have a lead on this. Trust me, if I knew who did this to you, I would have killed them myself. No fighting, no beef. Like I said, just the issue with quitting the firm, but that could never escalate to something like this."

Dante chuckled as his heart skipped a beat. Her statement probably wasn't meant to arouse him or make him feel so damn good, but it did. Knowing his wife was not only loyal but willing to do whatever to protect him made Dante want to give her the world. He felt the same way about her, even though their relationship was fresh for him. Dante couldn't imagine how crazy about her he was before he lost his memory. It made sense, though; Dante may not have remembered how their love story started, but it was clear they had been close for years, and he felt that bond more and more each day.

"You know I would never let you do some shit like that, though, right? I'd go to war behind you before I ever let you do something like that for me."

Sade smiled before leaning forward slightly and giving him a lingering kiss. "I know, Dante, and I love you for that too."

"C'mere," he requested, wrapping his arm around her and lowering them both down to the bed. As she caressed his chest, Dante told her, "I love you too. I'm really grateful for you sticking by me. You're not going to regret it."

Dante didn't hear her laugh, but he felt her body shudder against him. "I know I won't. Your character is too impeccable for that. Now, go to sleep."

Dante was going to try, but as soon as they stopped talking, his thoughts spiraled again. Who would want to erase him from the world? What had he done to warrant that? Could it have been someone Sade was working to keep him away from? Dante wasn't sure, but he needed answers—soon.

DANTE

The Morning of the Accident

AS HE DID *every morning before going to work, Dante stopped by Fifer's Coffee for a white chocolate mocha and raspberry latte. It would be his first time checking his notifications since he woke up. Dante had a strict habit of not reading, watching, or listening to anything that would negatively affect his mood before having his morning coffee. Though most of his job relied on his abilities, he spent much time interacting with clients and always wanted to be kind and sincere.*

"Hey."

At the sound of a woman's voice, Dante set his phone on the table and gave her his attention. He looked her over, not finding her face familiar at all.

"Hello."

"I'm sorry to interrupt, but I was wondering if you work at Four Financial."

"I do." Dante used his hand to motion toward the empty seat at his small, round table. "Are you a current or future client?"

She sat across from him. "Current, but I don't think I'll be working with you all for long."

Concern filled Dante as he looked over her beautiful brown face. Being married had never stopped him from appreciating the opposite sex, and even though slightly irritated, this woman was beautiful.

"What's the problem? Maybe I can help."

"Well..." She shifted in her seat uncomfortably. *"I was pleased the first time I worked with you all. You helped me with my taxes and then a loan. When I came back to start trying to build my credit, that's when I started having issues."*

"What kind of issues?" Dante asked, quickly thanking the waitress who'd brought his latte over. He asked the woman if she wanted something, and she told him she'd already ordered.

"I was charged three times the amount I was told. When I called trying to get that issue corrected, I could never get ahold of anyone. When I finally did speak to someone, they sent me a receipt that proved the charge was accurate, but it wasn't what I was originally given."

"Hmm, that sounds like it may have been a software glitch. Do you have your original receipt?"

She nodded. *"I do. I have the original one and the updated one."*

"Okay." Dante pulled his wallet out and handed her his business card. *"Email me a screenshot of both receipts, and I'll refund the entire amount to you."*

Her smile was genuine as she accepted the card. *"Thank you. I really appreciate that."* She paused. *"Is it okay if I share your information with my sister too?"*

"She had an issue as well?"

"Yes. Honestly, everyone that I referred lately has. Like I said, I was pleased with your services at first. Maybe it's because I was working with someone different then. But everyone I've recommended to you over the past six months has had an issue."

"Send me their names and emails as well. I'll make sure I get everything straightened out."

Dante stood, ready to get to work even more now. He hated hearing that his clients were having issues. Though he was in business with three other people, Four Financial was his dream. His passion.

His baby. If something were going on behind the scenes that needed to be addressed, Dante would be the one to do it.

"Okay, I will."

"Who was the last person you worked with?"

"Well, I worked with Jessica, but that's not who sent my statements. I emailed a woman named Armani, I believe."

Dante smiled. "Imani. That's my wife. Don't worry; we'll take care of this for you."

"Thank you…"

"Dante."

Dante extended his hand for her to shake, and she accepted. "Thank you, Dante. I really appreciate your help. I hate to complain, but I don't have $5,000 to blow like that, especially on my credit."

"Five thousand dollars?" Dante repeated a little louder than he wanted to before chuckling. "Yeah, we're definitely gonna get that taken care of for you. No credit repair services should ever cost that much with us."

After saying their goodbyes, Dante grabbed his coffee and headed out.

"Five thousand dollars," he grumbled under his breath as he headed to his car. "How in the fuck did the software do that?"

Initially, Dante's priority for the day would be their tax statements. Now, he needed to look into this too.

SADE

Back to the Present
Two Weeks Later

IT WAS LATE March, and Sade and Dante had just gotten back into town from San Juan. Puerto Rico was one of their favorite places to visit because of its proximity. Admittedly, Sade would use her money to live on different islands every month if she had someone to experience that with. Now... she had Dante... and she couldn't believe how something so tragic could work out for her good.

As they walked hand in hand into Muggie's Grocery, Sade asked, "Are you sure about this, babe? We can go to a restaurant and grab something to eat. It's been a long day."

"Nah. I want some home-cooked food."

Nodding in agreement, Sade allowed her eyes to scan the grocery store. Now that they were back home, she was back on high alert. Words couldn't express how good and freeing it was fully relaxing in her relationship with Dante and not worrying about anyone recognizing him. The peace she felt had her wanting to consider asking Dante to move. He wasn't working, she could work anywhere, and they both had more than enough money saved to go wherever they wanted to go.

When she was alone, Vanzette was the perfect home. Now, Sade wanted more.

"What do you have a taste for?"

"Something southern and unhealthy."

Sade chuckled as she grabbed a basket. "Bet. Let's do... fried chicken, yams, mac and cheese, purple hull peas, and greens. We won't have to cook again for a whole week."

"What about dessert? I got a feeling you make great homemade cookies. Is that right?"

Her mouth dropped before she nodded. "I do. You love my chocolate chip cookies. I don't put a lot of chips in them, and I have a secret ingredient you love."

"Cool. So let's do that then."

"O—" Sade's mouth snapped shut at the sight of the neurologist the attending doctor in Memphis recommended for Dante's follow-up care. So far, Dante hadn't mentioned making an appointment, so she couldn't help but say, "There's Dr. Shane. Why don't we go say hello?"

Dante's eyes shifted in Dr. Shane's direction before he shook his head no. "Nah. He'll just ask me about the appointment I missed and try to get me to reschedule it."

Not replying right away, Sade turned slightly and leaned against the basket. "Why wouldn't you want to?"

"I feel okay. I don't feel like I need to go."

"But what about the symptoms you've had lately, Dante?"

"I'm about to go grab a few bottles of wine. I'll meet you so we can get everything and not stay here too long."

Not bothering to go back and forth with him, Sade merely nodded and watched as he walked away. Once he did, she couldn't stop from going to Dr. Shane. So far, Dante hadn't regained his memory yet, and she couldn't help but wonder if that meant he never would. If not, the only thing that would ruin her ruse was someone from their past seeing them together. Sure, there was the nasty inconvenience of him marrying another woman, but that was something Sade planned to take up with God and God alone.

"Hi," she spoke quietly. "Dr. Shane?"

He turned, giving a polite smile, but she could tell he didn't recognize her. Sade wouldn't take offense. She couldn't imagine how many people he came in contact with daily.

"I am, and you are?"

"Sade. I'm not a patient of yours, but my husband is. Well, he was supposed to be. You saw him in Memphis, and he was supposed to have his follow-up appointments with you here."

He scratched his jaw. "Memphis... I remember that. He was in an accident, right?"

"Yes!" Sade agreed excitedly. "That's him."

"How is he doing?"

"He's... He says he's okay, but he's been having symptoms lately, and I'm concerned."

Dr. Shane's expression turned serious. "What kind of symptoms?"

Sade rubbed her lips together as she thought over everything happening for the last two weeks. "Migraines, throwing up or being nauseated, his mood is sporadic. Those are the biggest ones. I think he's having flashes of memory, but he won't confide in me about them because he doesn't want me to worry. So I don't know if the symptoms are because of the memories, the head injury, or both."

"Hmm," Dr. Shane hummed, massaging his chin. "After the accident, there was blood on his brain, correct?"

"Yes. And it was swollen. That's why we had to wait so long for him to be seen by the hospital neurologist and you."

He nodded. "I need to get him in my office for some scans and tests. He could have a blood clot or more blood on his brain. If I remember correctly, he was dealing with high blood pressure too. We wanted to get a handle on that with a primary physician because it was stroke-level high. Now, I don't know if that's something he has struggled with or was because of the situation, but if it is possible, you need to get your husband an appointment with me and a general practitioner."

As far as Sade knew, Dante hadn't struggled with his blood pressure, or at least that he knew of. That was probably why his doctor emphasized avoiding stress and anger before he was discharged.

"I will do my very best. Can I..." She looked around, making sure Dante was nowhere around. "Can I ask one last question?"

"Sure."

"With him having small flashbacks, is there a chance he will fully regain his memory soon?"

Dr. Shane's mouth twisted as he sighed and shook his head. "I can't say for sure. The mind is a tricky thing. Sometimes, when damage occurs, it's permanent; sometimes, it comes back on its own. I'm less concerned about his memory and more about him having blood clots. Get that appointment scheduled for him as soon as you can."

Sade nodded and thanked him before walking away. Dr. Shane may not have been concerned about his memory, but Sade definitely was.

DANTE

A Few Days Later

IT WAS DATE night, and Dante had gotten to a point where he genuinely looked forward to them. Even though he wasn't working, Dante refused to sit around the house all day. Until the accident, he was sure he'd forever want to work with money and numbers. Now, it felt like he had the chance to start a different path in his life. He had half a million dollars saved in his personal account, so the need to quickly begin working again wasn't there. Dante decided to consider other ways to make money instead of immediately going back into finance, though a part of him felt like he'd always return to that field.

"How was your day?" Sade asked before taking a sip of her lemonade.

She looked beautiful, as always. Her hair was in its signature style, with big, bouncing curls. Her honey-brown skin was covered in an orange spaghetti-strapped maxi dress that complemented her skin tone perfectly. Every time Dante looked into her dark, under-turned eyes, he was captivated by them.

"Good. Productive. I met with a commercial realtor to get information on the available properties in town. Not sure what I'd do with the building yet, but I want to exhaust all possible options."

"That's great, babe. I always say your purpose is for the world, and your passion is for yourself. You did a lot of great work at the firm. That was your purpose. Maybe now's your chance to do something for yourself. Something you're passionate about."

Dante considered her words as he shifted in his seat. "You know I love having a good time and bringing people together. Are there a lot of lounges here? Maybe I'll open a thirty-and-up lounge and host different events nightly. That way, if I decide to get back into finance, the two won't conflict."

"There aren't a lot of lounges, so I think that's a great idea. We only have one here, actually, and it's more like a bar at this point. They don't host events, so that would definitely set you apart."

Nodding, Dante tucked that bit of information into his brain. "How was your day? You reopened your online storefront this morning, right?"

"I did." Sade smiled widely, doing a small dance in her seat. "I made double the amount of canvas paintings I usually make available and sold out in two hours."

"That's great, Smiley, I'm really proud of you."

Her low eyes grew even lower as her smile dropped. It seemed like a permanent fixture on her face. Sade's mouth opened slightly, eyes blinking rapidly. She cleared her throat, head hanging as it shook.

"Is everything okay?" Dante checked.

"Umm..." She chuckled softly, looking into his eyes. "Why did you call me that?"

Confusion filled him as he stared at her. "You have the most beautiful smile I've ever seen, not to mention those dimples. I've never seen a more beautiful sight than your smiling face."

Sade smiled warmly as her eyes watered. Her breath came out shaky as she wiped away a tear.

"Sade..."

"You... That was your nickname for me since we met. I didn't think I'd ever hear you say that after the accident."

As her tongue rolled across her teeth, Dante stood and walked over to her side of the table to comfort her. She stood, quickly making her way into his waiting embrace.

"Why did you call me that?" she asked, just above a whisper, holding him tightly.

"Seemed like the perfect nickname, Day. Maybe I knew that's what I called you, and it just came out naturally."

She put a little space between them, swallowing back tears as she looked into his eyes—almost as if she was searching for something. Dante wasn't sure what Sade was looking for, but he hoped she found it.

Their waitress putting their food on the table caused Sade to remove herself from his grip. They sat down, and like she always did, Sade took a picture of both plates before they held hands and said grace.

"Do you want to try this?" Sade asked, picking through her seafood bag. They'd gone to a seafood steakhouse, which provided a happy medium for both their appetites. Dante chose a steak while she'd gotten a seafood boil with crab, shrimp, and mussels.

Dante's eyes shifted to her hand as she lifted the shrimp from the bag.

"Do I want a shrimp?" he asked skeptically, to which she nodded.

"Yeah, it's not too spicy if that's what you're worried about."

Dante chuckled, shaking his head as he cut into his steak. "I'm allergic to shrimp, Sade."

"Oh." She laughed nervously. "That's right. I don't know how I forgot."

Dante eyed her skeptically before taking a bite of his steak. That wasn't the kind of thing anyone should forget about someone they cared about. But things happened. Maybe she was just caught up in him calling her an old nickname, and it slipped her mind. Regardless, Dante was going to let it go. At that point, he was glad he remembered the things about himself that he did. Initially, he hated forgetting details about everyone else in his life, but Dante was even more grateful for his self-awareness if this indicated the self-preservation needed to survive.

"What do you have planned for the rest of the day?" Dante asked, deciding to change the subject.

"Nothing. My maintenance day is tomorrow, so I might just chill. Maybe go to a bar tonight and grab a few drinks. What about you?"

Dante shrugged. He didn't know what to do, but he would do *something*. But it felt weird not having friends or at least cousins to hang out with. Dante was done trying to figure out what happened with his old crew. They hadn't stopped by the house or called Sade to check on him, so maybe his not knowing about them was for the best. He would, however, start going out more to make new friends. Though he still dealt with slight stiffness from time to time, his knees were feeling almost normal.

"Not sure. I'm going to get into something, though. Now that I'm moving around normally, I don't plan to be in the house as much."

Sade chuckled. "I'm surprised you lasted as long as you did. I'm proud of you, though. In case you don't remember, you love the downtown scene. It's not as lively and crowded as other cities, but it's really fun. That's where people around our age hang. Lots of bars, one has live music, and there is one club down there too. It's really just a huge party every weekend once it starts getting warm."

"That sounds like the move, then. It's been a while since I hit up a club or a lounge. I'm sure that'll be fun. Care to join me?" Dante asked, more so out of consideration and accommodation. Though he enjoyed their time together, he loved it when they were apart too. He didn't want to become so dependent on Sade because he felt like she was all he had, that he shifted from love to need.

"Thanks for the invitation, but you usually do your club hopping without me."

"Good." He released a breath of relief, smiling when she laughed. "I asked because it felt like the right thing to do."

"And I appreciate that, but trust me, you'll have more fun without me. Clubs aren't my thing. I love lounges, though. We go there together, but you used to club with your friends. Maybe you'll find some new ones when you go out tonight. Friendship always meant more to you than it did to me."

"Why is that?"

Sade shrugged, her expression softening. "I grew up feeling very alone, so I guess I just got used to it. I have associates, but I don't care to speak with them daily or see them often. That was always your thing."

That made sense, and Dante was glad Sade was honest and understanding. Things like that made him even happier that she was his life partner, and he hoped nothing would ever change that.

SADE

IN NO RUSH to get out and go into the beauty shop, Sade considered returning her sister Imani's several missed phone calls and text messages. Since Dante had come to her home, Sade had silenced her sister's notifications. The last thing she wanted was for Imani to call or text while she was with Dante and have to explain who she was and why she hadn't mentioned having a sister. At the hospital, Sade said her parents died, and her grandparents raised her, intentionally leaving out details about her sister, and Sade wasn't ready to tell the truth just yet.

On top of wondering what her sister wanted, Sade didn't know what to expect when she entered Michelle's salon. She hadn't seen Trina since their run-in at the restaurant, and Sade didn't know if Trina had taken her threat seriously. She also didn't know if Trina had gone to the police. Typically, their hair appointments fell on the same days every two weeks, so Sade knew there was a great chance that Trina was already inside.

Recognizing that fear was a lack of control, Sade reminded herself there was no point hiding in the car. Trina was going to do what Trina was going to do. If that led to Sade's arrest, so be it. It would be a hard lesson to learn to remind her to control her rage, but protecting her secret was worth it.

Sade stepped inside, eyes scanning the waiting area first. Patrice was there, as usual. Their eyes locked briefly, but there was no anger or curiosity in Patrice's. She merely gave Sade a head nod before returning her attention to her phone. Like always, Sade walked over to Michelle and spoke before going to the waiting area. Trina was in her chair, and she made sure to avoid Sade's eyes the whole time. Holding back her smile, Sade breathed a little easier. Seemed Trina was a hell of a lot smarter than she looked.

Purposefully putting space between them, Sade sat on the opposite side of the waiting area as Patrice. Their eyes only locked once before Trina left, Patrice went to the shampoo bowl, and Sade was in Michelle's seat for her preshampoo scalp massage.

To Sade's surprise, her appointment went by without any issues. She left the salon an hour and a half later with her hair feeling refreshed and a smile on her face. Once she made it to her car, she took a quick selfie and sent it to Dante before finally breaking down and returning Imani's calls. The phone rang twice before Imani answered with, "Where the hell have you been, and why haven't you been answering my calls?"

Sighing, Sade rested her head against the headrest. Imani was only calling Sade because her life was unraveling. Before everything went down, the sisters spoke once a month and saw each other only for birthdays and holidays. That disconnect affected her friendship with Dante too. Had it not been for Sade's twin nieces and Dante, Sade would have completely cut her sister out of her life.

"I've been busy. What's up?"

"You've been busy?" Imani repeated in an accusatory tone before scoffing. "So busy that you can't answer your sister's phone calls knowing my life is fucking falling apart? God, you are so selfish, Sade. I don't even know why I've been trying to talk to you."

Unfazed by her sister's dramatics, Sade sighed and shook her head. "I don't know either. It's not like we're close. I don't know what you want me to say or do, Imani."

"I want you to say my husband will be found, and I'm not going to jail over this bullshit! I want you to tell me that everything will be all right. I want you to invite me to Vanzette so I can get a fucking break! Every day, it seems like someone asks me about the firm, all these charges, or Dante being missing." Imani paused, breath shaky, and her emotion caught Sade by surprise. "I just... need to get away for a day or two. Can I come and see you soon? Please, big sister."

Sade groaned. Until now, Imani had never expressed an interest in visiting her in Vanzette, or anywhere else, for that matter. Sade had been living there since they graduated from college, and Imani hadn't even bothered to come to her housewarming. There was one way for Imani to soften Sade's heart, though, and that was by reminding her she was the older sister—even if just by one year.

Just three months after Sade was born, Imani was conceived. As close as the sisters were in their early years, one would think they would have been the best of friends, but that wasn't the case. Things changed in Sade's eighth-grade year. Imani was in the seventh grade and had a growth spurt that made her look like the older sister. On top of Imani's budding body, she was on the cheerleading team and more sociable and popular than her older sister. After winning two homecoming queen crowns back-to-back, Imani became one of the most popular middle school girls when she graduated.

Sade, however, thrived being in the background. Her looks and personality took a backseat to her sister's. She decided to focus on her studies and stayed to herself. In Sade's first year of high school, she wanted to be a ghost. Dante wouldn't allow that. The two became friends, and he brought her into his fold. Things were almost perfect... until Imani arrived. Then, everything changed.

"Fine," Sade granted. "Just give me a heads-up of when you want to come."

"Yay! I will. I need to get a few things situated with the firm and make sure Grandma and Grandpa can keep the twins, and then I'll let you know."

"Okay," Sade agreed unwillingly before disconnecting the call.

"Why did I say she could come?" Sade muttered under her breath. "If she finds out Dante is with me and that he thinks we're married, everything will be over."

As Sade started her car, she tried to think of a way to appease Imani and ensure she didn't run into Dante before leaving for Memphis. It would be tricky but doable. There was no way in hell Sade would let Imani know Dante was with her. She didn't believe Imani was worthy of Dante when they first started dating, and she for damn sure didn't believe her sister was worthy of him now.

At the sound of her car making a dinging noise, Sade shifted her focus to the dashboard. At the sight of her tire pressure being low for all four tires, Sade cursed under her breath and got out. All she could do was chuckle at the sight of every one of her tires being slashed. Trina was responsible for this. There was no doubt about it.

Leaning against her car, Sade considered calling AAA or Dante. If she called Dante, he'd question her about why her tires had been slashed, and that was a conversation she wanted to avoid. Instead, she decided to have her tires changed and not bother mentioning it to Dante. The entire time she scheduled her pickup, Sade thought of ways to make Trina pay.

SADE

Summer Break before Their Senior Year of College

SADE'S GRANDMOTHER, AVA, *oiled her scalp as they watched* One Life to Live. *At school, she longed to be with her grandmother, talking, cooking, or watching soap operas for comfort. Even before Sade's parents died the summer before her last year of high school, she found the most comfort with her grandparents, Ava and Barron.*

Though Sade had a healthy relationship with her parents and knew they loved her, they coddled Imani more and showed her more attention because she was younger. Even if just by a year, that year sometimes felt like it put decades between Sade and Imani. Sade felt she had to mature quicker while Imani could enjoy her childhood and innocence more. Not just by how she was able to dress, enjoy life, and have no responsibilities, but by how their parents cared for her as well.

Both in college, Sade was forced to work and focus on her studies while their parents gave Imani a weekly allowance. They said it was because Sade was more mature and able to handle it, but Sade didn't think that was fair. Since middle school, Sade sought solace from being alone at their grandparents' house, but when their parents died, they both had to move in with them. Now, Imani hardly came over, and Sade was grateful for that.

When a commercial break came on, Ava asked Sade, "What are your plans for the summer?"

"*Not too much. I might take a couple of trips, but that's it. You remember Nya?*"

"*The skinny little girl you went to high school with?*"

Sade chuckled. "*Yes, her. Well, her family has a rental house that she's staying in, so I might go with her. It's in the Hamptons, though, so I don't know.*"

"*Ooh, that's where all the wealthy people go. Chile, you better have yourself a good time there. Who knows? Maybe you'll catch yourself a man.*"

They shared a soft laugh.

"*Grandma, you know I'm not thinking about a man until I finish school.*"

"*I commend you for that, but you know it's all right to enjoy your life, right?*" *Sade's eyes rolled, knowing exactly where this conversation was going.* "*You need more than me and your grandpa and Dante. More than people you talk to every now and again like Mya.*"

"*Nya,*" *Sade corrected.*

"*Whoever. You need a community, Sade. And that should include a man of your own. Contrary to what you and Imani think, you can't share Dante forever.*"

Sade sucked her teeth as she lifted her head from Ava's lap. "*We don't share him, Grandma. He's my best friend and her boyfriend. Besides, he was my friend first. I can't believe she followed him to UT Chatt, knowing she always wanted to go to TSU. I feel like I'll never get away from that girl.*"

"*Now, now, that's your sister. And you know how I feel. If Dante causes that much hate between the two of you, neither of you needs to deal with him.*"

"*It's not Dante; it's her. She's always hated me. I don't even care anymore.*"

Someone knocked on the door before the screen door opened.

"*Who's that coming up in my house?*" *Barron called from the kitchen.*

Sade didn't have to get up and look to know he was seated at the coffee table reading a book with a cigarette hanging between his lips.

"It's me, Gramps. Tay."

"Come in here before you leave. Let me holla at ya."

"Yes, sir."

Dante gave Ava a kiss and a side hug before lifting Sade to her feet.

"Your ears must have been ringing," Ava said. "We were just talking about you."

"Uh-oh. Was it bad?"

Sade chuckled as she pulled her hair up into a bun. "You don't want to know."

Dante chuckled as Ava swatted them both out of the living room since her show was back on.

"What are you doing here?" Sade asked, following him outside.

"I need to talk to you about something."

They walked to his car, and when he opened the passenger-side door for her and Sade saw the white lilies, a pretzel from her favorite shop in the mall, and a teddy bear, she smiled. She tried to cover it with her hand, but Dante pushed it down.

"Let me see that beautiful smile."

His request only made her smile spread wider. "What did you do?"

Dante laughed. "Why you think I did something?"

"It's not my birthday or Valentine's Day, so you must have done something wrong."

Dante sucked his teeth before smiling. "Just get in the car, Smiley. Damn."

She rolled her eyes playfully and moved a few things around before climbing in. As he made his way to the driver's side, Sade considered what Dante could have wanted to talk to her about. Surprisingly, their summer had been pretty drama-free. That had a lot to do with the fact that Imani was in Atlanta. She'd be back in a week, though. Maybe that was what Dante's trip and treats were about.

When Dante got inside, he released a huff of breath and looked over at her. "You look nice today."

"Thanks," Sade replied absently, her mind too concerned with where this conversation was going. "What's going on, Tay?"

"Have you talked to your sister lately?" he checked, leaning his head against the headrest.

"Of course not. Why?"

"She's pregnant, Sade." Sade closed her eyes and pulled in a deep breath. It didn't calm her the way she thought it would, so she took another one. And another. "Day..." Opening her eyes, Sade stared into his. "I'm sorry."

Sade scoffed. Her hand and left leg shook as she looked away from him. "Why are you apologizing?"

"Felt like what I was supposed to say."

She clenched her jaw, hoping that would keep her tears from falling. It was bad enough that she never had a chance to be with Dante, and even worse, after sharing with Imani that she had a crush on him, Imani pursued him. Now, Sade was supposed to deal with the fact that they were about to have a baby together?

That was supposed to be her baby—not Imani's.

"Congratulations," she mumbled, gripping the door handle.

"I'm gonna ask her to marry me," he blurted, causing Sade to jerk her head in his direction.

"What? Why?"

"Because I wanna do right by her and my kid. I want them to have the same upbringing I did."

"Your parents loved each other and wanted to be married, though. Can you say that's the case for you and my sister?"

Dante licked the corner of his mouth and looked away. "It doesn't matter. I'm going to ask her to marry me. I just... wanted to let you know first."

Sade brushed a tear away before it could fall as she bobbed her head. "Okay. Thanks for the heads-up."

She opened the door, and as she got out, Dante said, "Don't forget your stuff."

Not wanting him to see her tears as they fell, Sade kept her back to him as she said, "I don't want it."

"Day, ple—"

She closed the door quickly, speed walking back into the house. Bypassing her grandmother, she rushed to her room and slammed the door behind her. The second her body connected with the bed, her tears erupted. A few seconds later, the door opened and closed. A body indented the bed beside her, but she didn't bother looking up to see who it was. At the feel of his hand on her shoulder, Sade moved so that it would fall. She turned her back to him, unable to face him.

"I'm not trying to hurt you, Day. You're my best friend. Why are you so upset? I thought you'd be proud of me for stepping up."

Sade laughed as she wiped her face. "For someone so smart, you can be really dumb, Dante."

"Look, I know you and Imani have your issues, but you're just gonna have to get over them. We're about to have your little niece or nephew, and I need you by my side. I want you to be my best woman at the wedding. Please don't be mad at me, Smiley."

Each statement he made felt like a dagger going deeper and deeper into her heart. Sniffling, Sade requested, "Just get out, Tay. Please."

"Fine, but I need you to promise me that whatever issues you and her have will stop coming between me and you."

"You really don't get it, do you?" Sade sat up and faced him. "You're the biggest issue we have. Imani only went after you because I told her I liked you, and now you're marrying her."

Dante's head tilted as his mouth opened in surprise. He snapped it shut and swallowed hard, briefly looking away.

"Why didn't you say anything?" he asked softly.

"Come on, Dante." Sade laughed bitterly. "You know I wasn't your type back then. Besides, you never had a problem pursuing girls you were interested in. Since you never flirted with me, I figured you didn't like me. I wasn't going to set myself up to be rejected."

"Sade." He chuckled, taking her hand into his. "I used to flirt with your dense ass all the time. Like all the fucking time. How could you not see that?"

Now... Sade was looking at him as if she didn't understand.

"You liked me?" she asked softly, but before he could answer, she hopped off the bed and put space between them. "It doesn't matter. You're with my sister, she's pregnant, and you're going to ask her to marry you. It doesn't matter. You need to just... go."

Sade left the room, locking herself in the bathroom so he couldn't come inside. As she sat on the toilet seat, she rocked back and forth as silent tears fell. Was he lying to spare her feelings? No. Dante had always been honest with her. If he said he liked her, he liked her. All this time, she had no idea. Imani hadn't taken Dante from her; she'd practically given him away. At that realization, Sade's silent sobs gained a voice. She covered her mouth, trying to keep them from getting too loud, but it was useless. There was nothing she could do to stop the years of pain that were finally being released.

SADE

ADMITTEDLY, SADE'S MOOD had been sour for the entire trip back to Vanzette. Not only had they thoroughly enjoyed themselves, and she didn't want that to be over, but getting out of town had the opposite effect on Dante. She hoped it would make him want fewer details about his past and the people involved, but that wasn't the case. A part of her loved the idea of Dante remembering himself but no one else from his past, but now, his desire to learn more was driving her crazy. Eventually, he would take matters into his own hands, which was the last thing she needed, so Sade had mentally prepared to create the life she wanted Dante to believe he had.

On top of that, Sade was nervous about her sister coming to town to visit. While she had her reasons for keeping Dante's whereabouts a secret, no one would care to listen or try to understand why. When she first found Dante, she didn't intend to lie and say she was his wife. Sade only said that to ensure she could find and see him. After that, the lie took on a life of its own. Learning that he had no recollection of her allowed Sade the opportunity to rewrite history. To finally beat her sister and get the man of her dreams. She didn't think she'd get away with it for as long as she had, but now, Sade was invested and too damn happy to let Imani ruin the life she was building with Dante—even if she was his real wife.

Real wife.

If Imani could even be considered that.

Dante and Imani's relationship had its fair share of ups and downs. And betrayal. And secrets. And lies. And disrespect.

It was Imani's fault that Dante was accused of stealing from customers and the government through his taxes. Imani had made it her business to keep Dante's charges at the forefront of everyone's mind. They didn't believe he was capable of what he was being charged with and accused of, but with Imani's "proof," it was easier for people to believe he was guilty. Now, the FBI and MPD have expanded their search. If Dante was alive and well, they were more convinced that he was avoiding Memphis and punishment.

As far as Memphis knew, Dante was on the run, avoiding federal prison, and Sade was content with keeping it that way. His parents had finally reached out to her, and she didn't answer. Sade couldn't stomach lying to them. They would find it odd that Sade wasn't back in Memphis trying to help them search for Dante. How would she be able to explain that? She couldn't, so Sade remained silent instead.

Imani made a grave mistake by telling Sade she was responsible for the theft and money laundering that Dante had been charged with. Without that piece of information, Sade probably wouldn't have had the balls to lie to her sister.

Her sister.

The pair hadn't treated each other like family since they were children. Imani's popularity led to her becoming insufferable while they were in school, to the point where the two had become enemies. Sade held more loyalty to Dante than her own flesh and blood, and she slept peacefully at night knowing that.

Once they had their bags back inside, Sade told him, "I've been thinking."

"About?"

"It's kind of selfish of me to try to convince you that you're better off not knowing the people in your life instead of letting you figure that out for yourself."

Dante's head tilted as he ran his hand over the waves in his head. "You had the right intention behind it. Besides, they aren't looking for me, so that makes it clear that they really don't give a fuck about me."

That wasn't true. At all. His parents and friends were tearing the city up, looking for him. His wife was too, but not because she missed him; Imani wanted Dante back home in Memphis so he could deal with the mess she'd made with their business. Without him there as the scapegoat, the spotlight was on her. No one had thought to check in Vanzette with Sade because they didn't think Sade would keep him away. They also didn't think he'd go to her if he were in trouble. Sade could understand that. To them, she was simply his wife's sister. But to Dante, Sade had always been one of his best friends.

"I understand and respect that, but I just wanted to let you know if you wanted to reach out to your parents, I could set that up for you. They don't live here, but I'm sure they'd come down if they knew about the accident."

Dante released a hard breath. "One part of me believes connecting with them might help me remember my past with you all. The other part of me is hurt because they haven't reached out to me in months. Even with me not having that same phone and number, they could have reached out to you." Dante paused, patting the couch for her to sit next to him. "Were you close to my family?"

Sade shrugged as she sat next to him. "I wanted a close bond with your mom, and we had that when we were younger. Not so much now. We get along, but it's not the kind of relationship where we talk. We have a good time when we're in each other's presence, but we don't put forth the effort to make it a daily or weekly thing."

After nodding his understanding, Dante took her hand into his and kissed it. "I'm accepting the idea of rebuilding my life and family here with you. I met some cool people at the club, and I want us to see about starting our family soon. For right now, I'm content with that, but if that changes, I'll let you know."

Sade nodded, remaining silent. There were days Dante didn't want to know more about the people he couldn't remember and others where it was what he craved. Though he appeared content right now, Sade would put a plan in motion in case he changed his mind so she could be prepared.

She stood, deciding, "I'm gonna shower and take a nap. I really enjoyed this time away with you. It was absolutely perfect."

"Yeah, I did too. You were so relaxed and carefree. I loved seeing that side of you."

"You don't think I'm like that at home?"

"Here, yes, but when we go out, no. You're often on edge."

"Well... I guess I just don't like going out here a lot, but I love traveling, so..." She shrugged and looked away. Sade wanted to tell him she was a loner, that she didn't go out much before him because she'd gotten used to being alone. That on top of him being her truest best friend—he was also a missing person, one whose identity could easily be revealed by one glance of a person who kept up with Memphis news. Instead of saying any of that, Sade added, "I didn't realize it was that noticeable."

"I notice everything about you, Smiley. Even the things you might not want me to."

He held her gaze for a few seconds. Though his face was expressionless, his eyes were playful, sending a chill down her spine. *What the hell was that supposed to mean?*

SADE

Right before Dante and Imani's Wedding

SADE CHUGGED THE *half pint of vodka before stuffing the empty bottle into her purse. She looked toward the ballroom, unsure what the hell she was doing there. Well, she was there because Dante had asked her to be. She told him she wouldn't be involved in the wedding, but, as always, Sade was willing to show up for her best friend in any way possible. Not just because she loved him but because Dante had that same energy behind her.*

With a sigh, Sade lowered the visor and checked her makeup. Satisfied with what she saw, she stepped out of her car and grabbed her custom-made suit jacket from the backseat. It was burgundy and form-fitting, just like the rest of Dante's wedding party. The only difference was, instead of her having black accents and accessories like they did, she had white ones to match his white tuxedo with burgundy accents.

Sade ran her hands down her bone-straight hair, then slowly trudged toward the church in her six-inch heels. When she entered, all eyes and smiles were on her. Whispers were permeating the foyer from guests who were probably just as surprised as Sade was to see her there. No matter how she felt about her sister, Sade would show up for Dante.

At the sight of her grandparents, Sade smiled genuinely for the first time that day. She walked over and gave them both a hug, fighting back her tears when her grandmother whispered she was proud of her.

How long would that pride last?

Sade made her way to the left. The bride and groom each had their own suites. She made her way over to Dante's and knocked. Deandre opened the door, and when he saw her, he pulled Sade into his arms and proclaimed, "There's my girl!"

Giggling, Sade hugged him back. "You know I wouldn't miss this, Daddy Williams."

"I'm glad." Deandre's tone lowered when he said, "He needs you."

Sade's heart sank. She stepped inside, unable to ignore the somber energy surrounding Dante while everyone else laughed and talked. She walked over, squeezing his shoulder as he stared at the floor. Dante looked up, and at the sight of her, his head hung again as he chuckled. He released a shaky breath before he stood and embraced her. Holding her tight, he confessed, "I've never been happier to see anyone in my life. I couldn't have done this without you, Smiley."

"There's nowhere else I'd be. You're my best friend, Dante, and I'm proud of you. You've grown and matured into an amazing man, and there's no doubt you'll be an amazing father and husband. I pray God honors this commitment the two of you are making and that He equips you to be life partners and lovers for the rest of your days."

Dante took her hands into his and kissed them both. "Thank you, Day. That means a lot to me."

At the sound of Imani's yell, everyone rushed out of the suite. Sade lagged, holding back a smile. She took slow steps toward the commotion, covering her mouth at seeing Imani's wedding dress. It was ripped to shreds in the front.

"You!" Imani screamed, pointing at Sade. "You did this! You hate that I'm marrying him, so you ruined Mommy's dress!"

"You ruined her prom dress when I wore it." Sade shrugged. "Now we're even." Imani charged toward Sade, but too many arms were wrapping around her. "Relax, Imani. I had a duplicate made just to teach you a lesson. The real dress is in my car."

"Ugh!" Imani groaned loudly as Sade yelled and headed outside. "I hate you, Sade! You make me sick to my stomach. Now is not the time to be playing these games!"

"Yeah, yeah, yeah," Sade grumbled, too amused to be swayed by her sister's anger.

Sade hadn't noticed anyone following her, so when she grabbed the dress and saw Dante, she jumped and clutched her chest.

"Jesus, Dante. You scared the hell out of me."

"You just couldn't resist, could you?"

She chuckled and shook her head. "Nope. And I don't feel bad about it one bit."

Dante's head shook as he laughed softly. "What am I gonna do with you, Sade?"

Her expression grew solemn as she looked into his eyes. "Not much of anything now." Sighing, she took a step away from him. "Me and Imani have our issues, but marriage is different. I think we should restructure our friendship after today. She's your wife and... We have to respect the role you're giving her. I know we've been friends for what feels like forever, but... Maybe we should put some distance between us after today."

His tongue rolled across his cheek as he took a step toward her. "I don't want to agree, but you're right. I have to prioritize her and the baby, and I don't want her beefing with you to cause tension daily in our home."

"Glad we're on the same page."

"Can I tell you the real reason I asked you to be my best woman?" Sade nodded. "I knew this would be the closest I'd get to have you in marriage. At my wedding. I wanted you on my right because I know you'll never be on my left as my wife."

"Dante, please..."

"You deserve the truth. I've never given you anything less."

She looked away, willing her tears not to fall. "Go on and get ready, Tay. I'll be in there shortly."

He looked her over for a few seconds before kissing the center of her forehead and walking away. Once Sade was composed, she headed back inside to give Imani the dress. When she tried to walk into the bridal suite, her grandmother stopped her with, "Are you going to behave?"

Sade chuckled. "Yes, ma'am. I promise."

Ava nodded and stepped to the side so she could enter. Imani was in her robe, seated in front of a vanity mirror. Sade handed her the dress, but before she could walk away, Imani grabbed her wrist and stood.

"I'm hurt," Imani confessed, and it caught Sade by surprise. The sisters had never really expressed their feelings to one another, and even when they did, it was usually anger or happiness.

"Why?"

Imani's eyes rolled as she told everyone, "Get out." Once they were in the room alone, she admitted, "Mommy isn't here. Grandma is, but... you're the closest person I have to Mommy. We shared her womb. I was just hoping today would be a day we could be normal sisters. I wanted you here with me, Sade."

Sade's tone was low when she asked, "Are you being sincere?"

"Yes," Imani seethed, tightening her grip on Sade's wrist. "Look, I know I haven't been the nicest sister..." Sade chuckled before she could stop it, causing Imani to drop the hold she had on her wrist and turn her back to Sade. "I'm trying to be mature!"

"All right, all right. I apologize." Sade stepped in front of Imani so she could look into her eyes. "I know we called ourselves calling a truce after Mom and Dad died, but neither of us have been taking it seriously."

"I can agree. I know I had a lot to do with that. You always tell me I'm not easy to love."

Sade's body crumbled along with her heart. "I shouldn't have said that."

"It's true. I haven't made it easy for you or anyone else to love me."

"Is there a particular reason why? I mean... you were a little troll when we were kids, but... it seems it's gotten worse since we've been adults."

Sade held her breath, waiting for her sister's response.

"I don't know," Imani said softly. "In the beginning, it was because Mommy and Daddy treated you with more respect. I couldn't voice that then because I didn't know that's what it was, but that was it. They treated you like the mature, responsible daughter, and they coddled me and made me feel like I couldn't do anything right by myself. They would always tell you to watch out for me, making me feel like shit. I wanted my independence, so when we got to high school, I wanted to distance myself from you as much as possible. I figured if I treated you like shit, you'd let me do my own thing. I didn't realize how blessed I was to have a big sister, especially one so close in age."

Sade's eyes watered as she laughed silently. "It's funny because it was the opposite for me. I hated they coddled and spoiled you and let you stay young and innocent. All this time, we've been at each other's necks for what they did."

"I know we'll probably never have the typical sisterly bond, but... Can we at least take our truce a little more seriously?"

"Of course," Sade agreed. "I want to be in my niece or nephew's life and... I'd love to have a real bond with you finally."

"Good." Imani breathed deeply, then requested, "Will you walk me down the aisle? Then you can go stand with Dante."

Sade laughed when Imani rolled her eyes. "I'd be honored to walk you down the aisle, sis."

"Yay! Okay, well, I'll knock when I'm ready. It shouldn't take me long to get into this dress."

"Okay. I'll be right outside."

Sade left, hoping this would be the beginning of a new start for her and her sister, and she was even more relieved that she'd put boundaries between her and Dante. He may have been her best friend, but he was about to be her brother-in-law, and no matter the amount of love she had buried for him, she'd have to put Imani first.

PATRICE

Back to the Present

PATRICE WAS SO tired she could barely keep her eyes open. She was convinced a man was living with Sade and was determined to see who. There was no doubt in her mind that it was Dante, but until she had proof, Patrice didn't want to involve the police or Imani.

Back in high school, Patrice and Sade weren't friends. In fact, Patrice was a mean girl who taunted Sade while her own sister bullied her. Patrice may not have vocally disrespected or teased Sade along with Imani, but she and the rest of her friends laughed and egged Imani on the entire time.

As an adult, Patrice could admit the way they treated Sade was wrong. Even though they called her the ugly duckling between the two sisters because of her odd style, braces, and glasses, Patrice and many other girls had always been jealous of Sade because she was so beautiful. Weird but beautiful. She'd always had the same long, thick hair, dark, gorgeous eyes, and a bright smile. A smile that her sister's bullying had dimmed throughout the years.

Patrice remembered the first time the two had physically fought. Imani was with her cheerleading friends and a few football players, and they were making jokes about Sade. As often was the case, Dante came to her rescue, getting most of them to back down. This infuriated Imani because they were dating, and she believed Dante should be on her side no matter what. Thinking her big sister wouldn't lay a finger on her, Imani poured her milk on Sade's hair and shoved her pizza in her face. After that... it was on. No one could pull Sade off Imani until she'd landed five blows to her head and face.

The two sisters didn't try to fake a relationship at that point. It wasn't until their parents died in a car accident before Imani's junior year that the two decided to try to mend their relationship. Their parents had met in college, both studying international business. Their parents traveled so much that their grandparents pretty much raised them, which was also a reason for the conflict between them. While their parents often favored Imani and spoiled her, their grandparents did the same for Sade. Rumor had it their parents left a shitload of money to Imani, three times the amount they'd left for Sade, but Sade was grateful and never complained. Regardless of the amount, it provided a great life for her, so she was grounded and pleased.

They all went to college together, and though Sade and Imani made amends, they didn't hang out the way you'd expect sisters to. They spoke to each other in passing and spent holidays together based on their social media pictures, but that was about it. As adults, Patrice didn't care to have a friendship with either. In her maturity, she realized the way they'd treated Sade was wrong back in the day, and that was why she tried to be friendly and cordial when they were in the same space.

Now... Patrice's intuition was telling her that Sade was up to something, and she was determined to figure out what. Maybe it was a piece of loyalty to Imani because they were close in high school, or perhaps it was a desire to do the right thing. Whatever the case, if Dante were in Vanzette, Patrice would find out.

Patrice had been riding by Sade's home once a week, hoping to see Dante, but she'd been unsuccessful. At first, she planned to let it go, but when Trina mentioned Sade having a husband, her suspicions went into high gear. Sade wasn't married, and if she was hiding a man, it had to be for good reason. Either she was sleeping with her married friend... or she was hiding Dante.

Just about ready to give up, Patrice started her car and prepared to drive around the block one last time. When she passed a house whose owner was at the mailbox, Patrice stopped to speak to her. How Sade's home was situated, her acres of land kept any of her neighbors from easily accessing her property. There was a chance the woman had no idea who Sade was, but she at least had to ask. With her luck, maybe the woman had seen Sade with a man and could describe him.

After rolling her window down, Patrice greeted the woman with, "Hi."

She looked up from the mail she was going through and lowered herself slightly to look into the car. "Hi. Do I know you?"

"Um... no." Patrice put her Mustang in park. "My name is Patrice. I'm an old friend of your neighbor on the left, Sade. Do you... know her?"

The woman nodded skeptically, crossing her arms over her chest. The gesture made it clear to Patrice that she must be careful with her words. "I do. Why? What is this about?"

"Do you know Sade's husband?"

"Husband?" The woman chuckled and shook her head. "I didn't know she had a husband, but that doesn't mean anything. Sade and I talk in passing, but we aren't close. Maybe we'll have brunch once a month, but we talk about surface-level things. She hasn't mentioned getting married to me, but now that I think about it, we haven't had our monthly brunch since last December. I just assumed it was because she was busy."

"Have you seen a man at the house?"

The woman looked in the direction of Sade's home. "Why? Is he your man or something? I'm not comfortable getting in other people's business."

"No, nothing like that." Patrice sighed, unsure how much she wanted to share. "I think she has a man there that she's hiding, and if she is, it's because he's doing some shady, illegal things, and he has a wife, but it isn't her. I don't want to call the police or his wife until I confirm he's there. She told me a friend was staying with her and that he'd left, but someone else I know said they saw her out with a man, and he said they were married. Either way, both men are married. One is from our hometown, and his family is worried sick about him because he's missing."

"Well, if he's there, he's there willingly, right? Maybe he doesn't want his family to know where he is."

"Maybe, but that's not sitting well with me. I think there's more to the story."

"I'm sorry, but I don't know what to tell you."

"If you could just confirm that there's a man there and give me a description, that would be great."

Her head shook as she sighed and uncrossed her arms. "I really don't want to get involved."

"Okay. I understand." Patrice looked around the car before grabbing an old receipt and pen. "This man has twins and a whole family looking for him. He was possibly in an accident that left him unable to move around on his own for a while. He has possible brain damage, so he might even have amnesia. I understand your hesitancy, but I honestly think something wrong is going on. If you change your mind and want to help me bring this man back to his family, please give me a call."

She looked at the receipt briefly before taking it and telling Patrice, "I'm Willow. If I see anything suspicious, I'll call you, especially if she's keeping a man there with a family and has no idea who he is."

Patrice released a sigh of relief, patting her heart. "Thank you, Willow. Call me anytime."

Willow agreed before nodding and taking a few steps back. Patrice made one last circle around Sade's home before leaving. With her packed schedule, she didn't have the time to stop by as often as she wanted to. Now, she felt like she had an ally. Patrice hadn't wanted to give Willow too many details, but she was confident mentioning Dante's family and amnesia were the keywords needed to unlock her curiosity. She'd be calling soon with confirmation that there was, in fact, a man living with Sade, and as soon as she did, Patrice would send her a picture of Dante and Imani before pulling down the fairy tale Sade had created for herself.

SADE

SADE LOOKED AROUND the parking lot again before putting on her shades and casually heading into the hotel. She'd asked two actors, Carmen and Denzel, to meet her to discuss their role as Dante's fake parents. Sade had gone as far as having a few family pictures altered so that Carmen and Eric were in them with Dante instead of his actual parents. While Sade hoped she wouldn't have to use them, this was the best way for her to be prepared.

After knocking on the door of room 315, Sade inhaled a deep breath and took a step back. Her conscience wanted to make her believe she was taking this too far. That she'd be better off just telling Dante the truth. Then he'd kiss her, or make love to her, or tell her he loved her, and Sade would be recommitted to her plans all over again.

Denzel opened the door, favoring Michael Ealy. He didn't look like Dante's real father, but they did have the same curly hair and light skin. It made it easier to put Denzel's face on Deandre's body in the pictures.

"Good morning," Denzel greeted, extending his hand for Sade to shake.

"Good morning. Is Carmen here yet?"

"She is." Denzel extended the door wider, allowing Sade entrance. Carmen stood, smiling widely at the sight of Sade. Carmen looked a lot like Dante's mother, Olivia. They had the same cinnamon-brown skin, thick, shoulder-length hair, and almond-shaped eyes. Carmen and Denzel had been an acting duo for years. They had a chemistry that Sade was confident would make them the perfect fake parents for Dante.

"Hey, Sade," Carmen greeted.

"Hey. How are you?"

"I'm well. How are you?"

"I'm... grateful." Sade smiled softly as she walked to the table and sat across from Carmen and Denzel. "Thank you both for agreeing to play these roles. With Dante not having his memory of his family, I want to try to recreate the same positive relationship he had with his real family, but with distance and boundaries. I know many people may not understand that, but I'm willing to do whatever it takes to spare him from pain."

While Carmen nodded in agreement, Denzel briefly looked away. Not that it mattered, but Sade wondered if Denzel disagreed with what she was doing. If he did, she needed to be sure it wouldn't affect his portrayal of a caring yet detached father, especially since she'd already paid half their fee.

"Is there a problem, Denzel?" Sade asked, crossing her legs under the table.

His mouth twisted to the side, and his head tilted as he sighed. "There isn't a problem. I'm just not sure you'll get the outcome you want."

"Why do you think that?" Carmen asked before Sade could.

"She wants us to present ourselves as parents who care but aren't present. Who are detached. I don't think that will give Dante peace; I think it will make him want to fix our relationship more or resurrect old wounds that will torment him even more because he can't remember what he believes he should in order to heal. If he wants to fix our bond and closeness, are you willing to pay for that to happen? And if this makes him feel worse about himself because he doesn't have the family he believes he should, are you prepared for the consequences that come with that?"

Sade cracked her neck and nibbled her bottom lip. "I've considered both outcomes. I know Dante. If he meets you and you show little interest in being in his life, he will let it go. It may hurt, but he will let it go when he realizes staying away from you is for the best."

"If you're sure," Denzel replied, his expression softening.

Sade went into her tote bag and gave them their own personal files filled with information about Dante and his birth parents. She spent several hours at the hotel before leaving, drained and hungry. Once she reached her car, Sade called Dante to see if he wanted her to bring him something to eat. He mentioned being out with a few of the guys he'd met at the club, and Sade was starting to have mixed feelings about that.

She knew that Dante was a sociable extrovert, and he thrived when he had human contact. But there was a risk every time he went out publicly that he would be recognized. It didn't help that Patrice lived in Vanzette and would easily identify him. All she could do was pray Patrice stayed out of her way because, at that point, there weren't too many things Sade wasn't willing to do to keep Dante to herself.

DANTE

"*Argh!*"

*Dante grunted, trying to guard his head from the windshield.
He flung back, eyes squeezing shut immediately as the airbag opened
and pushed into his face and chest. With ringing ears, he tried to stay
awake, but that was proving to be more and more difficult. As his eyes
fluttered, he noticed an arm reaching into his car through the broken
glass. He thought they were trying to help him... but he realized that
wasn't the case when their hand went into his pocket to grab his wallet.*

"*St-sto—*"

*Before he could tell them to leave his phone and wallet, Dante
blacked out.*

"Shit," Dante grunted, gripping his temple as a piercing pain
sliced through his brain. His head would hurt whenever he had
flashes of the night of the accident. What he felt went beyond
a migraine, but Dante could never describe it. Since he was in
the middle of the road driving, Dante quickly pulled into the gas
station parking lot in case the pain intensified. Usually, when it
did, he was unable to keep his eyes open.

After cutting off his car, Dante pulled in deep breaths. He'd
gone to view a few commercial properties for his lounge and ended
up stopping by the only lounge in Vanzette. Though the vibe wasn't
the best, Dante stayed until after midnight. The dance floor wasn't
used, and the live band had very little entertainment value, which

was probably why the place had gone downhill and only appealed to an older crowd. Dante saw the potential in opening a lounge there and was excited about starting a new business venture.

He was going to meet his parents in a few days, and Dante didn't know how he felt about that. When he mentioned wanting to go ahead and meet them the night before, Sade gave him their numbers with no hesitation. He called his father first, and instead of asking him why neither of his parents had reached out to him or his wife in months, Dante told them he needed to see them as soon as possible. They told him they could fly out to Memphis and drive to Vanzette, and as good as Dante thought that would make him feel, he felt nothing.

Nothing for them, at least.

He closed his eyes, trying to see the man's face that had taken his phone and wallet. The man was either driving the truck or a bystander who wanted to capitalize on the accident. Either way, Dante's mind wouldn't let him rest until he saw that face fully. He'd reached out to the Memphis Police Department, and they didn't have a police report on the accident, which he found odd because he remembered his doctor at the hospital mentioning what the police had said. They did confirm, though, that there were no cameras in the area, so Dante pretty much had no idea why he was in Memphis or who tried to kill him in that truck... if they *were* trying to kill him at all.

Dante considered if the attack was random. Wrong place, wrong time. Honestly, he had no idea which bothered him the most.

There was such a small number of things he felt he could control, but his upcoming lounge was one. Now that he'd checked out his competition, Dante's excitement had increased... until he got on the road after midnight and had another flashback.

His eyes opened, and he pulled in deep breaths before closing his eyes again and trying to return to that night. To that moment...

right before he blacked out. The arm, outstretched, was covered in tattoos. Dante couldn't make out his skin tone because it was dark, but the man was Black. He squeezed his eyes tighter, willing himself to see more, but there was no more.

No face.

No hair.

No scent.

Nothing for him to remember the man by.

"Fuck!" Dante roared, slamming his hand against the steering wheel as his chin trembled.

Around Sade, Dante tried his hardest not to express how conflicted he was mentally and emotionally over not remembering that day fully or the people in his life. He wasn't sure how he hadn't gone completely insane without his memories. Maybe it was his ability to convince himself on some days that he was better off without people who didn't care about him. But there were others where he wanted to be in their presence just to tell them off. Because no part of him believed he could go months without hearing from people he loved and cared about and not find that odd.

Dante's phone rang, pulling him out of his thoughts. He looked down at the dashboard, jaws clenching at the sight of Sade's name. He considered letting it go to voicemail for a brief moment until he fully composed himself, but he didn't want her to worry.

"Hey," he answered after connecting the call.

"Hey. I was just checking on you."

"I'm on the way home. I stopped by the lounge after meeting with the realtor."

"How was it seeing the buildings in person?" she asked with a smile lacing her tone. "Did you see anything you liked?"

"There are two options I'd love for you to look at with me before I decide. Both are lease-to-own, and I don't know how I feel about that."

She chuckled, and for some reason, the sound eased his nerves. Dante rested his head against the headrest, looking into the bare streets. Traffic was nonexistent at this time of night. The town was empty and quiet, and though that was peaceful, it just didn't feel... right.

"Why not, baby? Do you want something more or less permanent?"

"Less. I know it'll be a gold mine here, but I'm not sure I want to stay here. It doesn't feel like me."

"Well, even if we left, the lounge could remain and bring in profit."

Dante paused, not replying immediately. "And what about me not wanting to stay here? It doesn't feel like I belong here, Sade. Other than you, nothing about this town feels like me."

Sade sighed into the receiver. "I can feel that. We've gone out of town twice so far, and you're alive when we aren't here."

"How was I happy here before the accident? I guess I was more fulfilled because of work and friends. Without those things, I'm drowning, bae. I need to be in a big city or at least travel more to feel more fulfilled."

After a long, pregnant pause, Sade asked, "Where do you want to live? And when do you want to move?"

"I don't know. I haven't really given it much thought. Maybe New York or Atlanta. Somewhere in Cali or even Virginia. What about Memphis? It's not too fa—"

"No!" Sade yelled louder than he'd ever heard. She released a shaky breath and a sniffle before saying softly, "We left Memphis because we hated it there. It isn't safe, and the people there are horrible. We can go anywhere other than there."

"Fine. Let's look into New York and LA. First of the year, next year. That'll give me enough time to get the lounge up and running here."

"Okay, Dante. If that's what you need."

"What about what you need? What *you* want? Are you okay with this? I know I've said it before, but if you need to leave me..."

"I'm not leaving you, and I'm okay with us leaving. Home is where you are, so I'm good as long as I have you."

That lifted the corners of his mouth and put a smile on his face. "Okay. We'll talk more later. I'm on my way home."

"Okay. See you soon."

After disconnecting the call, Dante sat there for a few more seconds, giving himself time to process his feelings. Control. It seemed he needed that more than anything. If he couldn't control his mind or the concerns of others, at least he'd be able to control where he lived and how he made more money.

SADE

SADE HAD GOTTEN so deep in her painting that she didn't realize how much time had passed. Two days. Two days had passed, and it felt like she'd seen Dante for two seconds on each one. He was starting to lose his patience with small-town life, and Sade wasn't surprised. Dante had never been the kind of man to sit still for too long, even when their twins were born. Even when they were snowed in. Even when he had no clear destination in mind. Dante would rather drive around aimlessly for hours before sitting in the house doing nothing.

"What was I thinking?" she grumbled, looking at the splattered paint on her canvas. She chuckled with a hung head. "Dante will never be satisfied here or with just me. This is never going to work." Sade ran her fingers through her hair, unfazed by the dried paint on them and her face. "There are no exciting parties, no celebrities." Sade scoffed, tugging her bottom lip between her teeth as her eyes watered. "He thinks his friends and family don't care about him. I'm making him miserable just to say I finally got him. I don't deserve him, just like Imani."

Pacing, Sade shook her head, staring into the distance. "No, this could work in our favor. We can just... go to New York. No one knows us there. I won't have to watch our backs. It'll be fun. It'll be... just the fresh start we need. No Patrice, no chance of anyone recognizing him from the news. This'll be perfect."

The doorbell ringing caused Sade to jump. She didn't have guests. Ever. Instead of going straight down, Sade grabbed her phone and opened her camera app. Her brows wrinkled, and her bottom lip poked out at the sight of Willow. They didn't have any plans, so Willow had no reason to be there. Sade checked the time—1:47 p.m. With a low huff, she left her office to let Willow in.

By the time she reached the door, Willow had turned to leave. At the sight of Sade, she smiled and waved.

"Hey. Is this a bad time?"

Sade looked down at her attire, chuckling. She was dressed in an oversized white shirt and socks.

"Bad time for what? Is everything okay?"

"I was just... stopping by to see you. Catch up. I feel like we haven't spoken in months."

Sade squeezed the back of her neck. "We haven't. Things have been hectic for me. But um... come in."

Sade closed the door behind Willow, pulling in a deep breath. Unsure if it was her intuition or paranoia that had her untrusting of Willow, Sade wanted to make this visit quick.

"Are you hungry or thirsty?" Sade asked. "Can I get you anything?"

"Um... maybe just a glass of something to drink. Unless you wanted to grab something to eat?"

"I can fix us something real quick if you're hungry. I'm in a zone with the painting I'm working on, so I don't want to leave until I'm done."

"Yeah, sure. I can come back later. I should have called first."

"It's fine," Sade reasoned as she motioned for Willow to sit on a bar stool behind the island. "Let's see." She opened the refrigerator, looking for something that could be fixed quickly. "We can do tacos, shrimp bowls, or fried fish. Those are probably the quickest options."

"Tacos work."

"Cool." As Sade pulled out the ingredients she would need, she asked, "Are you okay? Not that I mind the visit, but it just seems very random."

"Well... there is something that I..." At the sound of the garage letting up, Sade's heart dropped, and Willow's mouth snapped shut. "Oh. I'm sorry. I didn't know you had a guest."

"Yeah, it's my husband."

"Husband?" Willow repeated before chuckling, and quite frankly, Sade was tired of that being everyone's response. "When did you get married?"

The garage door opened, and Dante sauntered inside. He looked from Sade to Willow, giving her a nod as Sade made her way over to him.

"Hey, baby. Are you hungry? I was just about to make us some tacos," she said.

"Who is us?"

"This is Willow. She's our neighbor on the left."

Dante nodded, making his way over to Willow. "Hey, it's nice to meet you."

"You as well."

"I ate lunch with the guys, but we can go out later for dinner if you'd like," Dante offered.

"Great, sounds good."

"I'll be upstairs if you need me."

Sade nodded as he kissed her cheek. She waited until he was upstairs to walk over to her hanging wine bar. After grabbing a bottle of chardonnay, she poured Willow and her a glass.

"When did you say you got married?" Willow pried, accepting the glass.

"I didn't." Willow continued to stare, eyebrows raised, and Sade knew what that meant. She didn't value Willow enough to care about her opinion, but she didn't want to risk her snooping or asking questions around town. "My husband and I have known each other and been together for a while. We had separated and have now decided to try to make things work again. This isn't something I care to discuss, so..."

"Yeah, no, sorry for asking. I just... figured if you'd gotten married recently, you would have mentioned it. I would have gotten you guys a gift. But that makes sense." She paused, head tilting as she slowly eyed Sade. "Why didn't you ever mention him if you were separated?"

"Yeah," was all Sade offered, resisting the urge to ask Willow to leave. Her questions felt intrusive, and Sade had no idea why Willow was so interested in her life suddenly.

"What's his name? I can still get you guys something. Maybe some custom towels or lights. I feel really bad now."

"You don't have to do that. It's not necessary." Snapping her fingers, Sade forced a laugh. "I actually forgot we have a counseling session this afternoon, so can we reschedule lunch?"

"Of course!" Willow agreed, hopping down off the stool. "Call me anytime. I miss you, girl."

Sade smiled, quickly leading Willow toward the door. "I will, for sure. It was great seeing you."

"You too. Tell hubby I said bye."

Sade nodded, gritting her teeth. As soon as Willow stepped across the threshold, Sade slammed the door shut and leaned against it. "What the fuck was that?" she whispered before putting her acrylic nail in her mouth to chew. Running her fingers through her hair, Sade sighed and shook her head as she returned to the kitchen to put up the food. Unsure why Willow was so interested in her marriage and reconnecting, Sade decided to visit her sooner rather than later to see where Willow's head was at. The last thing she wanted was for her neighbor's curiosity to get her into trouble. Maybe she'd need to keep Willow close to make sure she stayed one step ahead of her.

DANTE

WHEN SADE TOOK Dante's hand into hers, he wondered if she felt the clamminess, if she could feel his heart beating in his palm. Dante wasn't sure why he was so nervous. These were his parents. He should have been more comfortable with them than anyone else.

"Are you okay?" she asked sweetly, looking at the side of his face.

They were in the sitting room, waiting for his parents to pull up. The last time his father texted Dante, he told him they were five minutes away. Since then, he'd been rocking in his seat, wondering if he should change his mind. This was the day he'd been waiting for, the moment he could connect with his family, but now... Dante was filled with uncertainty. Something didn't feel right, but he couldn't place his finger on what.

"I am." Dante looked over at her briefly. "Just wondering if this was the best idea. I know you had your reasons for wanting to keep me away from them. You said they weren't any good for me, and now I'm wondering if I should have just listened to you."

"Some lessons have to be learned through experience. I know you want to trust me, but this might be something you need to experience on your own. It's not like your parents are bad people. You just aren't close to them."

Dante nodded, allowing his thoughts to run rampant.

Something didn't feel right.

As a gray Toyota pulled in front of the house, Dante stood. Sade did the same, running a hand down his chest and kissing him on the corner of his mouth. He watched as she left to let them in. She looked beautiful in a white, spaghetti-strapped, flowy dress. So beautiful he wanted to fly her to an island so he could watch her lie on the beach while the sun made her honey-brown skin even more radiant and beautiful. That should have been his focus—his wife, getting her pregnant—but instead, Dante was focused on motherfuckers who proved with their daily silence they didn't prioritize him.

Sade opened the door, greeting his parents vocally and with a hug. She ushered them into the sitting room, and, as Dante looked them over... he felt nothing. No happiness. No relief. No peace—nothing. Not even anger. Or frustration. Dante felt absolutely nothing. His nostrils flared as he released a hard breath. Disappointment consumed him as his parents made their way over to him.

Why didn't he feel anything toward the people who gave him halves of themselves?

"It's so good to see you, son," his mother said, extending her arms for an embrace.

Dante hugged her, but he couldn't help but say, "So good, you hadn't bothered to call or text me for months? I was in a whole accident and lost my memory; damn near could have lost my life, and neither one of you knew."

"We apologize," his father said. "We can admit that we haven't been the most active parents, but we felt like if something bad were to happen, one of you would have reached out."

"It wasn't my responsibility to call and tell you that. You're my parents. You should have reached out to me way before now."

"You're right. You shouldn't have had to call to say that," his mother said, sitting in the chair on the right of the sofa. "Your wife should have."

"If she didn't, it was obviously for a reason," Dante defended, sitting on the couch so he'd be next to her. "Why didn't she feel comfortable calling and telling you that?"

His mother cupped her hands in her lap, looking toward her husband to answer.

"The truth is, we kept our distance, and you both did the same. We grew apart when you graduated from high school and left for college. In our attempt to give you space to grow and experience life, you pushed us out of it in the process."

"So you're saying it's my fault?"

"I'm just telling you what happened, son. We could have put forth more effort, but after you left home, we started doing things we could not do while raising you. We all could have done better, and if you'd like us to, we can start now."

Dante chuckled as disbelief filled him. Since January, he'd been waiting for this moment. Now, three months later, it felt like time wasted. Being around his parents didn't fill him in any way. It only made him value the life he was creating with his wife more.

His loyal wife.

The one who stood by his side through the good and bad, sickness and health. Every time he went against what she said or suggested, Dante regretted it. She was truly his helpmate.

Rubbing the space between his eyes, Dante sighed. "This was a mistake." He stood, placing a kiss on Sade's forehead. "I'm sorry y'all wasted your time and money coming down here."

"Dante," his mother called, stopping him from leaving the room. "We're glad you're alive. If you do decide to try again, you know how to reach us."

All Dante could do was chuckle. She missed the whole point of his frustration. He shouldn't have had to reach out. If he were a father, there wouldn't be anything other than God that could separate him from his children. On the off chance that they did push him away when he found out they were in an almost fatal accident, he would have been by their side every step of the way... not telling them to reach out to him if they wanted to try again. Hell, they wouldn't have had a fucking choice.

"Thank y'all for stopping by. I appreciate it," he heard Sade say as he headed for the stairs. The stash of weed he'd gotten from one of the guys at the club, Lathan, was in the upstairs entertainment room, and Dante needed a hit—desperately. He made his way inside, grabbing the stash out of the closet on the left, then making his way to the snack station in the cabinet on the right. As dope as their home was, Dante often felt silly for not being more content and satisfied. Despite all the ways to occupy himself inside, it still hadn't truly felt like home.

That wouldn't matter anymore. Once the lounge was up and running and Dante brought in more income, they would leave this house and Vanzette to start fresh. Maybe building a home together, decorating it, and being a new city was just what he needed. Even with the half a million he had in his personal account, Dante wanted to ensure he was financially stable enough so that Sade wouldn't offer a dime for anything. Whatever she'd gotten from her parents' death was hers and hers alone. No matter how often she offered it, Dante would never touch that money.

The front door opened and closed, and not long after, Sade was peeking her head into the entertainment room. Dante took a pull off his blunt and gave her a wink that made Sade smile.

"You okay?" she checked.

"Yeah, I'm good."

"I'll give you your space, but I'm here if you need me."

He nodded, patting his lap as he grew more comfortable in the recliner. Sade sat on his lap and wrapped her arms around his neck.

"Thank you," Dante muttered before kissing her neck, making her shiver and cave against him. "You tried to spare me from that, but I didn't listen. I thought I would feel connected to them, but I didn't feel a damn thing." Dante cupped her chin. "The only time I ever feel something is when I'm with you."

"I'm honored to provide that for you, but I don't want you to feel that only with me. I know you want connections outside of me, and you deserve that."

"I'll get it." His head bobbed as hope filled him. "With people who truly want that with me. Until then, I'm at peace just focusing on me and you."

"Yeah?" she cooed softly, straddling him.

Dante licked his lips, lowering his eyes to hers. "Yeah." He pushed her hair off her shoulders and kissed the right one. Then her neck. And her lips. Dante's hands slid up her thighs, gripping and kneading them as she rocked against him.

"Baby," she pleaded softly, her head flinging back as his hands caressed her breasts. "I want you inside."

Dante wasted no time lifting her dress and pushing her panties to the side while he unzipped and unbuttoned his pants and pulled his shaft out of his boxers. As soon as her wet, warm walls sheathed him, Dante sighed in relief.

This... her... Sade—*she* was his home.

WILLOW

NERVOUS, WILLOW'S LEG shook while waiting for Patrice to answer the phone. She'd texted Sade earlier to see if she wanted to have dinner, but Sade told her she already had plans with her husband. Sade offered to do lunch the next day, and Willow agreed, but Patrice insisted she go inside the home while Sade was gone and see if she could find anything suspicious.

In the beginning, Willow was unsure about snooping for Patrice. She planned to come clean with Sade and tell her what Patrice had asked her to do. When she met Sade's husband, and Sade gave her the excuse she did, Willow figured she was up to something. From the looks of it, the man was comfortable with her, so Willow wasn't sure about the whole amnesia thing, but Patrice wasn't ready to let it go.

Yet again, Patrice's phone went to voicemail, and Willow groaned. "I'm about to say fuck this shit," she decided, and just a few seconds later, Patrice returned her call.

"Hello?" she answered quickly, stepping out onto her porch.

"What's up? I'm at work."

"Sade is about to leave. What am I supposed to be looking for?"

"Any pictures of them together. Take a picture of him at some point too, if you can. Really, I'm looking for anything with his information on it—any important documents. Also, get him to tell you his name, not her. And make sure you ask him how long they've been married and where they met."

Willow nodded and rolled her eyes. "And you're absolutely sure there's a good chance this man is your friend's missing husband?"

"Yes, Willow," Patrice stressed with irritation in her voice. "Based on how you described him, it sounds like Dante. I need concrete proof, though."

"I'll see what I can do, but I really don't want to be involved in this, Patrice."

"I hear you. Just... Go over there today. When you get back home, let me know what you find. If nothing, just let me know when he's there and you see him out, and I'll pull up on him myself. I'll just have to leave work if necessary."

"Fine," Willow agreed, ready to be done with this already. After disconnecting the call, Willow shoved her phone inside her pocket and headed down the stairs. She pulled in a deep breath, covering her ears with the headphones around her neck. Dressed in a pink Puma sports bra and biker shorts, she decided to go for a walk. That way, if Sade and her husband saw her by their house while leaving, it wouldn't look suspicious.

As she started walking down the street, Willow's heart raced. All she could think about was getting caught and arrested for breaking and entering. What would be her excuse? A random woman she didn't even know told her the neighbor she'd been living by for years was housing a man who was missing in another city? No one would believe that. She chuckled as she thought about it because she couldn't believe it herself.

At the sight of a car backing out of Sade's garage, she slowed her steps. Her husband was driving, and when they passed her, Willow waved. Sade waved back, and her husband gave her a nod. Willow's head shook as she grumbled under her breath.

"This is crazy. Clearly, that man is exactly where he wants to be," was what Willow said, but that didn't stop her from continuing toward the house.

Instead of going through the front door, Willow entered through the patio. She remembered Sade mentioning how she often forgot to lock it when she went out for her morning workout routine. As she made her way through the house, Willow rubbed her hands together, unsure of what she was looking for. If he were a missing person, he wouldn't have a birth certificate or anything like that lying around. At the most, she'd be able to look for pictures and possibly get some hair or a toothbrush in case Patrice had a way to test his DNA.

Willow went from one room to the next in search of the master bedroom. When she finally found it, she looked around, surprised by the lack of photos of the married couple.

"That's odd."

"What's odd?"

At the sound of Sade's voice, Willow gasped as her heart skipped a beat. She turned to face Sade, who was smiling sweetly as she stared at her.

"Sade, I—"

Before Willow could finish, she was struck in the head and knocked out instantly.

Willow's head was throbbing as she groaned and tried to open her eyes. When she did, they landed on Sade. She was seated directly across from her with her head buried in her phone. Willow looked around, eyes widening, when she realized Sade had her arms and legs tied to a chair. With a rag between her teeth, Willow was unable to speak. She muttered against it, gaining Sade's attention.

Sade smiled, sitting up in her seat.

"Hey, sleepyhead. I wasn't expecting you to sleep for so long. I must have struck you, huh?" With a chuckle, Sade crossed her legs. "When I saw you on my camera app, I knew you were up to no good, so I had my man turn around so I could catch you. Do you want to tell me what you were doing in my house, Willow?"

Willow nodded, hoping Sade would understand and release her before more damage could be done.

"Where are we?" Willow asked after Sade tugged the rag from her mouth and down her chin.

"You're in my shed. I would have put you in the basement, but I didn't want to risk you making noise and Dante hearing you. Well, he won't hear you regardless after I give you this."

Sade lifted the syringe that rested on her thigh.

"Sade... please. I can explain everything."

"Go ahead," she granted, her voice low and sweet.

"A woman approached me a while ago and asked if I'd seen a man living with you. She said his name is Dante, and he's missing in Memphis. That he has a family that's looking for him, and he was in an accident. That he may have amnesia. She asked me if I could find pictures of you and him in the house or something with his name on it. I told her I didn't want to get involved, but she made me feel bad for him because she said he has kids and may have possible brain damage. But when I met your husband, he seemed fine, so I thought maybe she was just confused..." Willow's words slowed as her brows wrinkled. "But you... you just called him... Dante. That's the man she said everyone is looking for, isn't it?"

Sighing, Sade leaned back in her seat and crossed her arms over her chest. "Who had you all up in my business, Willow?"

"Patrice. Her name is Patrice. She's expecting me to call her, so if something happens to me, she'll know I was at your house last."

"You know..." Sade laughed as she stood. Her hands were on her hips as she stared at Willow. "Patrice has been a pain in my ass since we met in high school. Back then, she didn't speak up to help me. And now, she won't mind her own fucking business to save her damn life. Well... yours too. There's no way I can let you leave here knowing what you do."

"Sade, please..." Willow swallowed hard, her head shaking adamantly as her eyes watered. "I promise I won't tell anyone that Dante is here. Not even Patrice. Just let me go, and we can forget this even happened."

"Do you think I'm stupid? As soon as I let you go, you're calling Patrice, and then you both will go straight to the police."

"Sade, I swear—"

"Shut up!" Sade roared before sending a stinging backhand to Willow's left cheek. "You bitches in Vanzette just don't know how to stay out of other people's business. Now, you have to pay for it." Sade grabbed the syringe from the chair, telling Willow, "This will put you to sleep for about twelve hours. I need to figure out how long I will keep you here and what I want to do with you. Even if I kill you, I can't do it here. You really fucked up my plans with your nosy ass. Now I have to figure out how to get rid of your body."

As tears streamed down Willow's cheeks, she remained silent, but when Sade grabbed her arm and placed the needle against it, she begged her to reconsider. Her cries went through deaf ears as Sade pressed the needle into Willow's arm. Before she knew it, Willow was out cold—again.

PATRICE

"I SHOULD HAVE DONE it myself," Patrice grumbled, stuffing her belongings in her purse. She was getting ready to leave for her second shift at the clinic and hadn't heard from Willow yet. There was the possibility that Sade hadn't left home yet, which gave Willow the perfect opportunity to go down and sneak a picture of the man she was with.

Unable to take the lack of updates any longer, Patrice sent Willow a text that said, If they haven't left yet, go down there and get a picture of him. If they have left, go to the house and see what you can find. I need to make my next move on this ASAP! Patrice grabbed her keys and was about to head to the garage, but when her phone vibrated, and she saw the call was from Willow, she dropped everything on her bed and quickly answered the call.

"Please tell me you have good news," Patrice begged.

"What good news are you waiting for exactly?"

Patrice's head tilted at the sound of the voice. It wasn't Willow, but it was familiar. Unfortunately, she couldn't place the tone. Her steps slowed as she paced in front of her bed.

"Willow?"

She chuckled softly. "It's Sade."

Patrice's heart raced, and her knees weakened, forcing her to sit on the edge of her bed. "What are you doing with Willow's phone?"

"The better question is, why are you sending her into my home?"

Patrice's nostrils flared, and her nervousness was quickly replaced with frustration. "Because I know you're hiding Dante! I'm not stupid, Sade. He's been missing since January, and you ironically have a man who used his name after an accident? A man introducing himself to people as your husband when we both know you aren't married!"

"You don't know shit!" Sade roared so loudly that Patrice had to pull the phone away from her ear. She released a shaky breath and lowered her voice when she added, "Now... You sent Willow into my home, making her a trespasser and you a coconspirator for setting her dumb ass up. I have every right to blow her brains out and say I thought she was trying to steal from me."

"Sade, please, leave her out of it. She was just trying to help me."

"And see, that's what I don't understand." Sade laughed, and the innocent tone she used made Patrice's flesh crawl. "Why are you suddenly so concerned with me? What's it to you if I married a complete stranger or I'm dating someone who prefers to present himself as my husband? You haven't given a fuck about me since you moved to this town. Now, it's like you're obsessed with me."

"I'm just trying to do the right thing," Patrice reasoned, standing. "Dante needs to be at home with *his* wife and children, not with your crazy ass. He didn't want you then, and if he were in his right mind, he wouldn't want you now." Patrice chuckled, snatching her purse and keys off her bed. "I don't even know why I'm trying to talk sense into your crazy ass. I'll just call the police and tell them I think you have a man there that's considered missing. If you know what's good for you, you'll release Willow before they arrive."

"That was cute. The police can't search my home without a warrant, and you have no evidence to give to them to get one. If you know what's good for you, you'll watch your back and stay the hell out of my business."

Sade gritted the last part, causing Patrice to hang up the phone. She stared at it for a few seconds, trying to decide her next move. If Sade had harmed Willow and the police found out she was behind it, Patrice didn't know what to do.

"The hell was I thinking?" Patrice asked softly, pulling gently at her hair. "If anything happens to that girl, it will be my fault. God, I have to convince Sade to let her go."

Patrice dialed Willow's number as she headed out of her bedroom, hoping Sade would answer. She didn't. Cursing under her breath, Patrice hung up and dialed again. And again. By the fourth ring, she got in her car and grumbled, "I need to go over there. Ain't no telling what Sade's ass will do."

"You got that right, bitch." At the sound of Sade's voice, Patrice tried to turn in the driver's seat, but it was too late. Sade was behind her, strangling her with a thin cord. "I'm willing to do just about anything to keep Dante now that I finally have him... and that includes killing you."

Patrice struggled against the seat, trying and failing to pull the cord from around her neck. As she strived to breathe, she felt her eyes water before they bulged and rolled into the back of her head.

"All this because you stuck your nose where it didn't belong." Sade's voice sounded farther and farther away. "Crazy thing is, my sister doesn't give a fuck about you." Sade chuckled, tightening her grip on the cord and cutting deeper into Patrice's neck with it. "She had sex with your boyfriend during your senior year of high school. Don't worry, though. I'll punish her for both of us."

Patrice's body finally went limp. Her chest caved. When she released her last breath, it was to the melody of Sade's giggles.

SADE

SADE LOOKED AROUND the Airbnb, making sure nothing was out of place. Finding one available for rent in Vanzette wasn't easy because not many people saw their town as a tourist destination, but she'd been able to do so. When Imani finally gave her a day and time for her visit, Sade planned to get the rental property in case she spent a few nights with her. It would have been the first time the sisters were in each other's space for more than a couple of hours since they were in high school. Sade had already prepared to tell Dante she would do a solo staycation for inspiration on a new adult coloring book line she was considering.

With all the plans she made, something was telling Sade that Imani's visit wouldn't last long, especially since she wouldn't have the twins. They were the only valid reason Sade entertained her sister. The two had made amends after their parents died, but that did nothing to change Imani's attitude and personality. She was still the same spoiled, selfish, cruel woman she'd always been, and Sade couldn't stand being around her for long. Still, she packed a bag and had her excuse ready for Dante in case Imani stayed overnight.

Since Sade didn't want to risk Imani running into Dante, she'd already prepared to keep Imani in the house until she left. It was tricky enough to keep him away from Patrice and Trina. Patrice was officially out of the way, and as suggested, Trina had been keeping her distance. She'd even changed the date she got her hair done after flattening Sade's tires. Sade wanted to get even, but since Trina hadn't told the police about what happened in the restaurant bathroom, she let it ride.

After pouring herself a glass of wine, Sade headed to the living room area. She couldn't understand why Imani even wanted to be around her. Sade wouldn't be a shoulder for her fake tears. If anyone knew the genuine way Imani felt about her husband, it was Sade. Just as she grew comfortable on the couch, the doorbell rang. Inhaling deeply, Sade cut the TV on and headed to the front door. As soon as she opened it, Imani pouted and hugged her. It took everything inside of Sade to wrap her arms around her sister.

It was crazy how Sade had gone from being excited about being a big sister, even if it was just by a year, to despising Imani.

"Sissy, what am I going to do?" Imani asked, tightening her grip on Sade.

Sade sighed, pulling Imani into the house and closing the door behind her. Imani was distraught, all right. Not over Dante's well-being but what his being missing meant for her. There was no doubt in Sade's mind that Imani's visit would revolve around her, not Dante, which was one of the main reasons Sade kept his true identity a secret. She never trusted Imani with Dante.

"Come on inside. I'll pour you a glass of wine, and we can talk," Sade suggested as genuinely as she possibly could. More than anything, she was concerned about the search for Dante and if they had any leads. Obviously, none were leading them to her and Vanzette, and she wanted to keep it that way.

She'd already killed a woman for this man.

There was no turning back now.

The sisters walked into the living room, where Sade put the TV on a random movie on Netflix for background noise. Making her way to the kitchen, Sade shook her head and chuckled under her breath while pouring Imani's wine. The things she wanted to say to her sister...

Back in the living room, Sade looked over her sister, suddenly feeling like the ugly duckling all over again. Both sisters were beautiful, but Sade had to grow into her looks. Imani had always been beautiful with her tall, curvy figure, smooth, medium-brown skin, pouty lips, and coffee-brown slanted eyes. She started growing locs in middle school. Now, they were down to her knees.

Imani presented herself as the upgraded version of Sade before they even realized it in school, and Sade had hated her for it ever since. She was already self-conscious about her glasses, braces, and thick hair... and Imani's presence at school only intensified it. Their grandparents told them to stick together and have each other's backs, but that had never been Imani's intention. She wanted to be with the in-crowd, and the in-crowd picked on smart, quiet people like Sade... so Imani did too.

Having her younger sister come to her school and bully her, along with others, was probably the most heartbreaking experience for Sade before they lost their parents. She was already alone, having only their grandparents for emotional intimacy and support, and Imani's choice of strangers over blood only made Sade feel even lonelier.

Worse, Imani knew how much Sade had a crush on Dante, and as soon as she found out, she pursued him. Dante was the man back in high school. He played football and basketball, had excellent grades, and came from money. All the girls wanted him. He and Sade established a friendship early on because she was too nervous to express her desire for anything more. Besides, Dante had a type—the popular cheerleader—and it wasn't long before Imani became just that.

When Imani told Sade they were dating, she tried to kill her. She literally wrapped her arms around Imani's neck and tried to kill her. Sade probably would have succeeded if it hadn't been for their grandmother pulling her off. And as she stared at her sister now, Sade wished she had.

"So what's up?" Sade asked casually, leaning back on the couch and crossing her legs.

"Aren't you going to show me around the place?" Imani looked around, taking a small sip of her chardonnay. "This is... cute. It's way too small for me, but I guess it fits you."

Deep breaths, Sade, she told herself. *Deep... fucking... breaths.*

"Yeah, well, I didn't think you'd want to waste time with that or small talk. You seemed really upset the last time we talked."

"First, have you talked to Patrice? She was blowing my phone up yesterday. I called her back, but she didn't answer. I figured she was at work. She's trying to pay off her house so she can move, so she's been working like crazy. We talked last week, and she was staying at her job basically so she could pull in all the hours she could."

Sade shook her head slowly while gritting her teeth as her nostrils flared. "Patrice was your friend, not mine. We spoke to each other in passing, but no, I haven't talked to her."

"Hmm, I wonder what she wants. She said it was important. Something about Dante. Hopefully, I can see her before I leave. Maybe I'll just pull up at her job."

"That's not a good idea," Sade replied quickly, setting her wineglass on the coffee table. "That's not the kind of job she can just stop working to talk if she's with a patient. Besides, she does a lot of house calls. I wouldn't want you to waste your time or gas."

"You're right," Imani agreed. "I'm trying to track down every lead someone gives for Dante, but a lot of them are coming up empty. No one has seen him since that night."

"How are the twins?"

Imani huffed, tightening her grip around her glass. "Girl, they are so upset, and it's getting on my damn nerves. I might ask Grandma to keep them with her for a while when I get back."

Sade scoffed. "What did you expect, Imani? They miss their father."

As soon as the words escaped her mouth, Sade felt like shit. Her nieces were the only true casualties in this. Mila and Nila were twelve years old. Mila was quiet and reserved, but Nila was more outspoken, like her mother. Sade loved them both. The only thing that made her okay with keeping Dante away from them was the fact that he wasn't their biological father. He thought he was, but he wasn't. And Imani didn't even remember telling Sade that truth. It was during a drunken Thanksgiving night when she spilled the beans, and Sade had been storing that piece of information to drop at the perfect time ever since.

"Still, it's annoying. All they do is ask me repeatedly when he's coming home. I keep telling them I don't know. It's stressing me out."

"What exactly are y'all doing to find Dante?"

Imani shrugged. "I don't know. I'm letting the police handle that. He wasn't there when they went to the office to arrest him. They found his car wrapped around a pole, but he wasn't in it, so no report was filed. I think he's on the run because of the charges and doesn't want to be found."

"Did you check hospitals, Imani?"

Imani shook her head. "I did, but they didn't have any record of him being there that night, so I just assumed he made a run for it."

Sade held back her smile. Her persistence got her the information she needed. Imani wouldn't tirelessly call and visit hospitals for information like she did. It worked in her favor that whoever ran into Dante took his wallet because the police couldn't file a report with his name listed, which gave her the perfect opportunity to present herself as his wife.

"What if he was actually hurt in that accident? Do you care about that at all?"

Imani sucked her teeth and shook her head. "Why are you acting like you care? If you cared about how I was dealing with everything, you would've showed up for me like you always do." With a roll of her eyes, Imani pulled in a deep breath. "But if he were hurt, he would have been in the car, and the police would have called and told me. I know Dante's ass was running from the police. He probably hopped out of the car and ran somewhere else. Ain't no telling where he's at now."

"Of course, I care about you, Imani. You're my sister."

"Then why didn't you come to Memphis for me?" For a fleeting moment, Sade swore she saw her eyes water. Imani looked away briefly, and when they locked eyes again, they were dry. "I'm under a lot of pressure, and our grandparents aren't any real help. I needed you."

Sade chuckled nervously. Her mouth opened and closed, but no words would come out. It surprised her that Imani was being honest about this, but it shouldn't have. No matter how at odds they were, Imani often became a needy little sister when under enormous amounts of pressure. Sade had been so caught up in the bad things Imani had done that she hadn't considered how things would affect her mentally and emotionally. Dante had been her priority, and protecting him was most important... even if at the expense of what little fragile bond she had with her sister.

"I know you've been calling, but I honestly didn't think you would care if I showed up for you or not. You know how things get between us when it comes to Dante. I figured this would be one time it would be best if I kept my distance. I'm... here for you now, though."

Imani's mouth formed a pout, but her face returned to its regular, unbothered expression in seconds.

"Fine."

"So how would you feel if he never came back? Would you miss him?"

Imani chuckled so long and hard she leaned forward in her seat, and it was then that Sade realized her sad, needy little sister was gone. "Would I miss him? All men are replaceable. Eventually, the twins will forget his ass ever existed if I find the right replacement. I'm worried because..." She snapped her mouth shut and swallowed hard. "I don't feel comfortable talking to you about this. I hate I told you about it from the beginning."

"What are you talking about, sis? You know you can tell me anything."

Imani sighed as her chest caved. "I wasn't completely honest with you about the business."

Sade held her breath. Right before the accident, Imani frantically called Sade for advice. It was one of the rare times she almost had a conscience. She told Sade she'd done a terrible thing, and Dante was about to pay for it. After several minutes of coaxing, Sade finally convinced Imani to come clean. Imani told Sade that she'd been stealing from clients and not filing their quarterly taxes. Sade was unable to persuade Imani to tell the truth. As soon as jail time was mentioned, Imani decided to let Dante take the fall.

Instead of trying to convince Imani further to do the right thing, Sade let her ramble on, determined to save Dante however she could. She planned to tell Dante about Imani's plan and was glad he'd called her that night, but the accident happened, and he couldn't remember a damn thing. Sade didn't plan on telling Dante about the charges he was facing because then she'd have to tell him about Imani and their other business partners. The less he knew, the better.

"What did you leave out?"

"I wasn't just stealing from clients; I made fake clients and statements too. I've also been laundering money for this drug dealer and—"

"Imani!" Sade yelled, no longer able to maintain her composure. "What the hell were you thinking?"

"I was thinking it was a great opportunity to make more money!"

Sade laughed as she stood. "How much fucking money do you need? Mommy and Daddy had already left your ass five million dollars. What the hell did you do with that?"

Imani huffed, gently yanking Sade back down on the couch by her wrist. "That's not important. What's important is there are civil and criminal charges against Dante that he needs to come back home to face. If he doesn't, I'm next in line. The FBI already made it clear that someone will pay for this, and if it's not him, it will be me. Plus, the dealer doesn't want to stop just because we've been caught. He's expecting me to find another way to clean his money. I just... I need my husband to come back home, sissy, and I don't know what the hell to do."

Sade massaged her temples as her head shook. She chuckled. "So you're not here because you miss Dante and you want him to come home or that you're worried about his safety? You're here because you want him to go to jail for you."

Imani's face was covered with confusion. "Yes, exactly." Sade's laugh was vocal this time as Imani continued. "Look, I know you had a thing for him, and the two of you were close, but he was the most popular guy in school. I knew I'd be the most popular girl in school if I dated him. Same for college. I wasn't expecting to get pregnant by his ass, but I saw it as a permanent check, so it was cool. Then he asked me to marry him before the twins were born, which meant alimony if we ever split. You know I've always been about the money, Sade, so I'm not sure why you're so surprised."

"You know what? You're absolutely right. I don't know what I was thinking."

Meanwhile... Sade had killed Patrice and had Willow drugged in her shed just to keep Dante. Imani had never deserved and appreciated him, and this conversation only fueled Sade to continue to do whatever it took to keep them apart.

As the two stared at each other, Sade had to keep herself from jumping across the couch and strangling her sister again. There was no one else around them this time. This time, she'd succeed. There had never been a part of Sade that believed she could cause people harm, but Imani brought out this side of her.

Imani was the reason she'd kidnapped Willow and killed Patrice.

Imani was the reason she was hiding in Vanzette, refusing to let people in and get close. If her own sister betrayed her and treated her like trash, Sade believed strangers would too.

Imani was the reason she couldn't have her happily ever after with Dante while they were younger, and now, thanks to Imani's selfishness... Sade would finally get that happily ever after with Dante today, whether or not he knew the true reason for it.

"So what exactly do you want from me, Imani?" Sade asked, already feeling drained from their interaction. "Just a place to crash so you can get some peace? If so, you could have gone anywhere in the world. You got the money for it."

"I was hoping you'd try to help me find Dante."

"I can't do more than the police have. Are they tracking his phone and cards?"

"Yes, but they are coming up empty. The cards haven't been used, and his phone can't be tracked."

"And you still don't think that means he's hurt or even dead somewhere?"

Crossing her arms, Imani remained silent as she thought it over. "Maybe he is. That could work in my favor too. If I can convince them he's dead or hurt, maybe that will keep them from trying to bring the charges against me. Maybe they'll be buried right along with him," Imani squealed and stood, tightly hugging Sade's neck. "Initially, I insisted he was alive and well because I wanted him caught so he could face these charges. I shouldn't have done that, but I can fix this. You're so smart! And you're right.

There are literally millions of places I can go instead of being stuck in this boring-ass town with you. I might take a friend's private jet to an island for a week or two. Play the grief-stricken wife."

Sade stared at Imani for a few seconds before asking, "Where did we go wrong?"

"What do you mean?" Imani asked, sitting back down and giving her phone her attention.

"We agreed after your wedding that we'd work on our bond. That we'd treat each other better. I hear you say shit like this, and I can't help but feel like I failed you somehow."

Imani's eyes lifted toward the ceiling as she released a hard breath. "You didn't fail me, Sade. I never let you get close enough to have any real impact on the way I think or act. You're right; we tried to be normal sisters after the wedding, but it didn't work." Imani set her phone down and looked at Sade. "The great thing about our parents was that they spoiled and raised me in a way that made me not give the slightest fuck what anyone else wants, thinks, or feels. I can say and do whatever I want to keep me happy. If that makes you or anyone else unhappy, I have the smallest capacity to care. Most times, I don't care at all, just like now. I'm about to plan a trip and get away so I can do what's best for me. Maybe if you stopped caring so much about other people and their feelings, you'd be happier too."

As Imani made her plans on her phone, Sade stood and headed to the master bedroom. She'd suffocate if she didn't get away from her sister soon. What Imani did at that point didn't matter to Sade. She could have had Dante legally declared dead for all Sade cared. That would have only made things better for them. She'd plant the bug in Imani's ear before she left and hoped her sister would execute the plan. If she did, the media's attention would shift elsewhere, and there would be less of a chance for Dante to be recognized...

SADE

IMANI LEFT AROUND midnight to catch a flight to Jamaica, and Sade could not have been happier when she left. The whole time she was there, she complained about her kids, tried to brainstorm ways to make more money, expressed fear of being unable to clean the drug dealers' money, or tried to figure out the process for getting Dante declared legally dead. When Sade made it home, she desperately needed something stronger than wine. She'd stopped by one of the only two liquor stores in Vanzette and grabbed a bottle of tequila.

Before going inside, she went to the tool shed she was using to hold Willow and gave her a new dose of the sleeping serum she'd purchased. When Trina and Patrice first started giving Sade hell, she looked into all kinds of weapons and ways to keep people silent. She never thought she'd have to use any of it on Willow. Willow was awake but so drowsy she could barely hold her head up. The good thing about the serum was there were no adverse side effects. All it would do was make her sleep. As long as Sade kept food in her stomach, Willow would be okay.

Sade still hadn't wrapped her mind around killing Willow, but she would if she had to. Patrice was an easy kill because of their history, but it was different with Willow. If Sade believed Willow wouldn't tell the police or someone she trusted about Dante and being held captive, Sade would have let her go. At that point, the only two options were killing her and paying her to leave.

In the kitchen, Sade poured herself a double shot of tequila. Based on Imani's words and reactions, she wasn't the one responsible for trying to kill Dante. Now that Sade thought about it, it made sense for Imani to want him alive. Killing him would have meant killing her scapegoat. Imani didn't want Dante dead—she wanted him in jail.

So, who had been watching him and ran him off the road?

Who wanted him not only dead but unable to be recognized and mourned?

Sade couldn't think of a time Dante mentioned having any enemies, but honestly, Sade didn't know everything about him. Dante did love to gamble, specifically poker. Did he owe someone money who was tired of waiting to collect?

Sighing, Sade leaned against the counter and nibbled her lip. It was the first time she'd looked into the living room. Dante was seated by the fireplace in nothing but his boxers, staring at her. She smiled. It didn't matter how hot it got at night, Dante always kept the fireplace on.

"Hey, I didn't see you over there," Sade said.

"Yeah, I spoke, but you didn't hear me. What's on your mind, Smiley?"

Sade turned and chugged the tequila before taking slow steps in his direction. Instead of sitting next to him, she sat on his lap. He loved having her close. Physical touch was his love language; words of affirmation were hers.

"Nothing that I want to talk about just yet. I think I can handle it on my own, but if I can't, I'll let you know. What's up with you? Why are you just sitting here without music or the TV on?"

"I was thinking and waiting for you."

"Is everything okay?"

"I wanted to get you some new lingerie, so I went in your drawer to get your size. I found the birth control pills, Sade. You wanna tell me why you're taking them if we have been trying to have a baby for the last three years? Are the pills the reason you haven't been able to conceive?"

Sade's head hung and shook. She released a long sigh as her arms dropped from around his neck. Before she could stop them, her eyes were watering.

"No," she muttered, sniffling. "The pills aren't why we haven't been able to have a baby."

"Then why are you taking them? Do you not want children?"

"I do," she quickly answered as he lifted her head and wiped her face. Rubbing her hands together, Sade said, "I started taking the pills after the accident. You weren't confident about us, and I didn't want now to be when I got pregnant, so I got on the pills to be safe. I knew it would be hard enough for you dealing with your injuries and amnesia. I didn't want me being pregnant to be a bigger issue on top of that."

"I can respect and appreciate that, but that was something we should have discussed together, Day."

"You're right. I'll stop taking them if you want."

His head tilted. Slowly, his eyes scanned her face. "Are you sure that's the *only* reason we don't have any kids? If something happened that you don't want me to know about, you can tell me, bae."

What was she supposed to say? That he had children with his real wife, and they'd just started having sex? That she hadn't gotten off the pill because she feared he'd regain his memory and leave her?

"That's it. I can toss them now if you want. But only if you're sure."

Dante lifted her hand and kissed it. "I have the most perfect wife. I want to give you everything you desire and deserve. If we're on the same page about this, I want to get you pregnant as soon as possible. Throw that shit away."

Unable to stop her smile from spreading, Sade nodded in agreement.

"Okay. I know it's still in my system, but we can get started on that baby tonight."

Dante chuckled as he stood, wrapping her legs around his waist. "Practice makes perfect."

It felt almost too good to be true to hear him say those words. Not only did she finally have her man, but he also wanted to give her a baby.

SADE

SADE RAN HER hands down Dante's chest. He was about to go to the gym, and Sade wished he would have worked her out first. Every time he went somewhere alone, Sade grew nervous, but she'd learned that although Dante was friendly, he wouldn't allow anyone to disrespect her. If they tried to discuss her with him, especially while she was gone, Dante would shut that down almost immediately. He'd always protected her as her best friend, and now, he showed that same protection as her "husband."

"What are your plans for the day?" Dante asked, stuffing his change of clothes and headphones into his gym bag.

"I don't have any. I might go shopping or something."

"Alone?" Sade shrugged. "Bae, you've got to find your community."

Your community.

Sade's eyes closed at the sound of that statement. Her grandmother used to say that to her all the time when she was in college. Ava and Barron tried to let Sade and Imani find their way to each other. When they realized the sisters would probably never have a healthy relationship, Ava tried convincing Sade to find other people to join her tribe. Ava always told her that "her community" needed more than her self-love.

She stressed the importance of believing in a being bigger than her, having herself a life partner, and, at minimum, three people she could celebrate with, grieve with, and trust with her secrets. Whether they were family or friends, Ava wanted her granddaughter to have that community, and even after all these years, Sade didn't believe she had that.

Unfortunately, she'd gotten used to being alone. There were people she conversed with on social media and made small talk with, and there were even women she'd made time to grab brunch or dinner with... but her community? No. Sade still didn't have that.

"I'm okay," Sade told him, crossing her arms over her chest. "I like to be alone, and when I don't want to be alone, I want to be with you."

"Did we have this conversation a lot before I lost my memory?" Dante asked, heading toward the garage.

"Yes," Sade answered truthfully. "You hated I didn't have deeper connections with women. I had many male friends, but those kind of tapered off when we got married. We still talk but don't hang out as often now."

"Hmm." Dante leaned against the Maxima. He seemed to gravitate toward that one, and Sade appreciated that because it was the most low-key. Dante had been looking into SUVs to purchase and had a Hummer at the top of the list, but the selection in Vanzette was limited. From the looks of it, he would have to buy one online and have it delivered. "What's the reason for that?"

"For... what?" Sade asked skeptically, though she already knew where this conversation was going.

Dante gave her a soft smile. He didn't respond right away as he looked her over. That was new, or maybe that was a trait of her romantic partner, Dante, that she didn't get as his best friend. Back in the day, Dante would say whatever he was thinking and didn't really care how it came out or was received.

"Your lack of connection with women, Sade."

"Are we really about to talk about this right now?"

"Yeah. We can go back inside if you'd like."

Dante pushed himself off the car, but Sade placed her hand on his chest to keep him from going back inside.

"That's not necessary, babe."

Sade thought over ways to be as honest with him as possible. She couldn't very well tell him her relationships with women were difficult because of her mother and sister. How the women she was supposed to be closest to filled her with such insecurity, anger, and mistrust that they made her want to stay away from women altogether.

Because then, he'd tell her she needed therapy and ask her why she lied about being an only child whose grandparents raised her.

"I don't trust or feel comfortable around women. Women I've been closest to betrayed me and made me feel insecure or like I wasn't good enough. I've allowed myself to be pulled out of character trying to one-up women who have hurt me, and I don't like that version of myself. There's a lot of trauma there, and I know that. I also know not all women are the same, but when you deal with something all your life, it's not an easy mentality or set of habits to break. So, I choose not to have close friends as a means of self-preservation, and I'm really okay with that. There are women I hang with occasionally, and it works because they know their place in my life, and they serve it well, just as I do for them. We might not talk daily, but those bonds are sincere and ones that I can trust. I'd rather have two or three women I know will show up for me when I need them than fifty who I can't rely on just because we talk daily."

"Come here," Dante demanded softly, pulling her in for an embrace. Sade cocooned herself in him, surprised that discussing this with him was causing an emotional response. It wasn't the first time she explained why she didn't have friends with someone, but this felt different. Was it because it was Dante? All this time, he'd been given a pass of sorts. Though he caused a lot of grief between Sade and Imani, he always appeared fair. And when he wasn't fair, he was on Sade's side.

Was there a part of her that resented Dante for his role in their toxic relationship? Did she wish he would have just let both of them go? Her head shook at the thought, and she held him closer. She would have had no one but her grandparents if she didn't have Dante when they were young.

No.

She needed him.

Always had, and probably always will.

"I understand if whatever happened is something you don't want to discuss, but you know you can talk to me about it, right?" Dante cupped her cheeks to look into her watery eyes. "I'm here, Smiley, and nothing you can say will make me love or respect you any less."

"I know, and I appreciate that." Sade sniffled, pushing back her tears. "I don't want to talk about it, but I know I could trust you with it. It's fine, really. I'm a loner by nature. If I meet a woman I get a genuine vibe from, I'm okay connecting with her. It's just not a necessity for me, like most people. Trust me, Dante, I have all I need in you, my grandparents, and my monthly brunches."

Dante eyed her skeptically before nodding and releasing her. "I guess I have to get used to having a wife who isn't as social as me. But I want you to meet Lathan's wife if you're interested. I don't want to hang with them alone all the time. I want you there with me sometimes too. Only if that's something you'd be comfortable with."

"I'll think about it," Sade agreed.

That could work either way, depending on who his wife was. There were only two hair salons in Vanzette, so if they were young, there was a great chance she'd at least seen her before, even if she didn't know her. The malls, barbershops, and salons were where everyone in the town typically got acquainted.

"That's good enough for me."

Dante placed a quick kiss on her lips before pulling the car out of the garage. She went back inside, deciding to check the mail before getting comfortable and binging a new show. The mall wouldn't open for another two hours, so there was no rush for her to start getting ready. By the time she'd reached the mailbox, Dante was reversing out of the driveway.

"You want me to bring you back something to eat? I'll probably get a smoothie and salad from the gym café."

A car slowing its speed caught Sade's attention. When she realized who it was, her eyes bucked, and her heart dropped.

"Fuck," she grumbled, quickly turning toward Dante. He needed to leave... now! "Um, you can just bring me an acai bowl and some green juice," she requested, stepping directly in front of the window. "Bye, babe, I love you!"

"I love you too," he replied, rolling up the window.

As he turned out of the driveway, her grandparents stopped in the middle of the street. Her heart raced as she prayed they hadn't gotten a good look at his face. If they did, all of this would be over.

"The fuck are they even doing here?" she grumbled, looking from one car to the other.

SADE

THANKFULLY, DANTE HEADED down the right side of the street, not paying any attention to the car behind him. Her grandfather turned into the driveway as Sade checked the mail. Keeping her eyes on the back of the Maxima, she made sure Dante didn't look in his rearview mirror to see the car and turn around. If he checked to make sure she was okay since Sade didn't mention having any guests, her fairy tale would be over. Her grandparents wouldn't go along with or approve of what she was doing, no matter the excuse.

As they exited the car, Sade relaxed a little more.

"To what do I owe the pleasure of this surprise?" she asked, hugging her grandmother first, then her grandfather.

They'd both aged gracefully, probably because of the lack of manual labor. Her parents had left them a nice amount of money because of their vital roles in Sade and Imani's lives. And even before they died, her mother had retired them as thanks for raising her as well as they did. Sade would look from her parents to her grandparents and wonder what shifted between the generations that made her parents prioritize work and money as much as they did.

"Well, we haven't heard from you in weeks, so we figured we'd stop in and check on you on our way to St. Louis," Ava answered.

"Grandma, I just texted you yesterday."

"You know that's not what she means," Barron said, wrapping his arm around her shoulders. "You used to come and see us at least every two weeks and call us every other day. Now that the new year has started, you've been a ghost. What's up with that?"

"And who was that leaving this house?" Ava added.

Sade chuckled as she opened the front door of her home. They wasted no time making themselves comfortable in the living room. Not immediately diving into their questions, she offered them both food and drink as she'd been trained to do when guests arrived. As anxious as they seemed to be to know what was going on with her, neither rejected her offer, so Sade ended up fixing them a quick, light breakfast of eggs, toast, and seasoned turkey bacon with fruit. As happy as she was to have her grandparents near, Sade also rushed to get them out of the house.

Dante usually spent a couple of hours at the gym; she needed them gone by the time he returned home.

"You said you're on your way to St. Louis?" she confirmed, sipping her orange juice while they ate at the dining room table.

"Yeah, your great-aunt Celeste invited us to come for a spell so we could get out of the house," Ava answered.

"How long are you going to be there?"

"Just a week."

"Maybe less," Barron added, not to Sade's surprise. Her grandfather hated being out of his home for too long.

"Well, I'm glad y'all stopped by to see me. I've been really busy with work, but I miss you both."

"Are you working on a new book?" Ava asked.

"Yeah, but the inspiration hasn't been flowing lately. I think I have too much on my mind. So that's what's making it take so much time. The block."

Barron suggested, "Maybe you need to get away. Find inspiration elsewhere. You wanna go to St. Louis with us?"

Sade chuckled softly with a shake of her head. "No, but thank you for the offer. I do need new inspiration, though. It'll come to me. I have faith in that."

"And work's the only reason you haven't been reaching out like you used to?" Ava asked before putting a piece of melon into her mouth. "Or does that man have something to do with it too?"

"How do you know it was a man?" Sade asked with a teasing smile.

"I saw his silhouette, but I didn't see his face. How is he?"

"Can we hold off on the details? Just until I know for sure this is going to last?" Sade requested, looking at both of them.

"Is he staying here with you? If so, he—"

"Grandpa," Sade interrupted softly. Respectfully. "He's giving me more than enough money to cover my bills, and he has his own place too. He's serious about us."

That was classic Dante. Even with his uncertainty about them, as soon as he had access to his bank account again, he handed Sade money weekly and sometimes daily. It felt good to finally have someone care for her, even though it wasn't required because they were family. Their relationship wasn't one-sided at all. Dante showed up for her in ways Sade had never considered. And he was so caring and thoughtful. Considerate. Always wanting what was best for her.

She'd finally gotten a lover out of her best friend, but as she considered never being able to share this new source of happiness with those closest to her, Sade was filled with sadness. There would never come a day that she could make this make sense. Would they have to hide out forever? And what about children? Somehow, having everything she'd always wanted with Dante being a possibility was no longer enough. What good was it to have him if she had to hide him the whole damn time?

"Okay, I'll take your word for it now, but I want to meet him soon."

"Yes, sir," she agreed, standing and giving them both kisses on the top of their heads before refilling their juice and coffee.

They continued to talk and eat, and though they didn't want to eat and run, Sade insisted they get back on the road so they wouldn't be arriving late in St. Louis. Barron agreed, and they headed out about ten minutes before Dante returned home. It was a close call, one that had Sade wondering just how long she'd be able to keep this up.

DANTE

"YOU'RE GONNA HAVE to give me more than that, Sade."

Dante hadn't told her, but he had been looking into a few finance and accounting positions in Vanzette and Memphis. While he still desired to open a lounge, he also couldn't deny his love for numbers and money. He didn't remember what led him to no longer work with his old friends, but Dante was ready to return to what he loved. Maybe that would help him shake off the feeling of not belonging that had been nagging him.

The position in Memphis was a chief financial officer position, and with his experience, they were willing to start him out at two hundred thousand a year. Dante thought Sade would be happy, but she got upset as soon as he mentioned Memphis.

"Sit down and tell me why you don't want me to go on this interview in Memphis."

She released the cutest huff that would have made Dante smile if the circumstances had been different. Sade sat next to him at the patio table. It was April and finally warm enough for him to sit out there and be comfortable. The view of the lake always filled Dante with peace. He saw himself living in a condo or high-rise apartment, but small-town living had been good for him... to a certain extent. More than anything, being at war with his own mind made Dante question his surroundings.

"We don't like Memphis," she said with a pout. "That's why we left."

"Why don't we like Memphis?"

Her eyes rolled, and she crossed her arms over her chest. "Dante, can't you just trust me and not go on the interview?"

"No." Sitting up in his seat, Dante considered his words carefully. "On some things, I follow your guidance and lead because I need you to be my memory. I'm still a man, and I need to be in control of my life. You can't tell me not to do something like I'm a child, not provide a reason for why, and expect me to go with it."

Sade scratched the corner of her eye before squeezing the bridge of her nose. "You're right. You're absolutely right. I know we've talked about this before, but I can't help but go into protector mode about you. You're my husband, and... I'd die if anything happened to you. We still don't know who came after you, and I guess I just don't want you to go there, and they try to kill you again."

"Then you *do* think it was intentional and not a random accident or robbery after the fact?"

Sade's expression softened. "I just don't know why someone would rob you after they hit you unless they were on something or in desperate need. Seeing you lying in that bed..." Her head shook. "I don't want to see that again, Dante. I'm sorry for being clingy and trying to tell you what to do. I just don't want anything to happen to you."

Dante took her hand into his. He couldn't deny the sincerity in her tone or her eyes.

"Whatever happened that night, I'm sure I was caught off guard. If someone did target me, they took the cowardly way out by hitting my damn car at night. I can't live in fear and don't want you to either. God spared me, and I'm going to live my life. So unless you can give me a valid reason why I shouldn't go to this interview, I'm going."

Her head and leg shook. "No, I don't. So... I guess the only thing left to say is good luck on your interview."

Before Dante could respond, their doorbell rang. He stood to answer, walking quicker at the sound of hard knocking.

"Who the hell is that?" Sade asked, wrapping her satin robe tighter around her.

"I don't know, but it better be an emergency as hard as they are knocking on this damn door." Dante felt the frown changing the shape of his face as he quickened his pace. He opened the door, his mouth going slack at the sight of two police officers. "How can I help you?"

He lifted his hand from behind to keep Sade from meeting him at the door. Not only did he want to protect her, but he didn't want them looking at her body while she was in her robe.

"We are doing a wellness check on your neighbor..." The white officer looked down at his small notepad. "Willow Green. A family member was worried about her because they hadn't heard from her in several days. We're just checking in with neighbors to see if you all know anything."

"Willow?" Dante turned and looked back at Sade. "That's the woman I met last week, right? Apparently, she's missing."

"Yeah, that's her. Last time we talked, she was preparing for a late-spring-break trip. I think she's in San Juan, but I'm not 100 percent sure."

The Black officer nodded and said something into his walkie-talkie as he walked away.

"Okay, thanks," the white officer said. "We will relay this message to her family. If you hear from her anytime soon, tell her to check in with her family."

"We will," Dante replied, waiting until the officer left to shut the door. "You don't think anything happened to her, do you?" he asked, walking over to Sade. "She seemed cool."

Sade shrugged, running her hands down his chest. "I doubt it. She's probably just enjoying her vacation." Dante nodded, figuring that to be true. "Listen... I'm sorry about earlier. I support you and every decision you make. Congratulations on the interview. I already know you're going to get the job."

"Thank you, Smiley. Your support means the world to me."

As Dante wrapped his arms around her waist, she said, "Why don't we go dancing tonight to celebrate?"

"That works. I planned to meet the guys for drinks, but I can reschedule."

She giggled and nodded. "I'm tickled by how quickly you made new friends. I figured you would because you're a people person, but it always tickles me when you mention the guys, like you've been knowing them for years."

Dante chuckled. "I guess that's a gift. Being able to connect with people quickly, you know?"

"Yeah. It's one of the things that made me fall in love with you while we were in school. You saw me and became my friend when it felt like no one else would. I was crazy about you over that."

"I refuse to believe people didn't want to be your friend, Sade."

Her eyes playfully rolled as she smiled. "You'd be surprised. But fuck that shit, though. I'm about to shower and get dressed so I can start my day. I want to finish as much work as possible since we're going out tonight."

"All right, Day. How are the sketches for the adult coloring book coming along?"

"I had to pause them since the inspiration wasn't flowing. Who knows? Maybe I'll be inspired by people watching and being in your arms tonight."

Dante's eyes lowered to her ass as she headed up the stairs. He would have followed her up if she wasn't on her period and had his way with her. He was going to the interview in Memphis regardless, but he felt better having her support.

DANTE

"How are you adjusting to all that?" Lathan asked.

Dante finally felt comfortable enough to share with him, Pete, and Kurt that he had amnesia. It was odd to them that they'd never seen him around town over the years, and Dante chalked it up to the fact that he probably didn't spend much time in Vanzette before the accident. Learning that he had amnesia had them all asking him a million questions, it felt like, and Dante was starting to regret he'd even told them. What was supposed to be a night of drinking and watching the game was starting to feel like an interview.

"I'm more settled now," Dante admitted. "In the beginning, it was hard, I can't lie. My wife has been patient with me, so that helped."

"And you don't remember anything about her at all?" Pete asked.

"Nope." Dante shook his head before taking a sip of beer. "I didn't remember anything about her, or anyone else, for that matter."

"Cool. I was about to say, is she *really* your wife?" Kurt asked with a chuckle. "But if you don't have any memories of anyone, that's less creepy."

"Yeah, I mean, she had pictures of us and shit. Memories to share. And she knows me well. I've never questioned her genuineness or integrity. My wife is for me. Not a lot of people would tolerate the things we've gone through. I'm grateful to have her."

"Man, I don't know if I could do it," Lathan said. "I think my ego would be too bruised if my wife didn't remember me. I'd have to start all over again and risk it not working because we've changed and no longer fit." His head shook. "I might just end it before it even began again, so I commend her for sticking with it. You're definitely lucky."

Pete and Kurt agreed before Dante asked, "What does your wife do here? I'm trying to get Sade out of the house more, but all she wants to do is brunch."

Lathan chuckled as he grabbed a few chips out of the bowl. "She's almost the same way. Veronica is a homebody. I can get her out of the house every once in a while."

"Does she have sisters or friends that she hangs with here?"

"Two friends. Her sister is in a different state. You want to put them together so they can link?"

"If she's down. I know I'll probably have to coax Sade into it. She needs to come up out of her shell."

"I feel you. I be saying the same shit about Veronica. It's cool that she's so to herself, but sometimes I want to do stuff as a couple that we can't. Kurt and his wife have hosted three couples vacations we haven't been able to attend because V wasn't comfortable not knowing any of the women."

"Wait, you're married too?" Dante confirmed, directing the question to Kurt.

Kurt nodded. "Yeah. Pete's the only one that's single. My wife is more of an extrovert than V, though. She's out and about in Vanzette or Memphis literally all weekend. I be having to make her ass sit down and rest."

Dante chuckled. He'd keep Sade away from Kurt's wife for now, but he wondered if she'd get along with Veronica.

The idea of group outings and couples trips appealed to him, and he hoped Sade would be okay with it too. He and Lathan agreed to talk to their wives about meeting before their attention returned to the game, and all Dante could do was hope this didn't blow up in his face.

The Next Weekend

Dante watched as Veronica and Sade gave their attention to their phones. At the beginning of the evening, the conversation flowed freely. Veronica was actually excited about meeting Sade, and Sade felt the same way. They talked and got to know each other for a few minutes, then shut down. At first, it irritated Dante. Now, he found it amusing. Neither woman wanted to gain a new friend, and now, Dante had no choice but to accept that.

At least now, if they went out as a group, Dante hoped Sade and Veronica would talk and cling to each other. That, at this point, would be a success.

"I think we're about to head out," Dante announced as he and Lathan waited for another round of drinks at the bar. "I know they both would rather be at home."

Lathan chuckled. "I agree. They tried, though. I'm proud of V. Normally, she would have asked me to take her home by now, so that's a good sign."

"Yeah. They might not be talkative, but I guess this is a good start."

When they made their way over to the table, Dante told Sade, "Here. Take this shot, then we can go."

Sade's grin made him laugh as she grabbed it and chugged it down.

"It was nice meeting you both," Sade said, practically leaping from her seat.

"You too," Lathan said as Veronica took her shot.

"Text me and let me know how you like the show," Veronica said.

"I will. I think I'm going to like it. Maybe I just didn't give it a chance in the beginning."

The ladies embraced before Sade grabbed Dante's hand and quickly led him out of the bar.

He chuckled and shook his head, doubling his steps to keep up with her. "You win. I will not try to make you a new friend anymore."

"Thank you very much. She's cool, though. I don't think we'll be talking regularly, but we can talk if you ever want to have a party or something, and she's there."

Dante opened the door for her, tapping her ass as she got inside.

"What do I get for getting out of the house at your request?" Sade asked with a seductive tone.

"Whatever you want."

Her hand slid up his thigh, cupping his dick. "This?"

"You know you can always have that."

Sade giggled as he closed the door before jogging over to his side of the car. It didn't matter how many times they had sex now. The next time always felt like the first time. Dante couldn't get enough of Sade in every way possible.

SADE

SADE WAS SURPRISED when Veronica asked to meet her for lunch, but she agreed. Instead of going to a restaurant, Sade invited Veronica over. She'd just finished setting out wine and a charcuterie board when the doorbell rang. Sade closed her kimono over her SKIMS lounge dress and scurried to the door. At the sight of Veronica behind it, she genuinely smiled. There was something about Veronica putting forth the effort instead of it coming from their husbands that made her heart light.

"Hey," Sade greeted after opening the door and letting Veronica in.

"Hey, how are you?"

"I'm well. You?"

"Same. You have a beautiful home. I didn't know we had any lakes in Vanzette."

"Technically, we don't," Sade agreed, leading Veronica over to the dining room table. "It's man-made. I had it built when I bought this land."

"Cool. I'm really glad we met now. I love sitting out by bodies of water."

Sade laughed as they sat across from each other. "Well, you're welcome over any time."

"I know what you're doing," Veronica said.

Sade's smile dropped. "What do you mean?"

"With Dante. I know exactly who he is." Veronica poured herself a glass of wine, remaining silent so her words could settle in Sade.

"I don't know what you mean, Veronica."

She chuckled. "I know that's Imani's husband—the man missing from Memphis. Obviously, you don't recognize me. Could be because I was three hundred pounds heavier while we were in college. I went to UT Chatt and graduated the same year as you and Dante."

Scratching her scalp, Sade looked down at the table. There was a butter knife in each of the different flavored preserves, but they weren't strong enough to kill her, though they would do some damage. If she tried to strike, Veronica would probably make a run for it.

"Why didn't you say anything before?" Sade asked, trying to buy herself some time to devise a plan.

"I didn't think it was my place. I support your business. That's why I was so excited to meet you. I always buy your books for my nieces and nephews, and I even give them away to my patients. I own the pediatric clinic on Glistening Boulevard. So when I first saw you with Dante, it caught me off guard, and I needed time to process it." Veronica took a sip of her wine. "I thought about going to the police or Imani, but she was so cruel to me. She talked about me every day that she saw me. And she didn't just crack jokes about me. She made the other girls with her do it too." Her eyes watered as she stared into the distance. "I thought UT Chatt would be a safe space for me, but Imani made my life miserable there. So I said... Why would I do something to help her? You look happy, and Dante does too, so I won't ruin that. Your secret is safe with me."

Sade swallowed hard as Veronica stood. She popped a walnut into her mouth before saying, "You need to go through your pictures and remove the ones of you and other men over the years from your profile. It will look suspect if you're telling people you've been married for years, but there's proof on your page that you've dated throughout that time."

Sade's mouth dropped as she watched Veronica down the rest of her wine.

"Th-thank you, V. I... thank you."

Veronica's smile was soft as she said, "Just be careful and be happy. Both you and Dante deserve that."

Nodding, Sade wiped a falling tear as Veronica headed for the door. Once she closed it behind her, Sade sighed in relief before hopping up and grabbing her phone off the island. She'd completely forgotten to delete past men from her profile, but Veronica was right. The right person getting a hold of that would have destroyed everything she'd built.

SADE

SADE STARED AT Willow. She was refusing to eat. When Sade lifted the sandwich to her lips, Willow shook her head.

"If you're going to kill me, you might as well just do it now."

"There's another alternative that keeps you alive, so you need to eat."

Willow's head tilted as she eyed Sade. "What's the other alternative?"

"You have to eat first, then I'll tell you."

Willow considered her words briefly before agreeing and letting Sade feed her. When she finished, Sade had her to call her mom. Willow promised her she was okay, out of the country, and having poor service. When her mom asked her why she didn't tell them she was leaving town, she said it was a spur-of-the-moment thing. A free trip with a friend she couldn't turn down. Her mother accepted the lie and told Willow to call her when she returned home, and Willow agreed.

After the phone call, Sade prepared to leave, but she did want to keep her word and tell Willow the other option besides death.

"I am considering letting you go and paying you off, but there's no guarantee you won't take the money and still go to the police."

"I wouldn't." Willow's head shook adamantly. "You don't even have to give me any money. I'll still leave. I want no part of this."

"You obviously did. You agreed to be Patrice's pawn. Now, look at you."

Willow tightly squeezed her eyes shut. "That was a mistake. One that I will forever regret. If you let me go, I promise I won't say anything."

As soon as Sade pulled out the syringe, Willow's head shook. "Please, don't give me that. I promise I'll be quiet."

"No. You betrayed my trust for a woman you didn't even know. We've lived by each other for years, and you just... took Patrice's word as truth against me."

"Th-that's not true, Sade. I didn't believe her. That's why I was looking for proof that she was wrong."

"You're lying. If you didn't believe her, you would have told me what she said the minute she first brought it to you."

Distress covered Willow's face as she shimmied in her seat, but Sade had her bound so tightly that she could not get out.

"Sade, please. I don't care what you're doing with Dante or anyone else. Your secret isn't worth my life. Just tell me what I must do to prove you can trust me, and I'll do it. I promise."

Sade briefly considered her words before sticking the syringe in her arm. "I'll think about it. You really hurt my feelings, Willow. Why didn't you have faith in me?"

Willow's eyes lowered, and her head bobbed back as she fought to stay awake. Drowsiness immediately took over her. Her mouth opened and closed, with no words coming out. Sade watched her until she was back asleep.

"I knew something was wrong because Patrice never misses work. All she could talk about was paying off her house so she could sell it and leave Vanzette. Now, she's gone."

Sade stared at the TV and listened to the news anchor. Patrice had been found. When she didn't call or come to work for three days straight, her boss went to her home to look for her. He lifted her garage door when she didn't answer and found her in her car. Sade had taken her phone and purse to make it look like a robbery, and from the news anchor's commentary, that's what the police were leaning toward. Sade would be free and clear if no one questioned why nothing in the house was taken.

Massaging her temples, she lay back on the couch. It felt like things were stacking and preparing to crash down. Her intuition told her to take Dante to another city and get the hell out of Vanzette. Between his upcoming job interview, Willow, and Patrice, Sade didn't know how much longer she could hold her secret together. There was never a time she questioned if Dante was worth everything she was doing, but now... she was...

Trina Roe: I know what you did.

Sade stared at the message she'd gotten from Trina on Facebook for a few seconds before considering whether she wanted to reply. It was odd to Sade that Trina was messaging her, seeing as she'd gone to great lengths to avoid Sade in person. Curious about what Trina was referring to, Sade sent her a message.

Sade the Artist: What exactly are you talking about Trina?

Trina Roe: I don't think this is something you want to discuss online.

Sade the Artist: I'm not about to play games with you. Say what you have to say, or get out of my inbox.

Trina Roe: Patrice.

Trina Roe: Meet me at Covington's tonight at 6. We need to talk.

"Shit," Sade muttered, standing from her seat. There was no way she'd get any work done now. She left her office, waiting until she made it downstairs to message Trina back and tell her she'd be there.

"What the hell does she know about Patrice?"

Sade's leg bounced as she anxiously waited for Trina to arrive. She was seven minutes late, and it was taking everything in Sade not to leave. There was no telling what she thought she knew about Patrice, and Sade was almost too scared to find out.

After what felt like forever, Trina waltzed her way into the bar and sat next to Sade. She waited for the bartender to take her drink order before saying, "Patrice warned me about you. She said she was suspicious of you holding that man hostage and that it was because of you if anything happened to her. Imani... that's your sister, right?" Sade's head jerked to the left in her direction, causing Trina to smile. "I'll take that as a yes. Patrice told me to contact Imani Williams and tell her that Dante Williams is here with you if she dies or disappears. According to Patrice, the man I think is your husband is really your brother-in-law. If that's true, I will need a hell of a lot of money to make me forget that conversation and information."

While a part of Sade wanted to beat around the bush and stall, quite frankly, she knew that wasn't wise. She couldn't deny any of what Trina had said. If she lied, all Trina would do was call Imani, and everything would blow up in her face.

"How much do you want?"

"Hmm..." Trina's pointer finger bounced against her chin. "One hundred thousand, and you'll never be bothered by me again."

"What's my guarantee that that's the truth?"

"I'll leave town. There's nothing holding me here besides family, and they can visit me. I can leave as soon as you give me the money."

Sade sighed and nodded in agreement. "Fine. You have a deal."

"Good. Now, don't think you can try anything crazy. My cousin is watching us in this bar, and he will trail me home. He doesn't know what this meeting is about, and no one has to... as long as you give me that money."

Sade smiled. *Look at her... thinking she's running shit.*

"Okay. You need to delete our messages. Nothing can tie you to me. You will also need to delete whatever Patrice gave you with that information. After tonight, don't call me again. I'll meet you at the Rotting Cellar next Friday night at seven with the money. And please, don't be late."

Without waiting for Trina to respond, Sade left as her anger rose. Too many people... too many loose ends. There was no way in hell she trusted Trina not to try to hit her up for money again. She would have to die—soon.

The Next Friday
733 Oakley Street

Sade checked the address one last time before getting out of her car. She'd parked a block away from Oakley Street. After giving Trina the money, Sade had Veronica follow her while she stayed behind to ensure she'd be on camera long after Trina left. Since she last saw Trina, Sade tried to convince herself that it would be safe to let her live, but she couldn't. Trina was annoying as fuck and needed to be dealt with.

Getting out of her car, Sade headed down the street, her head hung low in case any cameras were nearby. She walked the block it took to get to Trina's house. Veronica had already checked to make sure no other cars or people were there before leaving. All the lights were off except one.

Sade walked toward the back of the house, smiling at the sight of the opened window. She climbed inside what had to be Trina's bedroom. Not wanting to alert Trina to her presence, she felt her way around the room until she made it outside. With the way the house was designed, light from the living room also illuminated the hall.

Quietly, Sade tiptoed down the hall, pulling her knife from behind her back. She stood behind Trina briefly before grabbing her hair and tilting her head. Trina was quicker than she expected... but not quick enough. When she'd punched Sade in the nose, the blade slid across Trina's throat. She watched for a few seconds as the life faded from Trina before the feel of blood running down her nose gained her attention.

"Shit," she whispered, cupping her bloody nose.

Sade ran down the hall, making sure none of her blood dripped in the process. Instead of stopping in the bathroom, she cut on the light in the bedroom with her elbow in search of the money. It was on Trina's dresser, so she grabbed it and hopped back out the window. Sade pulled her shirt off and used it to cover her nose as she briskly walked down the street.

"This has got to be the last one," she murmured, unable to take having another person's blood on her hands...

DANTE

AFTER SADE WOKE Dante up with a sloppy, slow head, she gave him the warmth of her pussy to start his day. As much as he enjoyed being inside of her, the mood was instantly ruined at the sight of Sade's shoulders caving as she sat on the edge of the bed and sniffled. When Dante reached for her, she got out of bed and quickly went to the bathroom.

Deciding to give her space, he went to the closest guest bathroom to shower and take care of his hygiene. When he finished, he met Sade in the bedroom, and she looked more like herself.

"I'm going to be okay. You know that, right?" Dante asked, sitting on the bed next to her. He didn't realize how nervous she was about him going to Memphis for the interview until this morning.

Sade nodded. "That's... easy to say, Dante. But we don't really know that."

"You know what I know?" Dante asked quietly, kissing her on the neck. "I know I am not leaving you again. Not anytime soon. I promise I will make it back to you, healthy and unharmed. Okay?"

Hugging his neck, Sade agreed with, "Okay."

Dante smiled softly as he held her, hoping she had as much faith in him as he had in himself.

171

As Dante walked down the hall, he gave himself the same pep talk he did in the car and on the drive to Memphis. Since the accident, he'd been more excited about this job than anything else. Regardless of how much money he had saved, Dante had always been a workingman, and having too much time on his hands didn't feel right. Plus, the more money he had in the bank, the better his chance of securing a loan for the lounge building.

Pulling in a deep breath, Dante ran his hand down his black tie and breathed deeply. He'd dressed classically for the interview—black suit and tie, white button-down shirt. His hair and beard were freshly trimmed, and the pussy his wife gave him had him walking with extra pep in his step. Seeing her cry broke his heart this morning, but Dante couldn't live in fear, and he hoped she chose not to as well.

He knocked on Ian Sanders's door and waited for him to let him in. Instead, Ian yelled, "Enter," causing Dante to open the door and step inside. Another reason Dante was so excited about working at Sanders Financial was that a pair of Black brothers ran it.

At the sight of Dante, Ian stood. "Damn, it's good to see you, man! How have you been?"

Ian walked around his desk, pulling Dante in for a handshake and a hug. Dante chuckled, returning the gesture.

"I'm sorry, man. Do I know you?"

"Dante, don't act like you don't know me, brother. What the fuck is going on with you?"

Dante ran his hand over his head. "Look, man, I'ma keep it a buck with you. I was in a car accident in January. Though I remember things about myself, I don't remember anyone else."

Ian's mouth dropped, and his brows hitched. "Damn. I'm so sorry to hear that, brother. We went to college together. We pledged together. We were in each other's weddings. Is any of this ringing a bell with you?" Ian asked as he grabbed his phone off his desk.

Dante's head shook as he scratched his eyebrow. "I'm sorry, but no."

Ian gave Dante his phone, pointing at a picture of them. "This was your wedding. Me and Eric threw your bachelor party in Vegas. It was a time, man. To this day, I can't go back and not think about the shit we did there."

Ian's laugh went in one ear and out of the other as Dante stared at the picture of him and Ian with a woman that wasn't Sade. But she was in a wedding dress... standing next to him. Holding him. Like *she* was his wife.

"Who is this?" Dante asked, pointing at the woman in the picture.

"That's Imani, your wife. Well, she was. I don't know if you two got divorced or not. We lost contact after college. That's why I was so excited to see your résumé come through."

Dante's head shook as he processed Ian's words. "You're saying I married her in college?"

"Yeah." Ian chuckled. "Have a seat. It seems like I need to give you a history lesson."

Though Dante chuckled, his nerves were getting the best of him. What Ian was saying didn't make any sense. Weakly, Dante plopped down in his seat.

"When did Imani and I get married?"

"Right after she had the twins. Right before senior year."

"Twins?" Dante repeated, sitting up in his seat. "They were mine?" he reasoned. "I have kids?"

Ian's frame weakened as he sat back in his seat. "Yeah, man. None of this is ringing any bells for you? Where the hell have you been since January?"

"Start from the beginning," Dante requested, ignoring Ian's question. "I'm married to someone named Imani, and we have a set of twins?"

"Yeah. Like I said, I don't know if y'all are still married because we lost touch, but yeah, you married her right before our senior year. She was a junior."

"And you haven't heard anything about me being missing?"

Ian's head shook. "Nah. I've been so busy trying to find new employees for the Memphis office that I don't have my ears to the streets for anything. I left town right after college and started my first financial firm in New York. I just moved back to Memphis about two weeks ago to start recruiting."

Dante's head was spinning. There was a chance something happened with this Imani woman because Sade did say they got married right after college. Did he have two kids out here that knew nothing about his whereabouts? Three months had passed since the accident. That was a hell of a long time to go without hearing from your father. He knew if not hearing from his parents drove him crazy as an adult, his kids were feeling twice the anxiety.

"I, uh..." Dante stood, looking around the office in a daze. "I have to get out of here. This is a lot that I need to process."

"I completely understand. If you want the job, it's yours, brother. Just call me once you've had time to decompress, and we can discuss the details."

With a nod, Dante extended his hand for Ian to shake. "I appreciate you, brother. Thank you."

As he headed out of the office, Dante massaged his chest. Something was wrong. Well, something had always been wrong, Dante couldn't deny that. Did Sade know about this other wife? If so, why hadn't she mentioned it? Did Dante keep that part of his life from her? He had more questions than answers at this point, and he was hoping Sade could help him sort things out.

SADE

SADE HAD NO idea what time Dante was going to get back from Memphis. To avoid driving herself crazy at home, she fed Willow, then headed out for some retail therapy in Nashville. By the time she made it home, Dante was already there. He was seated at the dining room table, tie loosened, with a glass of brown liquor in his hand.

Had he not gotten the job?

"Hey, babe," she spoke softly, taking small steps in his direction. "How did it go?"

Dante waited until she was sitting next to him to calmly say, "I'm only going to ask you this once, Sade. Please, tell me the truth."

Her heart dropped. Swallowing hard, Sade nodded.

"Of course."

"Was I married before you?"

Her ears rang. Mouth dried. "Why do you ask that?"

Dante slid his phone over to her, and at the sight of a picture of him and Imani on their wedding day, she gasped.

"Where did you get that from?"

"The guy I had the interview with was a friend from college. A good one, apparently." Dante swiped. "The whole time I was here waiting for you, I felt like shit. I felt like I'd lied to you about my life. Because that would be the only reason I would have kids and an ex-wife that you did not mention to me. But then I thought about it and said if that was the case, you'd know, because you said we went to school together." He swiped to a picture of Sade and Imani hugging, with Dante standing behind them. "So I told Ian to send me some of the pictures, and this is one of the ones he sent."

Tugging her ear, Sade looked away.

"You wanna explain this to me, truthfully, Sade?"

She wiped her tears quickly, knowing there was no space for them here. She wasn't the victim—Dante was.

"Yes, but I need your word that you will hear me out completely before asking anything or trying to leave."

Dante nodded, releasing a shaky breath. "Okay."

Sade expected her heart to race when the truth came out. It wasn't. In fact, it was beating quite slowly. So slow she was sure it would stop beating altogether by the time she was done talking.

"We did go to school together. We were best friends, but we were never lovers, and we were never married." She paused, giving him time to process that. "Imani is my sister. She's a year younger than me. Before she came to high school with us, things were perfect between us. Imani had always been spoiled and used to getting her way, and she wanted you when I told her I liked you, so she got you." Sade chuckled, wiping a tear that slid down her cheek. "She's always had a mean streak, so she was a bully in school. Being sisters didn't stop her from bullying me because I was quiet, dressed differently, and wore glasses and braces. You would always stick up for me, which made her hate me more. My sister and I fought a lot, and we just... never had a good relationship when we started going to school together. After our parents died, we made amends, but we still aren't close. I tolerate her, and she uses me. She's still rude and cruel and not someone I'd willingly spend time with if we weren't related."

"How could I have married someone so horrible?"

Sade shrugged. "She's beautiful, and she fit you perfectly back then. You didn't really care about her character, just her popularity and looks. You even told me in college the only reason you were marrying her was because she was pregnant. Both of you cheated on each other and had a toxic-ass relationship, but when the twins came, that changed. You tried to be the best father and husband you could be, and Imani took advantage of that."

His head shook. "Okay, so we had a bad marriage. That's no excuse for you to keep me from my family, Sade."

"That's not why I did it," she reasoned, covering his hand with hers. "You went into business with Imani and two other friends, Eric and his wife, Jessica. Imani has been stealing from clients, faking financial statements, and laundering money. She's setting you up to take the fall for it. I think you found out the night of the accident." Sade wiped away more tears as Dante looked away. "That's why I kept you here. She's trying to send you to prison for her choices, and you didn't deserve that."

"That wasn't a choice for you to make, Sade. Even if you felt like I didn't need to go back, you should have been honest with me about who I was and what was going on."

"But I... I got selfish, okay? It wasn't my plan originally. Being related to you was the only way they'd let me see you in the hospital, so I told them I was your wife. It felt so good saying those words, and I just... got caught up. I felt like I'd never have the chance to experience you in that way, so I took advantage."

"What did you plan to do when I found out?"

"Cut my losses, but pray you understood why I did what I did."

Dante chuckled as his head shook. He removed his hand from under hers, scooting his chair back to put space between them. "You kept me from my kids, Sade. That's unforgivable."

"They aren't your kids," she muttered. "Imani cheated on you. She knows they aren't yours, but she's not going to tell you. Get a DNA test done because I know you're not going to believe me."

"I have a hard time believing all of this, honestly."

"Look, I can give you the name of your business. Just Google 'Four Financial, Memphis, Tennessee, scandal,' and everything will come up. She's putting it all on you, Dante. You can't go back."

He stood. "My parents?"

"They are Deandre and Olivia Williams. They aren't the people you met. You do have friends and relatives that have been looking for you. I just didn't want to tell you because I didn't want them to tell Imani that you were here. If she knew, she'd send the police after you. There's no doubt about that in my mind."

"Do you think my wife is the one that tried to have me killed?"

Sade's head shook as she wiped more tears and stood. "No. I don't think so. She wants you to take the fall for this. She wouldn't risk going to prison by killing you."

"And she thinks I'm missing?"

"Yes. Well, she thinks you're running from the charges. She said she's going to try to have you legally declared dead, hoping it would make the FBI drop the charges against you."

Dante stared into her eyes as his watered. The sight was too much for Sade to bear, so she looked away.

"Out of respect for our friendship and you trying to protect me, I'm not going to raise my voice at you. But what you did was fucked up, no matter the reason. You've been lying to me for months, Day. You made me fall in love with you, knowing I was married to someone else. Your sister at that. No matter how foul she is, this is a reflection of *your* character, not hers. And regardless of if the twins are mine or not, they know me as their father. You've kept them from me for three months. Do you understand that?"

Sade nodded, gripping the edge of the table as her body weakened.

He was going to leave her.

She knew it.

Worse, there was nothing she could do about it.

This was her fault, and she knew this day would come.

"I understand. I was more loyal to you than any of them. I won't ever apologize for that."

He reached for her just to quickly pull away. "I'm so angry with you, but all I want to do is pull you into my arms and comfort you." Dante walked away, telling her, "I need to get away. I need to process all this shit and go to Memphis. See Imani. Give me her... my... address. I'm going there tomorrow."

"Dante, I don't think—"

He lifted his hand, silencing her. "You don't get to have any input on my life, Sade. Not anymore."

A low groan escaped her, as if his words literally hit her in her chest. "You're right," she whispered. "I'll text you the address and her number. Just... *please*... be careful, Dante."

Sade grabbed her purse and headed toward her keys. She went to the garage, getting in her BMW and speeding out quickly. She'd break if she had to watch him pack his things and leave...

IMANI

The First FBI Encounter

AS IMANI HEADED *toward her car with several shopping bags in hand, she was surrounded by four men and two women, all dressed in black. She dropped the bags, looking from one person to another as she walked backward.*

"Imani Williams," the younger of the two women spoke, flashing her a badge and ID. "I'm Agent Fields with the Memphis Branch of the Federal Bureau of Investigation." A black SUV pulled up behind them. "Can I get you to step inside of this truck?"

"Do I have a choice?" Imani asked.

"No, you don't."

As two agents picked up her bags, a third gripped her elbow and helped her into the SUV. When the door closed behind her, it sped off.

"What the hell? Where are you taking me?" she asked, looking from the man that was seated next to her to the two in the front seats.

"We're just going to ride around the parking lot and talk," the older man sitting next to her replied, handing her a manila folder.

Imani opened it, her heart dropping at the falsified documents she'd made along with pictures of her and Enrique—the dealer she'd been cleaning money for.

He placed a single piece of paper on top, and words like "fraud," "laundering," and "infringement" stood out most. "We have enough evidence to send you to federal prison for a really, really long time." He placed a business card in her hand. "Tomorrow evening, my director is expecting me to execute warrants for criminal charges against everyone included in the Four Financial fraud scheme. You have twelve hours to give me information on someone my director would consider more dangerous and valuable than you. Otherwise, you will be arrested and charged with several counts of fraud, corporate theft, money laundering, and tax evasion." As his hand rubbed across his mouth, tears slipped down her cheeks.

"Now whoever did this was very smart." She saw him stare at the side of her face out of the corner of her eye. "They made all these fake statements and charges in different names and ID numbers. But you know what makes us point the finger at you?" Imani's head shook rapidly as she wiped her face. He flipped a few pages and pointed at the picture of her and Enrique. "If you're cleaning his money, it's safe to assume you're the one that's been doing all this other stuff too."

"But I—"

"I'm not here to argue with you," he said, silencing her. "Like I said, you have twelve hours to give me someone more dangerous and valuable than you. Otherwise, you're going to prison. And how do you think Enrique will respond to that?"

The SUV stopped, and the doors unlocked. They ushered her out of the truck just as quickly as they'd put her inside. Imani weakly got inside of her Maserati. Just as she started the car, she hurriedly opened the door to vomit. After wiping her mouth, she closed the door and released a quick sob. Composing herself, she muttered, "No, bitch. Now is not the time to cry and shit. You need to figure this out—now."

Running the tips of her stiletto-shaped nails against her thighs, Imani thought of a way out. The only thing that definitely pointed to her was Enrique. Everything else was circumstantial. All she had to do was point the finger at someone else. Whose ID number and checks had she used most? Who was most responsible for withdrawing and depositing payments? Yes, it was her responsibility to pay their taxes quarterly, but it was Dante's responsibility to have the statements created and filed with their accountant.

Dante.

"No," she whispered, chin trembling as her tears fell. "I can't put this on him, but I don't have any other choice. I used his information the most because I had access to it. If it's him or me, I'm going to always choose me. I just have to make sure he won't find out."

After putting her car in drive and heading out of the parking lot, Imani dialed Adam's number.

"Yeah?" he answered after four rings.

"Where are you? We need to talk. Face-to-face..."

IMANI

Back to the Present

ADAM, ADMITTEDLY, WAS the kind of man Imani's parents would have wanted her to stay away from. In fact, her grandparents used to say, date the bad boys but marry the potential CEO. That was exactly what Imani had done when she married Dante Williams. Being with him set her up financially and provided her with the perfect father for her children. Except Dante wasn't their father; Adam was.

It wasn't Imani's intention to pawn her twins off on Dante. When she found out she was pregnant, she decided she would get a DNA test done and leave Dante if the twins weren't his. Adam was less stable with his rapping and drug dealing, but he was fun... and exciting... and the sex was amazing.

Dante proposed, complicating the situation. Then Adam was arrested, and that made Imani's choice even clearer. The DNA results proved Adam was the father, so she burned them and tried to forget she even knew Adam.

For a while, Imani was at peace with her choice. Their marriage was cool, they made a hell of a lot of money, and Imani was living a good life. However, after a few years, her desire for more excitement consumed her, and the cheating started all over again. Eventually, she met another drug dealer who was more interested in her business than her pussy, and that's when the money laundering started. It didn't help that the dealer was Adam's old supplier. Enrique ended up pulling some strings and having Adam released a few years early from prison as thanks for all the hard work Imani had been putting in.

Last year, she was sure her life was on the verge of becoming perfect. She was making more money than ever, Adam was out of prison, and Dante had no earthly idea she was getting ready to divorce him. Then... clients started complaining, and she learned about the civil case. Then... She was approached by the FBI with proof of her schemes. It felt like second nature to shift the blame on Dante when presented with the evidence, but Imani felt bad about it before and immediately after.

She'd talked to Sade and Adam, and Adam was the one that convinced her to let Dante take the fall so they could get to their happily ever after. Like a silly woman in love, Imani agreed. She wasn't expecting Dante to flee the city, and she for damn sure didn't expect the FBI to expect her to answer for his crimes.

Unintentionally, Imani sighed and rolled over onto her side to face Adam. She'd gone to his loft apartment to get a break from life. That's what Adam had always been for her—an escape. The one person she could be around, and her mind would be completely clear, even when they first met during her sophomore year of college. That wasn't the case tonight, though. Tonight, thoughts of Dante terrorized her.

At the sound of her sigh, Adam briefly looked up from his phone. In personality and looks, he was completely different from Dante. Adam was tall and wide with milk chocolate-hued skin. His entire chest and both arms were covered in tattoos. Prison had turned his body into bulging biceps and muscles. On his face was a mustache-goatee combo that drew attention to his plump lips. He had straight brows and dark eyes.

"What's wrong?" Adam asked.

"Thinking about Dante."

Adam dropped his phone onto the bed. "I just fucked you, and you thinking about the last nigga?"

Imani smiled as she shoved his chest. "Not in that way. He's missing, and I'm concerned about what that means for me. For us."

Adam's head shook as he sat up and rested against the headboard. "That don't mean shit for us."

Imani sighed as she sat up and shook her head. "This is already affecting me, Adam. They've already frozen our bank accounts to pay back what we owe. If Dante doesn't stand trial for this civil suit, it's going to fall on me. All my hard work to build my wealth is going down the drain because I got greedy. I have to find a permanent way out of this."

"His death was supposed to be the permanent way out of this."

Imani turned slightly to face him. "What do you mean?"

"I mean, I paid my cousin to kill his ass in a way that looked like a random accident. He's the one that ran into him in the truck. Dante going to jail wouldn't absolve you of any charges, but Dante being dead would have. If he goes down, you risk being charged for being his wife and business partner too. He was the first indicted. Who's to say they don't plan to come after the rest of you? If he would have died, the case would have died with him. Atlas swears Dante was damn near dead when he left him there, so I don't understand what the hell went wrong."

Adam's words came out so casually, Imani almost thought she'd heard him wrong.

"Did you just admit to paying someone to have my husband killed?"

"Yeah," he replied casually, grabbing the marijuana-filled cigar off the nightstand. "You got a problem with that?"

"Yes," Imani replied before chuckling. "Don't you think that's something you should have discussed with *me* first?"

"For what?"

"That's my *husband*, Adam!"

"And? You don't care about him enough to be faithful and not send him to jail, but you care enough about him to want him alive? Fuck outta here with that bullshit."

Adam stood and headed out of the bedroom. As much as Imani wanted to argue with him, it would have been pointless. Things had always been black and white with him. To Adam, because Imani said she was willing to do whatever it took to leave Dante and be with him, there were no rules or limits.

"Crazy-ass nigga," she grumbled, placing her feet on his cream carpet. "I don't know why I even got back with him."

Well, that wasn't true. Imani knew *exactly* why she'd gotten back with him. Because she was attracted to him, because he was the only man who could handle her, because he was just as greedy and ambitious as she was, *and* because he was the father of her children. Imani grabbed her phone off the nightstand to check her notifications. At the sight of her camera app notification, her heart dropped.

"Dante," she whispered, trembling fingers covering her lips. "You're back."

Dropping her phone onto the bed, Imani stood and quickly dressed. She was curious about where Dante had been and what he would say. Imani considered telling Adam that he was back, but now, she didn't trust him. If he knew, there was no guarantee he wouldn't try to get Atlas to finish the job he'd started. Before anything was done to Dante, Imani was owed answers—and she was going home to get them.

DANTE

Dante HATED TO admit it, but when he entered the home he shared with Imani in Memphis, it felt more like him. The innovation, upscale designs. The cream-and-white décor. The high ceilings and wall-to-wall windows.

His fingers ran across the pictures of him, Imani, and their twins on the wall by the front door. Mila and Nila, he'd learned from Sade. They'd just recently turned twelve, and Dante missed that. To keep himself from getting upset with Sade, he tried to block out that truth. Sade's actions were horrible, but her intentions were pure. No one had ever gone to such an extreme to protect him, and Dante didn't know how he felt about that.

After having spent months getting to know Sade on a romantic level, Dante wasn't sure why they'd never gotten together. He guessed he wouldn't know until he spent time with Imani. From the sound of it, Imani had bombarded her way into his heart and life, and Sade unwillingly stepped aside. That sounded like the kind of girl he would have gone for back in the day. The one that was loud with how she felt... and easy.

Dante promised Sade that he wouldn't tell anyone that he'd been with her all this time, especially Imani. From the sound of it, their relationship was already on shaky ground, and Dante didn't want to be the reason it crumbled altogether. As much as Dante wanted to call Sade, he resisted the urge. In no way did he want her to think he was okay with what she'd done, but he couldn't help the burning desire to hear her voice that filled him.

When he couldn't take it anymore, Dante pulled his phone out and called her, reminding himself to take the picture of them together off his wallpaper.

"Hey," Sade answered quickly. "I'm so happy you called."

"I just wanted to let you know I was here." And he wanted to hear her voice, but Sade didn't need to know that.

"Good. Have you... seen her yet?"

"Nah." Dante's head shook as he walked farther into the house and went upstairs. "She's not here."

The bedrooms were downstairs. Upstairs, there were two offices, one for him and Imani, a playroom for the twins, a home theater, and what looked like a mini-casino. This fit his vibe, and Dante hated that. He sat at the poker table as Sade asked...

"Are you going to tell her you know what she's been up to?"

"Not yet. I want to see where her head is at first. I know you said she's setting me up, but I just can't believe that. I'm going to tell her the truth, that I had an accident and lost my memory, and see what she says and does. Hopefully, she will do the right thing and come clean."

Sade chuckled. "My sister won't do that, but good luck. When she shows you her true colors, make sure you have a plan in place." She sniffled. "Bail money ready to go and lawyers on speed dial. All that jazz."

Sade was convinced Dante was going to prison, and that alarmed him. She knew her sister better than he did at this point. Was he playing with fire by coming back to Memphis?

"You really think she'd do that to me?"

"Yes!" Sade yelled. "You need to get out of Memphis ASAP, Dante, even if you don't come back here with me. Imani's going to set you up. Even if it's not immediately, she's going to turn on you."

The floor vibrated, signaling the opening of the garage. "She's here. I gotta go."

"Okay. I-I love you, babe. And I'm really sorry."

Dante's eyes closed as his jaws clenched. Instead of replying, he disconnected the call and made his way down the hall. He heard the clacking of heels before anything else. Imani made her way up the stairs before he could go down them.

"Damn," he mumbled at the sight of her.

He hated to compare the sisters, but he could see why Imani had gained his sight, even if Sade should have been the woman in his vision. Sade was beautiful but Imani was sexy. Between her heavily made face, curvaceous frame, and alluring scent... she was definitely the kind of woman that naturally drew men to her. Sade, however, had the kind of beauty that snuck up on a person. The kind that you might miss at first glance, but the moment you took a second look, she held you captive. Sade's beauty was sweet and innocent, and Dante probably didn't want that back in the day. He hated that now, but there was nothing he could do about it.

"Tay!" Imani yelled, pushing herself into his chest. "Where the hell have you been?" Before he could answer her, Imani was connecting her lips with his. He didn't want to kiss her back, but he couldn't help himself. Her tongue was swirling around his as she cupped his cheeks, and Dante couldn't fight his growing desire for her.

When they finally pulled away from each other, he said, "That was a damn good welcome home."

With a soft giggle, Imani took him by the hand and led him down the stairs to their bedroom.

"You didn't answer my question," she reminded, pulling his shirt over his head. "Where have you been?"

"I was in an accident and lost my memory. I went to rehab and physical therapy."

"You've been there the whole time?"

Dante nodded as she fell to her knees and pushed his shorts down. "Yeah. Once I was able to walk around and stuff on my own, I decided to look for work. I couldn't remember anything about my past, but I did remember details about myself and what I used to do. I came here looking for a job and the guy conducting the interview was someone who knew me. He told me some facts about myself that led me back here to you."

She took his shoes and socks off, looking up at him as she bit down on her bottom lip.

"So you don't remember me or our kids?"

Their kids.

She wasn't going to make this easy.

"No," Dante admitted.

Imani smiled. "Then why aren't you stopping me?"

"You're my wife. If you want to have sex with me, I'm not going to stop you."

Imani chuckled as she pushed his boxers down. "Good, because it's been a really long time, and I need you inside of me. We can talk later. I need my husband. Right now."

She stood, connecting her lips with his again. This felt like a distraction, and Dante would let her have that. He would let her have him. Physically, at least. As much as he hated it, his heart belonged to Sade, and there wasn't space there for Imani or anyone else, for that matter.

IMANI

FOR A BRIEF second, Imani felt guilty about having sex with Dante hours after having sex with Adam, but as soon as he was inside of her, none of that mattered. It didn't matter how much time had passed; Imani would never turn down her husband's dick.

As Dante rubbed cocoa butter into his skin, he said, "Where are the twins? I want to know about them, you, us. Everything."

"They are with my grandparents. I think I'm going to let them stay with them tonight. I don't want to overwhelm them or you."

"They didn't think I abandoned them, did they?"

Imani shook her head and made her way over to him. "No. They know you would never do that."

She stood on her tiptoes, placing a soft kiss to his lips. His hands instinctively went to her ass. No matter how disconnected they were mentally and emotionally, they were always on the same page physically.

"Can we just... chill today? I'm just happy you're here. I don't want to spend the day talking about facts and our past."

"I've been gone for three months, Imani. Don't you think I need to get back to my life as soon as possible? What about money? How have you been getting by?"

Imani palmed her face. Business had gone downhill since news about the civil suit spread, but they still had quite a few loyal clients working with them.

"Money wasn't an issue because I had quite a bit liquidated in cash, but all of our accounts have been frozen."

Imani said the words quickly before leaving the bathroom.

"Frozen? For what?"

"Um..." She sat on the chaise next to her side of the bed. "The FBI have proof that you've been stealing from clients and laundering money. There's also a civil case against you. You probably shouldn't even be here, Dante. If they find out you came back home, they're going to arrest you."

She watched his expression harden and nostrils flare as he walked over to her. He was naked, dick dangling and swinging as he charged over to her.

"Fuck you mean the FBI has proof that *I've* been stealing? I've never stolen *anything* in my life."

"Well, I know that, but someone is. If it's not you, it's Eric or Jessica, our best friends and business partners. Regardless, they have proof, and there's a 95 percent chance you're going to jail if and when this goes to trial."

Dante sat next to her, shoulders hung as he covered his face with his palms.

"You're telling me I'm in business with people that steal from our clients, are jeopardizing our business, and setting me up to take the fall?"

Imani rubbed his back before placing a kiss on his shoulder. "I'm sorry, honey, but yes. We need to get you out of the city."

She didn't want to tell him about Adam's plan to kill him, which was her real reason for trying to get him to leave. When he was missing, Imani believed him being dead was for the best. Now, she wasn't sure. Dante had already lost enough. He didn't deserve to lose his life too. The sooner she got him out of Memphis, the better, even if it did mean risking her own freedom.

"I can't leave. Not until I see my girls and my family. After that, I'll go, but only until I figure out who is trying to set me up and get proof." Dante took her hands into his. "When I do, I'm coming back home to you and our girls."

Imani sniffled as her eyes watered. That sentence, that goal, was impossible. If he found out who was setting him up, he'd learn it was her, and after that... there would be no more home.

DANTE

MILA AND NILA rushed over to Dante, almost knocking him over they hugged him so tightly. His laughter was warm as his eyes watered. He hugged them both, giving them kisses on the top of their heads before taking them by their cheeks and looking over their faces.

They looked like Imani... and Sade. Same shade of brown skin, same high cheekbones. Dante shook that thought away, determined to grab some hair for a DNA test. Sade didn't have a reason to tell a new lie, but who knows? Maybe she was trying to make Imani look worse to excuse what she'd done. The twins' paternity wasn't something he'd take either of the sisters' word for. Dante was going to find out that truth for himself.

"Where have you been, Daddy?" Nila asked with a pout. "I missed you."

"Daddy had a little accident, but I'm back now." His eyes shifted upward toward Imani. "For good."

Imani's eyes rolled as she crossed her arms over her chest.

Dante's phone vibrated in his pocket. As much as he wanted to let it ring, he'd reached out to a private investigator to help him figure out what the hell was going on. Though he was starting to trust Imani less and less, there was still the matter of who had tried to kill him. If it wasn't Imani... Who was it? He pulled his phone out, and relief filled him at the sight of the private investigator's name.

"I gotta take this phone call real quick, but as soon as I'm done, how about we spend the day together?"

While both girls excitedly agreed, Imani's head shook as she groaned.

Dante excused himself, answering the call with, "Hunter, what did you find?"

"Your cell phone isn't picking up on any cell towers. It isn't being used, and neither are your credit cards. Whoever took it wasn't taking it out of necessity. They took it because they didn't want you to have it when you were found."

"That throws a random robbery out of the way. Someone intentionally hit me and took my shit."

Unable to deny it anymore, Dante accepted that truth as his free hand slid down his face.

"The police didn't do a complete report on the accident. Whoever was first on the scene didn't follow up because you didn't have any identification. Apparently, they didn't care enough to check the registration in the car. They didn't do that until Imani found the car and filed a missing person report. I called a few junkyards to see where your car was taken. I found it, and it's still there if you want to go check it out. There probably won't be any fingerprints left behind but maybe it'll give you some memories."

Dante nodded, unsure if that was what he wanted, even if it was what he needed. "I appreciate that. Text me the location, and I'll follow up."

"Will do."

After Dante disconnected the call, he went back into the living room and found Imani there alone.

"Where are my girls?"

"I sent them to their room so they could freshen up." Imani stood and walked in his direction. Even on a random weekday with nothing to do, she was dressed impeccably in a gold dress, nude pumps, and gold accessories. "Listen... I'm not sure if it's a good idea to make them think you're here to stay. I thought we agreed after you saw your family tonight, you'd leave town."

"I'm not really feeling that agreement. I just got back. Is there a reason you don't want me here, Imani?"

Her head hung briefly, but when she raised it, Imani's smile was soft as she completely closed the space between them.

"I just want to make sure nothing happens to you. The FBI have been on me heavily. All it takes is one random pop-up or sighting, and they'll know you're back home. They might have the house or your family members' phones bugged."

"I considered that. That's why I haven't tried to get anyone's numbers to call and let them know I'm back. I'm going to pull up on my parents and make sure they understand the importance of keeping my return between us."

"This isn't a good idea, but I can't force you to leave. Just don't say I didn't warn you."

Dante wanted to ask her about her part in his charges, but it wasn't time yet. Instead, he asked, "How have you been without me? Mentally? Emotionally? I can't imagine how hard this has been for you."

He looked into her eyes as if he could see the wheels spinning in her head. It didn't matter what Imani said; it never felt sincere. Dante wondered if it had always been that way, or if the accident opened his eyes to the true her. Without their history and connection, there was nothing standing in the way of him seeing everyone in his life for who they truly were.

Sade.

His friend.

His lover.

His wife?

No.

His friend.

"I was going crazy, not knowing where you were."

Dante could believe that. Imani was smart with how she worded herself. He took her hand into his, kissing it, his mind taking him back to all the times he did that gesture to Sade. How she'd melt against him. Imani froze. Dante saw the exact moment her heart stopped beating.

"When I leave, will you come with me? Or at least visit on the weekends? You can bring the girls. I've already been away for months. I don't want them to think I'm abandoning them, Imani."

"I'll think of a story to tell them. It's best if we... stay away from each other. You don't want the FBI to think I was involved in this, do you?"

"Were you?" Dante checked. "You're telling me I did all this shit under your nose, and you knew nothing about it?"

"I... no. I didn't know. I trusted you, so there was no reason for me to go behind you with the statements."

"But you were responsible for filing our quarterly taxes, correct?" Imani nodded. "Why didn't you say anything if I wasn't giving you the money to handle that?"

"I don't know, Dante," she stressed. "What are you trying to say? That I *knew* what you were doing and just ignored it?"

He chuckled. "I'm saying I don't think I did this, and you're too willing to accept that I did, even with the knowledge that someone tried to kill me. Why are you so adamant about getting me out of the city instead of letting me stay and fight this?"

Her phone rang, and Imani rushed over to the coffee table to grab it. "I need to take this. Can we talk about this later?" Without waiting for him to answer, Imani accepted the phone call and headed outside.

Who is she talking to that she needs privacy with?

"My baby, my baby, my baby!" Dante's mother yelled, jumping into his arms.

Her legs went limp like linguine at the sight of him. Regardless of who was watching, this was what Dante needed. His people. A connection that made him feel like he belonged. This feeling was nothing like the people he met in Vanzette. This was real, and the love that reverberated from her onto him healed parts of Dante's shattered soul.

"Let me get to my boy," his father pleaded, pulling Olivia off him. As soon as Deandre's arms wrapped around him, Dante finally felt safe enough to release all that he'd been feeling. His mother's love may have been good for his soul, but his father's embrace was protection... safety.

Even without having memories to bind them, Dante felt his parents on a level that could never be forgotten.

They stood at the doorway for what felt like forever before they stepped farther into his parents' home. Imani was in no rush to give Dante the address, so he'd gotten it from Sade. She told him to let her know how it went if he was comfortable enough to do so, and Dante was considering giving her a call.

"Now, where the hell have you been?" Olivia asked as they all sat down in the living room. "We never stopped looking for you." He had a parent on each side of him, giving the stability he'd been missing for months.

"Long story short, I was in an accident, I had amnesia, and I just now figured out who you all were and how to get back home."

"Were you really running from the police? That's what Imani has been telling us."

"Yeah, but I don't know why." He paused and shook his head. "I mean, I know why, but I can't remember what was happening that night."

"Did you do what they are accusing you of?" Deandre asked. "Did you really steal from all those people?"

"Come on, Dad. You know y'all raised me better than that."

"Then what the hell is going on, Dante?"

He shrugged and ran his hands down his face. "I'm trying to piece everything together. Someone is setting me up, that's all I know."

"Do you have any idea who it could be?" Olivia asked.

"Yeah." Dante took a deep breath, unable to let the words come out of his mouth. "Imani."

"Imani?" his parents repeated in unison.

"Yeah." Dante bobbed his head. "She's the one that did all this shit, and she's setting me up to take the fall. I need y'all not to let anyone know I'm back home until I get this resolved. When I have proof it's her and find out who tried to run me off the road, I can get back to my life. Until then, I need to lie low."

"I have so many questions," Olivia said softly.

"And I'll answer them all... later. Right now, I need to make the most of the next two days. I leave after that."

"Where are you going?" Deandre asked. "Will we be able to get in touch with you?"

Dante's head shook as he stood. "I don't think communication is best. I'm risking being seen just coming by here. But I promise, once I figure this out, I'll be back."

His parents stood, and they both gave him a hug before he headed out. Not wanting to sit in one place for too long, Dante left, though he had no clear destination in mind. He'd given Ian several hundred dollars to book a hotel room in his name downtown just in case Imani had any ideas, and the FBI showed up at their home. Dante couldn't fathom his own wife setting him up, but there was no denying it at this point. Outside of the off vibes he'd been getting from Imani, she'd been omitting truth, shifting blame, and straight-up lying about some things since Dante came back.

"Sade was right," he grumbled, gripping the steering wheel tighter. At that recollection, Dante dialed Sade's number.

"Hey," she answered quickly with a smile in her voice.

"How... are you?"

"I'm good... now."

Dante smiled, biting down on his bottom lip. "I uh, you were right about Imani. She's not telling me the truth about any damn thing."

Sade sighed. "I'm sorry, babe. I know how much you wanted her to. Did you ask her about the twins?"

"Nah, but I got a few strands of hair out of their brush. I gave it to my private investigator for a DNA test. Should have the results back in seventy-two hours or less."

"Good." Sade cleared her throat. "I know you'll probably never forgive me for not being completely honest with you."

"Sade..."

"But I-I saw that as a one-time opportunity to finally experience you and love you the way you deserve." At the sound of her sniffle, his heart squeezed. "It was never my intention to—"

"I miss you, Sade."

She didn't reply right away. Before she did, Sade released a heavy breath. "I miss you too. So much."

"I can't act like what you did was okay," he said, to remind himself more than her. "But I... thank you."

"Dante..."

"I gotta go, okay?"

Sade sniffled before agreeing with a soft, "Okay."

He disconnected the call quickly, not wanting her to say anything to make Vanzette his next destination.

IMANI

IMANI WATCHED AS Adam played her footage from her home security camera of Dante coming in.

"You forgot I got the password to this shit?"

Obviously. When Imani first saw Dante on the camera, she completely forgot about Adam having access to it. Adam said it was his way of looking out for her and the twins while he wasn't around, but now, Imani wondered if he was watching to see if and when Dante would show up.

"I was going to tell you he was back, Adam."

"When? Because from the looks of it, you didn't plan on telling me *shit.*"

Imani rolled her eyes as she continued to roll his weed. "He has amnesia. He's harmless at this point."

"Nah." Adam's head shook as he sat back on the couch in his living room. "Even if he does have amnesia, he still needs to be handled. Permanently."

Imani's fingers stopped moving. She sat back on the couch and looked at him. "Why are you so dead set on killing him, Adam? He's back. I can call Agent Monroe and have him picked up. He'll be arrested and go to trial. Then all of this will be over."

"That's not good enough. With the feds taking our money, we need that insurance policy. Even with him in jail, it'll take us too long to make back the millions they seized. Did you forget

Enrique is expecting us to still clean and move money for him? We can't do that without a business, and you can't expect anyone with sense and wealth to fuck with you after this. We gotta do it on our own. Dante needs to fucking die."

"Wouldn't it make more sense for him to die *after* he's sentenced? I just want to make sure *I'm* not facing any charges, Adam."

Adam massaged his chin momentarily, thinking over their dilemma.

"A'ight, this is what we can do." Adam stood and paced in front of the muted TV. "If he has amnesia, he doesn't know about his offshore accounts, right?"

Imani shook her head. "I don't think so. I don't think he knows his attorneys here either. I'll have to link him back up with them."

"Good. We're gonna have Atlas finish the job, but it's going to look like a suicide. Atlas will have him record a video confessing to everything and making it clear that you were not involved or aware of what he was doing. He's going to say he wants the victims in the civil suit to be paid from his offshore account. Once he's done with the video, Atlas will kill him. But before that happens, I need you to make sure you have his offshore accounts information. We need to clean out all of them except one. That way, the civil suit will be handled, and you won't have to worry about facing federal charges."

"Okay." Imani thought it over for a few seconds before saying, "But this has to work, Adam. Are you sure you can trust Atlas? We don't need this coming back on us in any way."

"Cuz is cool. Don't worry about that. You just make sure you get that information."

"I will. I'll tell him I need it in case something happens that I need to cover financially. If he doesn't remember, I'll go with him to his attorney's firm and get it from them. Then I'll call you, and Atlas will have to do it before he leaves."

"Consider it done."

Dante hadn't come back home since yesterday, and Imani's concern was growing. Did he suspect her of something? Had he already left? Imani needed that money... soon. She wasn't completely honest with her sister when she went to visit Sade in Vanzette. Imani wasn't just anxious about getting Dante back because of the charges he was facing; Imani was getting low on money too.

Between her and Adam's extravagant purchases and traveling, giving the twins every materialistic thing they desired, and the raid, Imani was running low. It didn't matter how many times Imani insisted she wasn't involved just because she and Dante were married. The FBI wasn't as accommodating as Imani would have liked for them to be.

Had she thought it over more carefully, she would have set it up to where Eric or Jessica had to take the blame. That way, she could have been left out of it completely. Dante was the easiest mark, though, even if it did make her collateral damage. Imani had been able to get herself out of all kinds of trouble. She was sure this wouldn't be any different.

Both Imani and Dante agreed to limit phone conversation for the time being. There wasn't a doubt in her mind that the FBI had bugged her phone. She didn't have a number to reach him, so all she could do was wait for him to show back up or reach out to her. Imani considered calling his parents, but she doubted he was still over there. Still, she called Olivia anyway and hoped her mother-in-law would have some good news.

"Hello?" Olivia answered.

"Hey, um... I was wondering if..." Imani paused. "I was thinking about bringing the twins over but not if you have company. Is anyone over there?"

Olivia let a few seconds pass before she said, "Not today, no. We had company yesterday, but they left rather quickly."

"I'm sure you were glad to see them."

"More than you'll ever know."

"Do you know when they're coming to see you again?"

"No, I don't."

"Do you know if they are still in Memphis?"

Olivia sighed. "If they wanted me or anyone else to know, they would have said so."

"You're right." Imani released a frustrated breath. "I will talk to you later then."

"All right."

Olivia abruptly ended the call, and Imani couldn't help but wonder what that was about. She had never been the biggest fan of Imani, but Olivia was usually polite and pleasant. Kind.

"Hmm," Imani hummed, staring at her phone. "What do you know, Olivia? What do you know?"

The next morning, Dante finally returned. He made the twins breakfast before dropping them off at school. Though he promised not to get out of the car, Imani still tried to get him to change his mind. He didn't. At that point, Imani decided to give up the façade that she cared. If he was arrested, so be it. Adam would be upset, but their plan could still work. All it took was one inside connect with an inmate who needed commissary and they could have Dante killed there. Regardless, Imani was tired of playing the doting, caring wife. She needed his offshore accounts information and for all of this shit to be over.

When Dante made his way back home, Imani asked, "Where have you been?"

"I think it's best if I stay away. I only came back to see the girls."

"And what about me? Us?"

"Can I be honest with you?" Dante asked, leading her toward the sitting room. They sat across from each other in the white and gold thronelike chairs. "I don't trust you, Imani."

She scoffed, clutching her chest and feigning offense. "You don't trust *me*? Why not?"

"I don't know you. I don't feel anything when I'm with you that makes me feel like you're... safe. Do you have any idea why that's the case?"

Dante's gaze was unwavering, but Imani wouldn't fold.

"No, I don't. Maybe it's just the amnesia, but I assure you, you can trust me."

"I only want us to have this conversation once, okay?" Imani nodded. "Are you the one that's setting me up?"

Her eyes blinked rapidly before she laughed. Her hand wrapped around her neck as she avoided his eyes. When she did look at him, she asked, "How dare you ask me that? I'm your *wife*."

"Yeah, but I know I didn't do this, and I remember talking to someone who told me you did. That you set me up that night. Why would they say that?"

"I don't know. Maybe you should call them and ask."

"I would if I could remember who it was." Dante sighed, head tilted as he stared through her. "I want to trust you, Imani, but I'm feeling completely alone in this. I don't know what happened before my accident, but I know I didn't do this shit. So who the fuck did?"

"Look, I don't know, but it wasn't me. You need to talk to Eric and Jessica. Maybe it was one of them."

He looked away and chuckled. Then he stood, his head shook and shoulders slouched. "All right. Give me their numbers."

Imani wasn't expecting that. He walked over to her, giving her his phone. She put both of their numbers inside, hoping something they told him would make him suspicious.

"Are they still working at the firm?" Dante asked, accepting his phone back.

"No, they went into business for themselves. I haven't even been talking to them." Imani stood, taking his hands into hers. "Look, I get the paranoia and suspicion. I can't imagine how you're feeling right now. Not only are you facing some serious charges, but you don't even remember what you did to get them..."

"I didn't do this shit!" he roared, catching her off guard. "And you *know* it, Imani."

"If you didn't do it, who did?"

Dante laughed, putting space between them. "I don't know why I'm wasting my breath with you. You're not capable of telling the fucking truth."

"Why would you say that, Dante? I've never lied to you in my life!"

"Oh, so you didn't lie to me about the twins?"

Imani's chest deflated. Her knees weakened as she sat back down. Dante pulled a piece of paper out of his back pocket and tossed it at her.

"What's this?" she asked softly.

"DNA test results. They aren't mine."

Imani rubbed her eyes, as if she couldn't believe what she was seeing. "Why did you... who told you... You don't trust me?"

"No, I don't." Her eyes lifted to his. "So, if you lied to me about them, how do you expect me to believe you're telling me the truth about this?"

Her head hung, but Dante gripped her chin and lifted it.

"Dante, I can explain."

"I just need to know who their father is and why you lied to me."

"I can't tell you that. I'm sorry."

He nodded, taking a step back and crossing his arms over his chest. "I don't trust you. At all. I came back here with high hopes, but every time I talk to you, you show me more and more that you aren't worthy of my trust. You need to make arrangements for the girls because I'm going to find proof you set me up, and when I do, *you're* the one that's going to jail."

Her mouth opened but closed at the sight of his back retreating as Dante walked away.

"Shit, shit, shit," she muttered, standing and pacing while biting her acrylic nail. "Adam is going to fucking kill him, but I need that money first. I have to draw this out."

Imani waited until she heard the front door close to rush upstairs and grab her phone. Jail might have been the safest place for Dante until she figured out her next move. If he stayed on the streets, Adam would hunt him down... especially since Dante had threatened her.

DANTE

"MAN, I CAN'T express how happy I am to see you," Eric stated, giving Dante another hug. "I thought you were dead. Where the fuck have you been?"

They sat down on the burgundy couch on Eric's back porch. As soon as Dante called Eric, he told him to come through. Just like with his parents, the response from his return was genuine and appreciated.

"I feel like I've told this story a million times," Dante said with a smile, accepting the beer Jessica offered him. She cried as soon as she set eyes on him. These weren't people who were responsible for not only ruining their business, but his reputation too. They weren't involved in trying to take away his freedom. They couldn't have been. "I was in an accident the night the police came to the office. I have amnesia, so I don't remember anyone from my past. I was at a rehab facility all this time."

"Wait, so you don't recognize me?" Eric confirmed, sitting up in his seat as his elbows rested on his thighs.

Dante shook his head. "No, not at all. I recognize the vibe and the love, but no, I don't have any memories of you or your wife."

"That's not weird or scary to you?" Jessica asked.

"In the beginning, it was. I had a very hard time submitting and connecting with..." His mouth and eyes shut as thoughts of Sade permeated his mind. He gave her a hard time, and she was so gentle and patient with him. Her smiling face invaded his thoughts, causing Dante to bite down on his bottom lip and resist her.

I'm in love with her. Still.

Shaking that thought from his mind, Dante opened his eyes and licked the corner of his mouth. He looked from Eric to Jessica as he swallowed.

"It was hard," Dante settled on. "Now, I have peace being around people I know are sincere."

"Memories can be replaced," Jessica said. "We're just glad you're okay."

"That's true," Dante agreed, popping the top on his beer. "I want to run something by you. Please, be honest, and don't hold back. I know I haven't done what I'm being accused of, and I don't think either of you did it. That leaves my wife. Has she given either of you reason to believe she could set me up for this?"

Eric and Jessica looked at each other, then him.

"I suspected Imani was up to something and brought it to Eric," Jessica said as Eric covered her hand with his. "He didn't want to bring it to you because she's your wife, and we felt you'd take her side. We said we'd wait until we had proof, but before we could tell you, the civil suit was filed, and they tried to arrest you."

"Why'd you think she was up to something?"

"Three things," Jessica started, before taking a deep breath. "I accidentally walked up on a conversation she was having with a man who isn't our client, but he frequently came to see her. They were arguing about her inability to deliver his funds quickly. He said something along the lines of, if she can't handle cleaning such large amounts of money, she will no longer be valuable to him, and if she isn't valuable, she's dead. I heard her heels as they prepared to leave her office, so I all but ran down the hall to make sure neither of them would see me.

"Second, one of her clients goes to my church. When we do our annual Christmas offering, the pastor announces it. Of course, we put it in the business name, so she approached us because she said we'd stolen from her. We went outside, and she told me she was promised a 300-point increase with her credit in thirty days for $5,500. I told her that's not possible, nor is it something we offer, but she said she had proof."

Jessica paused and looked at Eric, who nodded for her to continue. "The contract had your name and signature on it, but it wasn't your ID number in the system. It was Imani's. She'd created the client's account to get all their information, then immediately deleted it, but I guess she didn't know the history would still be accessible."

Dante released a vocal breath before asking, "Can you still retrieve that history?"

Jessica shook her head. "It disappears after three days."

"Shit. And what was the last thing?"

"One of the assistants had mixed up our files. I went to her office to drop hers off while she was in the conference room for a meeting. She had several of your company checks and was writing them out to the names on her files. I didn't think much of it. I just thought you all were sharing clients, but after the FBI came to the office, I knew something was off."

"Would you be willing to testify to this?" Dante asked.

"Yes. Originally, we wanted to separate ourselves from it, but we can't do you like that."

"Professionally, we had to leave," Eric added. "But you know I got your back personally. Whatever you need, we got you."

Dante shook his head as he composed himself. Never in a million years did he think he'd have to prepare for a war against his wife, but that's where they were at that point. Maybe if she had come clean, things would have been different. But every time she looked into his eyes and lied, a piece of hope Dante had in her died.

"Thank you both," Dante said as he stood. "I'm gonna go to the office and see if that jogs my memories. I'll reach out soon."

Eric and Jessica stood, both giving him hugs and making him promise not to go ghost. He said he'd stay in touch and genuinely meant it. The more he talked to others, the more confident Dante was that he could find a way to prove Imani was behind this. No one was perfect. She had to slip up somewhere, and Dante was determined to figure it out.

DANTE

"*W*HERE ARE YOU?"

"*I'm leaving the office now.*"

"*How do you think I know you're at the office, Dante? Think. Who knows you're at the office and could be working with the FBI to send you to federal fucking prison?*"

As the elevator lowered, Dante considered his cousin's question.

"*No.*" *His head shook as revelation set in.* "*My wife wouldn't tell them I was here, and even if she did, it would be because she's scared. Not because she's trying to set me up.*"

Chelsea huffed. "*I know that's your wife, but she is not to be trusted, do you hear me?*"

"*She's loyal. She wouldn't—*"

"*You need to go downstairs and wait for them in the lobby. Do not speak without your attorney present. I'm going to help you in any way that I can, but if it comes down to you or her, which I know it will, you need to accept the fact that your wife is behind this, and she's setting you up to take the fall.*"

"Who was I talking to?" Dante asked, looking around his office.

All of his computers and files had been taken. There wasn't anything for him to go through to try to find some evidence against his wife. He'd gone to the junkyard in hopes that being in his car would bring back memories, and it did, but he still couldn't see the man that had taken his things. His flashbacks were happening more frequently, and they were less painful. All Dante could do was hope that night came back to him fully before it was too late.

Leaving his office, Dante went inside Imani's. He looked around, hoping something would strike up more of his memory. Sitting behind her desk, he allowed his fingers to slide against her laptop.

His eyes closed, and Dante inhaled a deep breath, willing images of that night to come back. Were his memories suppressed because of the accident, or because he didn't want to accept what he'd found that night as truth?

"What are you hiding?" he mumbled, going to her desktop when none of the passwords he tried on the laptop worked. That password was still the same, causing Dante to release a sigh of relief. Instead of going through the files on her desktop, he accessed her iCloud, where he found fictitious statements and invoices mirroring the ones in his office.

Refusing to believe his wife was the one committing fraud, Dante immediately logged out of her computer and went back to his office. For a while, he just sat there, staring out into the darkness. It was a little after midnight, and the downtown streets of Memphis were eerily quiet. Standing, Dante made his way to the large window on the side of his office. Hands stuffed in his gray slacks, Dante cursed under his breath.

If she's stealing from the company, there has to be a reason for it.

If she's stealing from the company, what else is she doing behind my back?

He tried to think of anything over the past few months that may have hinted at his wife's greed, but Dante was coming up empty. There hadn't been anything out of the ordinary—no big purchases or unaccounted for deposits of money. His mind played scenario after scenario of what his wife could have been into.

"No," he whispered, going out of his office to return to hers. "There has to be a reason. Maybe someone is setting her up to take the fall, just like they set me up to find these statements." Nibbling his bottom lip,

Dante paused in the hallway. "Who has the most to gain by getting my wife and me out of the business?"

With ringing in his ears, Dante squeezed his eyes shut tightly as that entire night replayed in his memory. He groaned, covering his ears as he rocked back and forth.

"Dante?" the woman answered, sleep thick in her voice.

"Hey, I know it's late, but I need to get out of Memphis. Can I crash at your spot until I figure out my next move?"

She cleared her throat. "Um... sure. Is everything okay?"

"No, but I'll talk to you about it when I get there. I'm heading your way now. Should be there in about an hou—What the fuck?"

"Dante?" she called, but he didn't reply as he ended the call.

He was too distracted by the bright lights of the truck coming straight toward him. Dante sped up, and the truck did too.

"What are you doing?" he asked, knowing they couldn't hear or respond. "Shit!" he roared, gripping the steering wheel and trying to prepare for impact with the truck. But nothing could have prepared him for that. As soon as the wide truck hit the back of his car, Dante crashed into a light pole.

Dante's body jerked, as if the truck was hitting him all over again. He leaped up from the seat, chest heaving as his eyes looked around the room.

Sade.

That's who he was calling.

Sade.

The *only* one he knew he could trust.

Coming back to Memphis was a mistake. He should have stayed in Vanzette with Sade and worked to bring her sister down.

"What have I done?" Dante asked. "I let go of the woman who loved me most. Cared about me most. Sade was more loyal to me than I was able to be to myself. If I lose her..." His head shook as he charged out of Imani's office. "I *can't* lose her."

SADE

IT WAS A little after midnight. Sade was in the middle of her bed, crying her eyes out. Her soul had been filled with dis-ease all day. There was no particular cause for it. That was a lie. It was loneliness. The kind of loneliness that came from having everything with the only one she ever wanted just to return to nothing. As she wiped her face, Sade stared at the last picture of her and Dante that she'd taken. They looked so happy in the middle of the dance floor.

Salsa.

A dance that forced them to be close enough for their hearts to join as one.

They'd spent the night dancing, and for some odd reason, Sade wanted to capture the moment.

Now... she was glad she did.

Sade was so deep in her grief and mourning the loss of her relationship with Dante that her phone vibrating scared her. She jumped before reaching over to her nightstand and grabbing it. At the sight of Dante's name, she gasped. Pushing her hair out of her face as if he could see her, Sade accepted the call.

"Hey," she answered, as always.

"Smiley..."

Her eyes closed and jaws clenched as more tears threatened to fall.

"Dante, is everything o—"

"I never should have left you. What you did was wrong, but I guess I'm wrong too because I want you."

"Dante, please. Don't fucking play with me."

He chuckled. "I called you that night, didn't I?" She nodded. "I'd just found some proof that made me question Imani, but I still didn't believe it. Then, my cousin called and confirmed it, but I still refused to accept it. I got in the car and called you, because you were the only person I felt like I could trust and talk to. That night, I was running. I felt like that was so out of character for me, and that's true. I wasn't running to avoid responsibility. I was running to get to you. I knew that if I just made it to you, you'd help me figure this shit out. I trusted you that much. You meant that much to me."

"That's true," she whispered, wiping her face.

"Why didn't you tell me before I left?"

"I didn't want you to think I was saying that to sway you. I knew what Imani had done, and I planned to tell you that night when you made it, but you never did."

"That's why you knew something had happened to me... because I never showed up."

"Yes. You ended the call so abruptly I... that wasn't like you. And when I finally found you and saw you in that bed, I just wanted to protect you, baby. I'm so, so sorry, but I—"

"You don't have to apologize anymore, Sade. I'm the one that should apologize. I'm going to make all of this up to you... not choosing you from the beginning, leaving you now. All of it. As soon as I get this shit taken care of, I'm going to divorce her ass and..." He paused, and his background was filled with the sound of sirens. "Fuck!"

"Dante?" Sade hopped out of bed. "What's going on?"

"The police and FBI are here. I bet that bitch had me followed. She knew I was going to talk to Eric and probably had the police waiting there for me."

"Where are you now?"

"I'm at the office."

"Are you going to try to make a run for it?"

"My running is over."

"Dante—"

"I'm facing this head-on, Day. I just... I need you to know that I love you. It should have always been you."

"Dante, wait, I—"

He ended the call, and Sade had to resist the urge to throw her phone against the wall as she screamed. She jogged to her closet, grabbing several pieces of clothing before heading for the bathroom. If Dante was going to face this, he wouldn't face it alone, and he for damn sure wouldn't face it with Imani by his side...

Sade beat against the door until Imani answered. She'd driven straight from Vanzette to Memphis with no stops. As soon as Imani opened the door, Sade punched her in the nose. Imani fell back onto the floor, and Sade straddled her, wrapping her hands around her neck. As Imani squirmed underneath her, Sade gritted, "I should've killed you when we were kids, bitch. Then *none* of this would have happened. You're going to rot for what you're doing to Dante, and I pray God lets me be the one to send your ass to hell."

"Auntie!"

Sade looked up, locking eyes with Mila as Nila ran over to her.

"Let Mommy go!" Nila demanded, wrapping her small hands around Sade's wrists.

Sade lowered herself to Imani's ear and said, "The only reason I'm going to let you stay alive is because I don't want to kill you in front of my nieces. Thank them when I leave, but I promise, you'll see me soon."

Sade stood, smirking as Imani scooted backward, coughing and clutching her neck. Sade looked from Nila to Mila, and their eyes on her put out some of the fire that was burning internally.

"I'm sorry, girls. Forgive me."

"You bitch!" Imani yelled before coughing and crawling toward Sade. "I'm going to fucking kill you, ho. You're lucky my damn kids are here, *and* you sucker punched me!"

"Fuck you, Imani. We can go outside and square up right now."

Imani stood, telling her twins, "Mommy is okay. Y'all go up to your room."

"But, Ma," Mila said, to which Imani yelled...

"Go!" Both girls stomped back upstairs to their rooms, and Imani waited until she heard the door slam to ask, "What did Dante tell you? Or better yet, what did *you* tell him? Are you the reason he no longer trusts me?"

Sade scoffed before running her tongue across her cheek. "Did it ever cross your mind that *your* actions are the reason he doesn't trust you?"

"That's bullshit! We were fine when he first came back, then he had the girls tested and started accusing me of setting him up." Imani paused, staring at her sister. She crossed her arms over her chest and placed the bulk of her weight on one side. "The fuck are you even doing here? If Dante lost his memory and has been missing all this time, how do you know what's going on with him? Who have you been talking to?"

Sade chuckled as she closed the space between them. Imani didn't flinch or move, but she inhaled a deep breath and shrunk a little to make space for her sister.

"Dante called me before he was arrested. Did you have him followed, Imani?"

Imani smiled. "I did. I knew he was going to go and see Eric eventually, so I called Agent Monroe, and he put an undercover on Eric's street for surveillance. They followed Dante to the office and arrested him there." Imani's head shook as she waved her finger in Sade's face. "Something isn't adding up. How did Dante know how to get in touch with you? Was it his parents? They always liked you more than me."

Sade considered if she wanted to tell Imani the truth or not. It didn't take long before she came to the conclusion that in this instance, the truth was going to hit Imani exactly where she wanted her to hurt.

"Dante knew how to get in touch with me because he was with me after the accident."

Imani's brows wrinkled, and mouth parted slightly. Frowning, she shook her head softly. "Whoa—"

"I found him after the accident and told him I was his wife. He's been in bliss with me since January. The only reason he came back to your ass was because some nigga told him about you at a job interview. But yes, I've been with Dante this entire time."

Imani rubbed her lips together before chuckling and squeezing the bridge of her nose. "You're one desperate crazy-ass bitch. The fact you even have the audacity to stand here and tell me you've been sleeping with my husband is beyond me."

"Dante has *always* belonged to me. You took him, knowing you didn't want him. It's my turn now, and you'd better damn well believe I'm not letting him go."

Sade turned to leave, but she stopped when Imani said, "Wait, Dante was with you in Vanzette?" She faced her sister. "That's why Patrice called me. She said she wanted to talk to me about Dante... and a day later... she was dead. You killed her, didn't you?" Imani clapped as she laughed and walked over to Sade. "You killed her because she knew you had Dante. Wow, Sade. You're some kind of crazy."

"I don't know what you're talking about, but if I did, I would tell you to take that as a warning of what will happen to you if you get in my way."

"You don't have the balls to kill me. No matter how much you hate me, I'm your sister."

Sade chuckled. "Yeah, okay. Believe that if you want, Imani. We're blood, but you've *never* been my fucking sister. You terrorized me for the sake of popularity. I have absolutely no love for you."

Imani's mouth twisted to the side as she nodded. Her expression changed none at Sade's confession. "I can accept that. I can even accept you being with Dante. But what you're *not* going to do is get him out of jail and try to put me in it. If you do, I will call the Vanzette Police Department. If I understand correctly, they ruled Patrice's murder as a robbery homicide. I wonder if that will change when I tell them about what you've been up to. Leave Dante where he is and take your ass back to Vanzette, Sade, or I *will* make your life a living hell."

"My life has been hell since the day you were born. Do your fucking worst."

Turning on her heels, Sade stormed out and didn't slow her movements until she was in the car. She slammed the door and beat against the steering wheel as she screamed. The last person who needed to know about Patrice was Imani, but she'd risk it if it meant getting Dante out of prison.

DANTE

DANTE STARED AT the account numbers and total amounts of money he had saved in offshore accounts in disbelief. He figured they were doing well based on the home he and Imani shared, but he wasn't expecting to have several million dollars saved, and that was what the FBI hadn't touched. He couldn't help but wonder how much they *had* seized.

After Sade paid his bail, Dante was released around three that morning. They went straight to Vanzette. He called Eric, who gave him their legal team's information, and one of Dante's attorneys agreed to meet with him in Vanzette as soon as the sun came up. Troy had gone over the affidavits and let Dante know what he was up against. He warned him that 95 percent of the time, charges weren't pursued unless they were confident they could win the case.

A lot of the evidence against Dante was circumstantial—forged signatures, fabricated client accounts with his ID number, checks made out to Imani's clients. Other than that, it was his word against Imani's. With Eric and Jessica's testimony, Dante believed he may have had a fighting chance, but he needed something more concrete. The smoking gun.

Since he'd officially been booked, processed, and released, Dante decided to go public with everything that had been going on. He gave his parents permission to tell everyone that he was alive, and he went on social media and gave a video statement of everything that had been going on. He added family and friends that he could remember, and already, the video had been shared hundreds of times. Imani had been tagged so much that she deactivated her Facebook page, and that was a start.

Once the truth was out fully, Chelsea dropped everything she was doing to come and see him in Vanzette. He wasn't expecting his cousin to admit to not only watching his back from the inside but risking her job in the process. Chelsea had worked her magic to ensure he and Sade had a fighting chance. With all the facial recognition software the FBI had, Dante wondered how he hadn't been found in all this time. It didn't help that right after he was missing, his face was on the news. Chelsea admitted to having a part in that.

After her phone call to him, she traced his phone and location and found out about the accident. When she went to the hospital, she saw Sade there and knew her cousin would be in good hands. At that point, she switched a few things around in their files and software to ensure Dante would never be found. And every time there was a hit for him in their system, Chelsea was alerted first to report it as a false lead. She knew there was a chance her superiors would eventually find out, so she resigned as soon as Dante came forward. Her reward? Dante's unwavering loyalty and enough money for her to start a new life wherever she saw fit.

"I just don't understand what I did so wrong for Imani to do this to me," he said to his father. "I don't accept the role of victim, but damn. Was I a horrible husband?"

"You didn't do anything but love the wrong woman, son. Your mother and I told you from the beginning that Imani was no good for you. We told you Sade was the one, but you were so caught up in Imani's looks and her popularity... how she fit you... you didn't care about her heart... her integrity. The day you came and told us she was pregnant, I told you you'd just ruined your life."

"What am I supposed to do with that, Dad?"

Deandre chuckled. "Let it motivate you to go forward. Do things right. Handle this case and prove your innocence, divorce her, and move on. What are you gonna do about my grandbabies? I know they aren't yours, but they are still mine."

"I don't know, honestly. I want them, but I know she's not going to let me have custody if I do somehow send her to prison."

"Do you know who their father is?"

"No."

"Find out. Maybe you can use that to your advantage. Get in front of a family court judge and prove you're the best option for them since they grew up with you as their father."

"I'll consider it. How do you feel about me being with Sade? I know you said y'all liked her back then, but all things considered..."

"I don't like that she hid you, but I get her reasoning for it. We accepted her not coming to help look for you because of her issues with her family in Memphis and you being missing was something that was too difficult for her to accept emotionally. It was odd to us, but we don't judge a person based on how they respond to a crisis. It hurt us not having her here, but now, we're grateful that she had you there. For that, we will always have gratitude for her. Would we have liked to be let in on what she was doing? Yes. But right now, son, we're just grateful you're alive. At the end of the day, the only person's opinion that matters is yours. And God. Fuck everyone else. Regardless of who you're with, you make sure you get divorced first."

"Yes, sir." Dante yawned and stood from the dining room table. "I've been up for over twenty-four hours now. I'll talk to y'all later."

"All right, son. Get some rest."

Dante disconnected the call and headed to Sade's bedroom. He found her in bed. Dante thought she was sleeping, but as soon as she heard his steps, her eyes opened. She gave him a soft smile

and extended her hand for him. Dante placed his hand inside of
hers and walked over to the bed.

"I didn't mean to wake you."

"I couldn't sleep. I've been waiting for you."

He undressed and got into bed, pulling her into his arms and
on top of his chest. Peace immediately filled him.

"I haven't felt this good and at peace since I left you," Dante
admitted.

"I can't believe you're here. I just knew you wouldn't want to
have anything to do with me."

"Honestly, I didn't want to want you. I wanted to hate you,
but I can't. I love you, Smiley."

"I love you too," she cooed.

"What's crazy is, the whole time I was here, I felt like I didn't
belong. When I got back to Memphis, that felt like me, but it no
longer felt like home." Dante tilted her head so he could look into
her eyes. "My home is with you, no matter where we are."

Sade's smile was soft as she lowered her lips to his. Kisses
turned into touches, and not much time passed before they were
connected at the center. Unlike usual, their sex was rough, and
hard, and deep. Maybe it was what they needed to prove they were
there, together, as one again. Whatever the case, Sade whimpered
as they came simultaneously.

As Dante spilled his seeds inside of her, someone incessantly
knocked at the door and rang the doorbell nonstop.

"Who the hell is that?" she asked.

Dante sighed as he pulled out of her. "Only the police knock
like that. They have to be here for me."

"No." Sade sat up on the edge of the bed. "They're here for *me*."

SADE

SADE'S EYES BOUNCED against the white walls of the room Detective Jones had placed her in. This was Imani's doing, and Sade was okay with that. Imani would get hers. There was no doubt about that.

Detective Jones came back in, putting a cup of coffee in front of her.

"Cigarette?" he asked, and Sade shook her head. No matter how bad her nerves were, she wouldn't start that habit. They had her grandfather in a chokehold.

"No, thanks. What is this about?" she hurried out as he sat next to her.

"This is about Patrice Combs. You know her, right?" Detective Jones slid a picture of Patrice over to Sade.

"Yes, we went to school together. We also got our hair done at the same place."

He nodded, sitting back in his seat. "Ms. Griffin, what do you know about Patrice's murder?"

Sade's head shook as she shrugged. "What was shared on the news. That it was a robbery homicide."

"That's it?"

She nodded. "Yes, sir."

Detective Jones sighed. He looked at her for five Mississippis before asking, "How was your relationship with Patrice?"

"We didn't have one."

"What about when you were in school?"

"Why?" she asked skeptically.

"Just trying to establish your connection with the deceased."

"We didn't have one."

"Are you sure?"

Sade released a hard breath as she nodded. "Yes."

"I'm going to give it to you straight. We received an anonymous tip that you were involved in Patrice's murder and that we closed the case too early."

"Is the case reopened?"

"Officially, no. Unofficially..." Detective Jones leaned forward, lighting a cigarette. "I had our team hack Patrice's iPad. Her iCloud is connected to all of her devices. We were unable to locate her phone because it's off, but we were able to access her text messages."

Shit.

"Okay?" Sade questioned softly, trying to keep her legs from shaking under the table.

"We found deleted text messages between her and Willow Green... your neighbor. The same neighbor that went missing around the same time Patrice was murdered. Do you know what the two had in common?"

Sade's head shook. "No, I don't."

"You, Ms. Griffin. They were discussing you and someone named Dante. Is that the same Dante that was at your home this morning?"

"I'm sorry, where are you going with this?"

"I believe you're involved with Patrice's murder and Willow's disappearance. I'm not sure how yet, but you are."

Sade's lips lifted into a slow smile as she crossed her arms over her chest. "You brought me all the way down here to tell me that?"

"I wanted to give you the chance to come clean."

"About what?"

He shrugged. "You tell me."

With a huff, Sade leaned back in her seat. "I didn't have anything to do with Patrice's murder, and the last time I talked to Willow, she was going out of town. If she's missing, she's missing in San Juan."

"But there's no record of her going there, Sade. No plane ticket purchases, no credit card usage. Nothing."

"She said it was a free trip with a friend, so, you should look into that, not me."

Detective Jones smiled. "You're going to make me work for this, aren't you?"

Sade laughed. "That *is* your job, right?" Before he could respond, she was asking, "Is that it? If so, I'd like to go now."

He nodded, licking his lips. "You can leave at any time. You're not under arrest... yet."

Sade stood and headed for the door, stopping when he called her name. "Yes?"

"Don't leave town."

With one bob of her head, Sade left. She was clever, but was she clever enough to escape this? Only time would tell.

"You wanna tell me what that was about?" Dante asked, watching Sade gulp down her glass of wine. She hadn't bothered to have lunch yet. Quite frankly, she had no appetite.

"No, not really," she mumbled, making him laugh softly.

"If this is going to work, we have to be honest with each other."

"I know that, but some things are better if you didn't know."

"Sade..."

Tugging her bottom lip between her teeth, Sade avoided his eyes as he walked over to her. Dante lifted her and placed her on the counter. He set her glass next to her and took her hands into his.

"Dante, I really don't want you to know."

"I can't help you if you leave me in the dark."

She waited a few seconds before saying, "They think I was involved with a murder that happened before you left."

His head jerked as he processed her words. "Why would they think that?"

"Because it was someone we went to school with. She and I weren't close. In fact, she was one of Imani's minions. They don't have any evidence against me, just an anonymous tip that I know came from Imani. She's trying to get me in jail because of you."

"Is there any way they can prove you were involved?"

His question caught her off guard. He didn't ask her if she did it. If she had motive. Did that mean he didn't care, or that he trusted her so much he didn't think it was possible?

Sade's head shook, then hung. "No, they can't."

Dante squeezed her thighs as he nodded. "That's all I need to know then. If they come back, we'll look into filing harassment charges. Don't talk to anyone without me or an attorney present."

He removed himself from between her legs and opened the refrigerator as she smiled.

"That's... That's it?"

He briefly looked at her over his shoulder, giving her a soft smile. "Yeah, that's it. You need to eat. What do you have a taste for?"

Hopping off the counter, Sade made her way over to him. Closing the refrigerator, she turned him around and pressed him against it. "You."

As she lowered herself in front of him, Dante released a low groan. She looked up at him, giving him a wink and a seductive smirk.

"You can always have that," Dante granted, gripping the edges of the refrigerator after she pulled his shorts and boxers down and took him into her mouth.

IMANI

IMANI WATCHED AS Adam loaded his guns. Their plans had been ruined, yet again. Now that Dante had been released from jail, Imani knew she had no way of getting access to his funds. At this point, there was no reason for Adam to keep him alive.

Learning that Dante had been with her sister all this time didn't surprise Imani. Those two had always been close. For some reason, Imani expected Sade to have some type of loyalty to her since they were sisters. Didn't matter how much bullshit they'd put each other through over the years, Imani was sure if Sade knew about Dante's whereabouts, she would have told her. What did pinch at Imani's heart a little was knowing Sade had finally gotten Dante. Imani didn't want him, but she didn't want her sister to have him, either.

Imani hated Sade simply because she'd come first. She hated sharing the spotlight with anyone. Their parents and grandparents always wanted the sisters to do everything together, especially since they were so close in age, and Imani couldn't stand that. The spoiled princess believed she was meant to be an only child, so she treated Sade as if she weren't her sister.

"Do you know where he could be?" Adam asked.

"I know exactly where he's staying. He's in Vanzette with my sister."

"You know the address?"

"Yeah, no thanks to that bitch. When I went to visit her, she gave me the wrong address. I looked at the last package she sent me, though, and her real address is on it."

"Cool. Write it down for me. I don't want it in either of our phones. And you need to stay here. Go through your normal routine. Make sure you start practicing how you're going to react to finding out your husband has been murdered."

Imani nodded, looking at her reflection in the mirror. "When we get this money, I can't wait to get my breasts done. They should be bigger."

"Your titties are perfect. Don't touch them shits."

Imani smiled as Adam walked over to her and pulled her into his arms.

"Are you excited about us being a family soon? The girls will need some time to warm up to you, but they'll come around quickly."

"It's going to be an adjustment, but I'm ready. I've waited thirteen years to get my family back. It's past time."

Adam covered her lips with his, and it wasn't long before he had her in the air and on his bed for a quick round of sex that had her legs shaking as she cried his name.

When Imani walked into her home and saw Dante sitting in the living room, her humming stopped, and the bag of takeout from her favorite restaurant dropped from her hand.

"We need to talk," Dante said. With his head motioning toward the couch across from the one he was seated on, he told her, "Sit down."

"H-how did you get in here?" she asked, taking slow steps toward him. "I didn't see you on the camera."

"I blocked the Wi-Fi, so don't bother trying to use your phone to call for help. It won't work."

She sat across from him, eyes bouncing around the room nervously.

"Look at me," Dante demanded, and Imani complied.

"What do you want, Dante?"

"I want to know why you've done what you've done. Why did you lie to me about the twins? Did you intend to ever tell me the truth about them?"

Her head shook as her eyes focused on the Glock next to him. There was no point in lying or playing games. If he was going to kill her, she'd might as well come clean.

"No, I didn't. How did you find out?"

With a small smile, Dante lifted his ankle to his knee and stretched his arms across the back of the couch.

"You drunkenly confessed the truth to Sade one night, and she told me."

"Shit, I thought I was just dreaming that. How long have you known?"

"I didn't find out until after the accident. She told me before I came back home."

"That bitch," Imani grumbled, adding this to the list of reasons why she hated her sister.

"Who's their father, Imani? Just tell me the truth."

Her eyes rolled as she shook her head. "Adam," Imani almost whispered.

"Adam?" he repeated before chuckling. "The nigga that was stealing cars and selling drugs while we were in college? *That* Adam?"

"Yes, *that* Adam. I was going to tell you they weren't yours, but he got arrested and you proposed so I kept that secret to myself."

"They deserve to know the truth."

"I agree. We planned to tell them after you went to prison," Imani informed him.

"We?" He sat up in his seat. "He's back in your life?"

"He is. He's…" Imani squeezed the back of her neck and looked away briefly. When she returned her eyes to his, she lifted her head a little higher and decided to fully own the truth. "He's the one that I've been working with. We're in this together. I planned to divorce you and be with him so my girls could finally have the chance to get to know their father."

Dante nodded, remaining silent for a few seconds before chuckling.

"So you have your future already planned out, huh?" Imani shrugged. "What did I do to make you hate me enough to do this?"

"I don't hate you; I just don't like you. All these years, even with you dating me and marrying me and thinking I was the mother of your children, you *still* chose Sade."

"Please don't tell me this is about her."

"It is!" Imani yelled, leaning forward in her seat. "No matter what we were fighting about, you always chose her. You never considered me a friend; you always hung out with her. I was the one you kept on your arm like candy, but she…" Imani's chin trembled as her eyes watered. This was the first time she'd ever expressed any insecurity toward her sister, and she hated how vile the words tasted as they came out. "She always had pieces of you I could never reach. Every time the two of you interacted, I hated her more and wanted you more. And even though you were attracted to me physically, I just… felt like there was a disconnect between us. We didn't connect the way I connect with Adam mentally and emotionally because you have that connection with her. Friends or not, she's always been that one for you, and I… yes. Maybe I *did* hate you for that."

Silence surrounded them, and it was loud. So loud, Imani almost wanted to beg him to speak.

"So…" He cleared his throat and shook his head, as if her words were stuck there. "Because I had a close friendship with your sister, you stole from our clients, didn't pay our taxes, set up false financial statements, and laundered money, then set me up to take the fall for it?"

Imani rolled her eyes. "I was going to do that shit anyway, but yes, I blamed you for it because of her... and because it was easier to pin those things on you instead of Eric and Jessica."

"Did you try to have me killed too? Were you the cause of the accident?"

She shook her head. "No. That was Adam. He paid his cousin, Atlas, to kill you. I didn't find out until after the accident and you came back."

Dante rested his head against the back of the couch and stared at the ceiling. "How are we going to resolve this, Imani? Because I'm not going down for this."

"I'm not either, so I don't know what to tell you."

Imani chuckled, but when he gripped the gun, she stopped.

"What if I have a way for you to come clean, and we both avoid jail time?"

That didn't seem possible, but Imani was curious enough to hear him out, anyway. Not like she had much of a choice. As long as he had that gun, Imani was going to comply with whatever he said.

"What is it?"

"If you tell the truth and record a confession, I'll give you all the money from my offshore accounts. You can take the kids and go wherever you want. Of course, I'd recommend a country that wouldn't allow the US to have you extradited. You'll need to give me a divorce as well. Both will have to be done before my first court date."

It was on the tip of her tongue to say no, but when Imani considered the drought she was in and the fact that Enrique was expecting her to continue to launder money for him, she couldn't help but ask, "You'd give me all of it?"

"Yes. Every million I saved and invested over the years. It'll be yours."

"And all I have to do is record a confession and give you a divorce?"

"That's it. I won't share it with the feds until you and the girls are safely at your new destination."

"Do you care if Adam comes?"

Dante chuckled and shook his head. "I don't give a fuck. What you do with him doesn't concern me."

"Actually..." Imani's palm smacked her forehead. "You need to cut the Wi-Fi back on so I can call him. He's on his way to Vanzette right now to kill you."

"What?" Dante jumped out of his seat. "Why didn't you say something sooner?"

"I thought you were going to kill me!"

"Do you think he'll hurt Sade when he sees I'm not there?"

Imani shrugged, watching him place the gun at his waist and pull his phone out of his pocket.

"I don't know. I told him I didn't care either way."

"You need to call him and tell him to stand down. If anything happens to Sade, the deal is off, and I'm coming back here to finish what I started with you."

After pressing a few buttons on his phone, Dante quickly made his way toward the front door.

"This isn't over!" Imani cried out. "I want this deal, Dante. I want that money!"

Dante ignored her, but Imani didn't care. She was too busy dialing Adam's number. She cursed as it went straight to voicemail. The third time she called and that happened, she figured it was because there was no service where he was driving.

"Adam!" she yelled, leaving him a voicemail. "Cancel the plan. Please don't kill anyone. Dante and I worked out a deal that keeps us out of jail and will make us rich. Do *not* go into that house. Come home and call me back ASAP."

Imani hung up and tugged at her dreads.

"You'd better not fuck this up for me," she muttered, dialing his number yet again.

Imani's shoulders slouched as she dropped her phone. "If Dante has amnesia... how in the *fuck* did he know who Adam was?"

SADE

Sade DIDN'T KNOW when Dante would be back, but she wanted to have dinner ready when he arrived. She'd decided on baked chicken, macaroni and cheese, and Brussel sprouts. Everything was done except the Brussel sprouts. Those would need to be fresh. She decided to make him some cookies too. A smile spread across her lips as she thought about being excited for his arrival.

This was a feeling, an experience Sade never thought she'd have again. Finally, it felt like all things were going right in her world. The truth was out, and she still had her man. Now, Dante needed to divorce her sister, and they'd be able to live out their happily ever after.

When Dante left earlier, he didn't give her many details, but he told her he had a plan to make his charges disappear. Sade didn't want to get her hopes up, but she prayed he would succeed. Her nerves had been rattled, waiting for him to know the outcome. She wanted to call her grandparents but since they had the twins, Sade didn't want to risk them mentioning the fight between her and Imani. It wouldn't have been anything new for her grandparents, but they would have chewed Sade out for attacking Imani in front of the children.

She'd see them soon enough.

Once all this foolishness was over, Sade planned to take a trip to visit her grandparents.

At the sound of a loud bang, Sade jumped and clutched her chest. It was followed by glass shattering.

"What the fuck?" Sade yelled, heading toward the entry hallway. At the sight of Adam unlocking the door from the inside, Sade gasped and covered her mouth. She ran up the stairs, but Adam was quick on his feet, tackling her and turning her over at the top of them. Holding her down by her wrists, he looked down at her with a smile.

"Where is he?" Adam asked.

"Who?"

He sucked his teeth. "Don't play with me, Sade. Dante."

"He isn't here. He's on his way to Memphis."

"For what?"

Sade shrugged, trying to get from underneath him. "I don't know, now get off me!"

"Nah. I came here for a reason, and I'm not leaving without something."

His left hand went to her neck while the right went to her lace panties underneath her gown.

"Adam, plea—"

Before she could get the words out, his grip around her neck tightened and silenced her. She swung at his chest and face, but the hits didn't sway him. Why wasn't she surprised? The man had just spent over a decade in prison. He'd probably fought men three times her size.

"If you make me fight for it, it's only going to get worse," he warned, ripping her panties off her body.

Sade whimpered, refusing to allow him to take anything from her without putting up a fight. She reached for his eyes, but he pushed down on her throat so hard her body convulsed underneath him. Just when she was about to surrender to the inevitable... footsteps sounded off downstairs.

"Police! Hands up, now!"

Her eyes closed as tears slid down her temples. They opened when she felt Adam removing his weight from her body.

"Fuck you!" he yelled, reaching for his piece. "I ain't going bac—"

"Gun!" one of the officers yelled.

Before Sade could crawl away, gunshots rang out. Adam's body fell onto her back, weighing her down as she screeched. Seconds felt like hours before men were pulling her from underneath him and asking her what had happened.

Once she gave them her statement, she asked them how they knew she needed help. They told her that Dante had called the station and asked for a unit to be sent to her home. They didn't know how he knew Adam was on his way there, and Sade didn't care, either. She'd find out later. In that moment, she was just glad he did, because he'd saved her from Adam in more ways than one.

"I wish I could bring him back to life just to kill him myself," Dante said, gently running his fingers across Sade's neck.

There was some bruising there from Adam's hand and a couple of scratches on her thigh from when he snatched off her panties. Other than that, she was okay... physically, at least. Sade didn't know how long it would take for her not to see him lying on top of her when she closed her eyes. There was no fear, though. Adam was dead, and there was nothing he could do to her now.

"I'm just glad he's dead. Thank you for having the mind to call, knowing it would take you a little while to get back here. If they wouldn't have been here, I..."

Her voice broke as she fought back tears.

"It doesn't matter. That's over. He's dead. I'm not going to let anything happen to you, baby. I got you."

"What do you think Imani's going to do? Do you think she'll renege from the deal now?"

Dante had told her about his visit to see Imani. How he'd recorded their entire conversation and planned to share it with the FBI.

"It doesn't matter. I have the recording. Even if she tried to say she didn't want to do it anymore because he's dead, I have what I need. I won't give it to them until she signs the divorce papers, but she's as good as done."

"God, I'm so glad this is almost over. I can't imagine how you feel."

He lay flat on the bed, taking her hand into his. "I don't really feel anything yet. I don't think I'll feel relief until she signs those papers, I give the FBI this recording, and she's arrested."

"That's understandable. I just hope she prioritizes money over Adam and doesn't draw the divorce out because he's gone. Imani has always put herself first. I hope that won't change now."

"From your lips to God's ears," Dante said, and Sade didn't respond.

All they could do was wait. As anxious as she would be, Dante's freedom, just like his love, were worth waiting for.

DANTE

One Month Later

DANTE HEADED TOWARD the picnic table where Imani was seated, grateful she didn't have the twins with her. It was late May, and she looked immaculate, as always, in her straw hat and white summer dress. At the sight of him and Sade, hand in hand, Imani lowered her shades and rolled her eyes before chuckling. Dante's grip on Sade's hand tightened as he looked down at her.

"You good?" he confirmed, to which Sade looked up at him with her signature smile and nodded.

"I'm great."

They sat across from her at the table, and Dante wasted no time handing her the divorce papers. He'd already signed, and his lawyer had tagged everywhere that Imani needed to sign.

"Hello, sister," Imani greeted with a smirk.

"Just sign the shit so we can go."

Imani chuckled. "Always so hostile. If anyone should be upset, it should be me. You're the reason the father of my children is dead."

"No, *he's* the reason he's dead," Dante answered before Sade could. "He tried to rape her. That doesn't sway you at all?"

Imani looked from Dante to Sade as she shrugged. "If it effects my happiness, I couldn't care less what happens to her."

240

Sade chuckled with a shake of her head as Imani finally signed the papers. When she was done, she handed them to Dante and stood.

"Is that it?" Imani asked. "When do I get my money?"

"When hell freezes over," Sade said as they stood.

Dante folded the papers under his arm, telling her, "Thanks for finally setting me free," which was the code he'd given the FBI. As soon as he said the words, several agents in plainclothes surrounded them. As Imani was handcuffed, she stared at Dante in disbelief.

"You set me up?"

"How does it feel?" Sade asked with a smile as Dante wrapped his arm around her waist.

"You motherfucker!" Imani roared as they dragged her away. "I can't believe you set me up!"

"You should be grateful that's all we did," Sade taunted, removing herself from Dante's grasp.

That didn't last long. He took her by the hand, telling her, "Come here," as he pulled her close. "Focus on me. She doesn't matter anymore." Sade's body relaxed against him. "It's almost over, Smiley. We're one step closer to our happily ever after."

Sade wrapped her arms around him as he placed a kiss on her forehead. "I cannot wait. I shouldn't have as much peace as I do knowing my sister's about to go to prison, but that girl has been a thorn in my side all of our lives. I'm so glad she's finally getting what she deserves."

Dante held her close as she wrapped her arms around him. His eyes closed, and he pulled in a deep breath, feeling the exact same way she did. He was grateful Imani was about to do time for the crimes she committed, but more than anything, Dante was grateful that he was finally able to live the life and have the love he deserved.

When Imani was first arrested, she tried to cut a deal by offering information on the attempt on Dante's life. Unfortunately for her, Atlas had struck a deal of his own. He confessed to running Dante off the road and agreed to testify against Imani and Adam in exchange for immunity. Atlas gave proof of several other financial schemes that Adam and Imani had been involved in, increasing Imani's time away from seven years to thirty-three. In exchange for a plea deal, Imani waved her right to a trial and settled for serving thirteen years without the possibility of parole.

Dante didn't think anything about that moment could make him sad... until he saw the looks on the twins' faces. They were already confused and upset over the fact that Dante wasn't their real father. Now, they had to deal with their mother being taken away. Imani may not have been the most present parent, but she gave what she had received from her parents, and no one blamed her for that. Though Dante offered to take the twins in, they requested to go with their grandparents instead, which made sense. Dante and Sade accepted that, promising to be there for whatever they needed.

After Dante opened the door for Sade, he went over to his side. She waited until he was inside to ask, "What now?"

He looked over at her and took her hand into his, giving it a kiss. "Well, we can stay in Vanzette. I'll open a couple of businesses there, and we start our life. Or, we can move somewhere no one knows us and reinvent ourselves."

"Hmm..." Sade's mouth twisted to the side as she considered the options. "I like the idea of going somewhere new. I can do my art and books anywhere. What do you say? New York, Cali, or Georgia?"

"Shit, why not all three? There's nothing stopping us. We have nothing but money and time."

"That's true." Her grin spread. "Let's do it."

"Let's do it," Dante agreed, starting his new Hummer. "Before we leave Memphis, why don't we stop by the mall and get one of those pretzels you like and ride the carousel? Have one last good memory here."

"You remember that?" She sat up in her seat and turned to face him. "How do you remember that?"

"I've had my memory back for quite some time," Dante confessed, holding in his smile.

Sade swatted his arm as she yelled, "What?"

"Bae," he called sweetly through his chuckle.

"Nuh-uh! What's quite some time, Dante Nathaniel Williams?"

Dante laughed harder, and though she was trying not to, Sade smiled herself.

"I regained my memory after my second flashback, but I didn't remember what happened the night of the accident until I went back to the office. It appears I was suppressing that because I was in denial about Imani, but everything else came back to me after that second flashback."

"That's when you started calling me Smiley?"

"Yeah."

Sade huffed and crossed her arms over her chest as she looked straight ahead. "Why didn't you say anything?"

"Because..." Dante tugged her face in his direction by her chin. "I wanted us to have a chance at forever too. To start fresh. To pretend as if the past didn't exist. I had always wanted you, Day, but I was just... dumb and stupid. If I told you I had my memory back, it would be over, so I let you do your thing. I guess I wanted the chance to experience you without the past being in the way." His fingers tapped the center console. "That's why I didn't want to go back to the doctor. I didn't want him to say everything was normal and that my memory should have been back. I didn't want you to get suspicious of me."

"You don't even know what I did to make sure you didn't find out," she almost whispered, her leg shaking. "And you already knew? The things I had to do." Sade's head shook as she rubbed her hands up and down her thighs. She pulled in a deep breath before chuckling. "I want to be mad at you, but I can't. We both lied, so I guess we're even."

She looked over at him and smiled.

"No more secrets, though, right?"

Sade looked at him for a few seconds before replying with, "Right. No more secrets."

SADE

As SADE WENT down one aisle to another, she hummed. It seemed all was right in her world. The truth had come out, and the world didn't cave in on her. Her sister was in prison and Adam was dead. Her nieces were where they were comfortable, with her grandparents, and that was really no surprise. Though Sade would have liked to have them with her and Dante, she understood how confusing this would be. More than anything, she wanted Mila and Nila to be in a healthy, loving environment, clinging to each other like she and Imani had never been able to do.

Once she gathered everything she needed from the grocery store, Sade headed to check out. She had gone to the local arts and crafts store earlier to get new canvases and paint. With the truth being out now, her creativity flowed again. Already, she had written twenty ideas for her adult coloring book. Sade always painted the ideas on canvases before digitizing them. For whatever reason, seeing the pictures painted helped her determine if they were good enough to be in her coloring books or not.

The left side of her mouth lifted into a smile as she thought about the work she planned to do when she got home. Ironically, Dante was the one that pushed her to get serious with her painting and drawing. She'd always been into it, even as a child, scribbling on anything she could find—including the walls of her home. That was probably the most considerate thing her parents had done for her. Instead of yelling at her for messing up the walls, they let her color and paint on them as she saw fit. Her grandparents, however, wanted no part of that. Barron had put large pieces of kraft paper onto the walls for her to draw on. When they were covered, he'd take them down and replace them.

At the thought of them, Sade dialed her grandmother's number. They were at Imani's trial, though they were upset with both sisters. They didn't agree with what either of them had done. In Sade's eyes, Imani's actions were worse, but to her grandparents, wrong was wrong, and a sin was a sin.

"Hello?" Ava answered, and Sade's smile widened at the sound of her grandmother's voice.

"Hey, Grandma. How are y'all?"

"We're good. Grandpa has taken the twins down to the bank to go fishing for some reason." Ava chuckled. "How are you and Dante?"

"Good. I'm grabbing a few things to make dinner, and you were on my mind."

Several seconds passed before Ava said, "You know I don't approve of what you did."

"Yes, ma'am, I know."

"You're going to have to pay for that. God won't bless that mess. It might not be in your relationship with Dante, but you're gonna reap what you've sown."

"Yes, ma'am," was all Sade could think of to say. There was no point in going back and forth with Ava about it. Besides, she was right. With everything that Sade had done to keep Dante, she was surprised nothing bad had happened to her yet. All she could do was trust that the universe knew her intentions were pure. Regardless of how she did it, Sade's goal had always been to protect Dante— getting to love him and receiving his love was just a bonus.

"Now, when are you coming over? I wanna see my girl."

Sade nodded and nostrils flared as her eyes watered. "I can come this weekend."

"Good. Make sure you bring something nice for the girls."

"I will. Tell them I said hello and that I love them. Have Grandpa call me when they get back home."

"Okay, baby. I will."

They said their goodbyes, and Sade disconnected the call. Grateful she'd reached out, she was content with how the conversation went. Her grandmother would never sugarcoat things or tell her she was right if she was wrong, and Sade had always appreciated her for that.

There were two people in front of her in line, so Sade browsed social media while she waited. She and Dante were no longer a trending topic in Memphis or Vanzette. While a lot of people said she was wrong for what she'd done, some understood when they learned of Sade and Imani's backstory. When Imani was sentenced, people cared less. People who barely spoke three words to her in high school spent hours giving think pieces and their experiences with the sisters during their teenage years, and all Sade could do was laugh.

When it was finally time for Sade to put her things on the belt, her phone vibrated in her tote bag. She let the call go to voicemail, not wanting to hold up the line. By the time she was done getting everything out of the basket, her phone was ringing again. Pulling it out of her purse, Sade figured it was a spam call since she didn't know the number. Sade returned the cashier's greeting and completed her checkout process, trying to ignore the incessant vibrating of her phone.

As she headed toward the exit, it started up again. With a growl, Sade answered with, "Who the fuck is this?"

At the sound of the recording letting her know an inmate was calling her, Sade clutched her chest. She pushed her cart over to the closest bench by the doors and sat down. Then she answered the call, surprised by her desire to hear her sister's voice. Her heart raced as she waited for the call to be connected.

What the hell did Imani want?

Is she okay?

A million questions swirled around in Sade's brain. Her eyes scanned the store, as if she felt Imani could see her. She put her acrylic nail into her mouth and tapped it with her teeth, holding her breath until she heard, "Hello?"

Her back straightened against the bench. "Imani?"

"Who else would it be?"

Sade's eyes rolled. "What do you want? Are you okay?"

Imani chuckled. "Don't act like you care. You're the reason I'm in here."

"Of course, I care. You're my sister. And I'm not the reason you're in there. *You* are. You chose to steal and clean money for that man and set Dante up to take the fall for it out of all people."

She sucked her teeth and huffed. "Look, I didn't call you to talk about that shit, okay?"

"Then what did you call for, Imani?"

"I want you to come and see me next week. You'll need to fill out the paperwork to visit. I don't know how long it's going to take to be processed, but I need you to come as soon as you can. We need to talk."

"Okay. Can you tell me what it's about?"

"No. Just fill out the paperwork and bring your ass here."

Imani disconnected the call, and Sade couldn't help but laugh. Even behind bars, Imani just *had* to call the shots. She sat there for a while, trying to wrap her mind around her sister's request. Sade didn't think anything could top hearing Imani's voice... until she walked outside and saw Detective Jones leaning against her car...

SADE

THE LAST TIME Sade saw Detective Jones, she was being questioned by him right after Dante had returned to Vanzette. Though he had no proof, Jones seemed to be convinced Sade was involved in Patrice's death and Willow's disappearance.

She took him in, ankles crossed, belly fat, as a cigarette dangled from his mouth. The sun caused his eyes to squint as he stared in her direction. Once she was just a few feet away, Jones flicked the cigarette away from her car.

"Need some help?" he asked, motioning toward her cart.

Sade wanted to say no, but if he was about to hassle her, the least he could do was put her bags in the trunk. With a bob of her head, she opened the trunk and allowed him to take the cart.

"If you followed me here, that's harassment," Sade said, making him chuckle.

"I don't need you to tell me what is or isn't harassment, Ms. Griffin."

"But I do need you to tell me what this is about. What do you want?"

"I want you to explain to me why every woman that came in contact with you this year is either dead or missing," Jones said, placing the last of the bags into the trunk. He closed it, then turned to face her. "When we got the call about the possible home invasion going on at your home, I looked into everyone involved."

He crossed his arms and ankles again. "Dante Williams, that's the man that had been missing for months in Memphis. He's the one that called in the possible attack. He's been staying with you. Amnesia, correct?"

She didn't answer right away, but when she did, it was with, "You seem to already have a story in your head, so you tell me."

"Sure." Jones pushed himself off her car again and stepped closer to her. "I believe he was with you the whole time, Patrice and Willow found out, and you killed them to keep your secret. Trina, I'm not sure about. She's connected to you and Patrice in only one way, so that might be a coincidence, but I've been in this field long enough to know there aren't coincidences when it comes to murders. I'd bet my life that Trina found out too, and you're responsible for her death as well."

"Detective Jones—"

"We've had three murders since Dante arrived in our town, Sade. Three murders. We haven't had three murders in three years, and now that he's here, we have three murders."

"Last I heard, Willow was missing, so Patrice and Trina make two."

Jones chuckled and ran his fingers down the corners of his mouth. "I like you. It's a shame I'm going to have to arrest you."

"For what? Do you have a warrant?"

"No." His head shook. "Not right now. I haven't put the pieces together fully yet, but I'm getting there. If you didn't kill these women, Dante did. I'm giving you grace now to go ahead and confess or admit to what you know. You slipped up somewhere, Sade, and I'm going to find it."

Sade ran her tongue across her teeth. "Well, good luck with that, Detective Jones. Until you have that warrant, stay the hell away from me."

"Oh, Ms. Griffin?" he called as she opened the door.

"What?"

"I thought I'd tell you, Patrice's case has been opened again. We've dropped the robbery angle. This was intentional, and we're going to figure out by who and why."

Her eyes blinked three times before she cleared her throat. "Like I said, good luck."

Sade jumped into her car with haste and sped off. "How in the hell are they going to reopen her case without any evidence? Or do they have evidence? Of course he's not going to tell me. I need to figure out a way to find out. I was careful, but you can never be too sure." She nibbled her bottom lip as her head shook. "God, what am I going to do? I don't want to let Dante in on this, but I should probably let him know." Her head shook again as she accelerated her speed. "No, I can't do that. If he was willing to send Imani to jail for stealing, he'd want me thrown under it for murder. Dante can *never* find out about this—ever."

IMANI

Before Her Phone Call to Sade

*W*HEN IMANI LEARNED *she had a visitor, she was surprised. Her grandparents made it clear they didn't approve of what she'd done, and all the friends she'd collected over the years immediately turned their backs on her when she was sentenced. Adam was gone, and it was the first time in her life that Imani truly felt alone. Thoughts of Sade feeling like this all of her life had plagued Imani almost daily, forcing her to consider writing to Sade countless times.*

Imani decided not to see the twins while she was in prison, but she did plan to call and write them often. If she was to be honest with herself, Imani took being their mother for granted. Losing her parents as suddenly as she did should have motivated her to be a present parent, but it was the opposite. For whatever reason, Imani was sure she'd have forever with her girls, so she didn't prioritize being present with them. Now that she was unable to be with them, Imani craved them the most.

She sat across from the stout, Black, heavyset man in an ill-fitting suit. Imani didn't recognize his face or have any idea why he visited her. Still, a visit meant she wasn't in her cage, so Imani was looking forward to what he had to say.

"Do I know you?" she asked as his eyes scanned her face.

He stared at her, almost in awe. "No, you don't, but I know your sister. You two look a lot alike."

Imani's eyes rolled. It wasn't the first time she'd heard that, but it irritated her just as much as it always did. Imani could admit her older sister had always been attractive; she just didn't put as much effort into it as Imani did, and that made Imani envious. When they were in school, Sade's glasses and braces and oversized clothes made her an easy target, especially when she'd wear her hair in braids to the back or those thick, puffy buns, but Sade had always been beautiful. Imani had made it her personal mission to point out every flaw in her sister she could find to separate them as much as possible. Sometimes it worked, but no matter what she said or did, it never changed their genes and similarities.

It never changed the fact that Sade was a mirrored reflection of her.

Her older sister.

The one meant to guide and protect her.

Imani had never wanted any of that, and just like the day of her wedding, she craved it now. It was funny how life worked that way. Whenever Imani was in deep shit or in need of advice, Sade would always come running. No matter how big of a fight they'd had before that call, Sade would always come running.

"What has she done now?" Imani asked.

"That's what I'm hoping you can help me figure out." He pulled out a small black notepad from his pocket. "I'm Detective Jones. We spoke months ago about Patrice Combs. You told me you believed your sister was responsible for her murder."

Imani remained silent. Yeah, she'd called and given them Sade as a suspect, but that was in the heat of her anger. Now that she'd settled into the mess of her life, Imani didn't really care to see her sister go to prison for anything, especially for killing Patrice. Patrice and Imani hung out in high school and kept in touch via social media in and after college, but Imani had never considered her a friend. Patrice was all too willing to agree with whatever Imani said or did, and Imani didn't respect people that didn't challenge her.

More than anything, Imani didn't believe her sister was capable of killing someone. They fought a lot, but she didn't think Sade had it in her. At the most, Imani figured a detective would pop up on Sade a time or two and scare her with questioning, but this was a bit extreme.

"Yeah, what about it?" Imani checked. "Did you arrest her?"

"Not yet." He sighed and rubbed the creases in his forehead. "We don't have enough substantial evidence to connect her to the murder, and I was hoping you could help me with that. Why don't you tell me why you believe Sade was involved, and we can take it from there?"

Imani's head shook as she sat up in her seat. "I don't want no part of this. If you want to build a case against my sister, you're gonna have to do it on your own."

He laughed quietly, but his smile fell immediately. "You're in here for the next thirteen years because of fraud, theft, and money laundering. You took a plea, right? And that was after you tried to set your husband, well ex-husband, up to take the fall. Dante Williams. The same Dante Williams that has been in Vanzette with your sister.

"I assume you called me because you were upset about that, and now, for whatever reason, you've changed your mind about helping. But it doesn't work like that." Jones sat up in his seat. "There's a direct link between your sister and three women, two of whom are dead, and one has been missing for months. If I can prove that you had anything to do with this or knew information and willingly withheld it, I can have additional charges added. Or you can help me, and I'll speak with the FBI about having your sentence reduced." He crossed his arms on top of the table. "Quite frankly, triple murder carries more weight than the petty shit you did. Are you willing to help me out now?"

Imani considered his words before saying, "My sister isn't capable of killing one person, let alone three. She's a fighter, but no, Sade wouldn't have done this. I was upset with her when I made that call, I can admit that, but I don't have any information that will help you."

"*I can accept that, but you have more information than you believe. If you can make me aware of any fights or engagements between Sade and Patrice, that would be a start. Also, if you could agree to a DNA sample, we could use yours to rule her out as a suspect or prove that she was involved.*"

Sitting up in her seat, Imani's head tilted so that her ear was closer to his mouth when she asked, "You're saying you have DNA evidence against my sister?"

"I'm saying there was hair in Patrice's car that wasn't hers. I'm saying there was the tiniest bit of blood on the other victim that wasn't hers. We ran it through our system and it's not a match for anyone that has a record. If you can give me a DNA sample, I can run it against the evidence we have. And if you have proof of your sister and Patrice being at odds, a voicemail, recording, text conversation... something that I can take to a judge for a warrant for your sister's DNA, that will work in your favor."

"And you can guarantee me less time in here?"

"Yes. Now, I can't say you'll get out now or anything like that. It depends on how valuable what you offer is. So I'm going to ask you again. Are you sure you don't have proof that your sister committed these murders?"

SADE

Back to the Present
Ten Days Later

FOR A LITTLE over a week, Sade had no idea what the hell Imani wanted to see her for. She had been anxiously racking her brain, trying to figure out what this could have been about. Unsure of what Imani wanted to talk about, Sade decided to wait until she was about to leave to tell Dante about the visit.

Sade waited until Dante had finished his call with Eric to go into his office space. Though they were looking for a new home, Dante was still making small changes here and there to make that one feel more comfortable.

"Hey, beautiful," he spoke, patting his lap for her to sit on it.

"Hey, handsome. What's Eric talking about?"

"He's trying to get me to work with him and Jessica."

"Are you considering it?"

"Not at all." Dante chuckled as he squeezed her thigh. "We're getting the hell out of Tennessee and not looking back. I loved working with them, but I'm ready for that part of my life to be over. I don't want anything to remind me of your sister."

"Well, how do you expect to be with me and not think of her?"

Dante licked his lips and smiled. "I don't see her when I see you. You two are so different I wouldn't believe you were sisters if we didn't grow up together."

Sade wanted to tell him she and Imani were more alike than he believed. Hell, maybe she was worse. There was no maybe. As far as she knew, Imani hadn't killed anyone like she had.

"It's funny that you mention her," Sade started, repositioning herself on his lap. "Imani called and asked me to visit her."

He released a long, slow breath. "And you're going to?"

"Yes. I'm about to head out now."

Dante's head bobbed once. His grip on her loosened before he released it altogether. "Why, Sade?"

She shrugged. "I don't know. She's my sister, and I want to know what she has to say."

Dante chuckled, gently pushing her off his lap. "Nothing good, I can promise you that. She's either about to say some shit to get in your head or start some mess."

"Maybe," Sade muttered with a pout. "But I-I'm going to see her, regardless of whether you approve. I hope you can respect that and understand."

"All right," he agreed. "You have every right. I might not like it, but I support you either way."

"Thank you, babe." Sade gave him a kiss and hug before preparing to leave. "Do you need me to bring you back anything?"

"Just you—exactly how you left."

Sade chuckled. "I'll do my very best."

Sade watched as Imani walked over to her. The guard released her arm and uncuffed her, then Imani sat down. Even in prison, she looked surprisingly radiant. Her locs were pulled back in two large French braids, which made Sade chuckle. Imani used to clown Sade every time her hair was braided, and now, her locs were in the same style. There was a scratch on her cheek just under her eye, and Sade couldn't help but wonder if it was because of a fight. Even if she didn't want it to, her protector spirit came out.

"The fuck happened to your face?"

Imani chuckled. "This is nothing. You should see the bitch that tried to take my time on the phone. I damn near choked her ass out with the cord."

"They ain't got guards in here watching over y'all?"

Her eyes rolled and head shook. "Get real, Day. These folks don't give a fuck about us. And you don't give a fuck about me. You've done worse than this to me."

"Yeah, well, I'm the only one you can fight. You know I've never let another bitch put their hands on you."

Imani laughed because she knew that was true. They may have terrorized each other, but not once had another woman been able to touch the other and there not be violent consequences.

"I never needed that, though."

"Yes, you did. You needed me just like I needed you."

With a groan, Imani rested her elbows on the table. "Don't start with the sentimental shit. That's not what I asked you here for."

"Then why am I here, Imani?"

"How much do you value your freedom?"

Imani's question caught her off guard. The sisters' eyes remained locked for a brief moment until Imani called her name.

"Huh?"

"I asked, how much do you value your freedom?"

"What kind of question is that?"

"An important one. So answer."

"I don't know." Sade shrugged, looking around the visiting room. Its white floors and walls somehow provided purity in the midst of so many people that were filled with darkness and chaos—herself included. "I value it a lot, of course."

"You know what's funny?" Sade wasn't given time to respond before Imani said, "You finally have everything you wanted. I took Dante from you, and you got him back. I'm in here and can't do shit. My girls can't come see me like this. You finally win, Sade."

"Okay, you know what?" Sade chuckled as she stood and rested her palms on the table. "I'm not doing this with you."

"Just... sit down," Imani requested, crossing her arms and sitting back in her seat. "Damn."

With a frown, Sade sat back down, eyeing her sister skeptically. "What is this about, Imani?"

"How careful were you when you killed Patrice?" Unsure if that was a trick question or not, Sade remained silent, making Imani laugh. "I asked you a fucking question."

"I don't know what you're talking about," Sade grumbled, preparing to stand again.

"Now is not the time for the little miss innocent act. That detective came to visit me, and he made me a very nice deal."

Now... Imani had her sister's attention. "Jones?"

Imani nodded. "Yep. Him."

"What did he say?"

"Basically, that you're connected to three crimes there, and he wants me to help him get evidence or enough probable cause for a warrant to get evidence. In exchange, I get a reduced sentence."

"What does he have so far?"

"Just my call and the connection of you, Patrice, and some other bitches. There was hair in Patrice's car and blood on someone else, but they ran it through the system, and they don't know whose it is. He wants me to give greater testimony and my DNA. Apparently, if they get a hit off me, that will prove the hair and blood are yours."

Sade's heart was pounding so loudly against her rib cage she heard it in her ears. She felt herself wobble in her seat. Had she not been sitting, Sade was sure she would have fainted. Inhaling deeply, Sade closed her eyes and counted to three. When her eyes opened, they rolled at the sight of Imani's smirk.

"Let me guess, you wanted me here to rub it in my face that you're going to help him get to me?"

Sighing, Imani shook her head. She leaned forward and looked around before saying, "I wanted you here to see how much your freedom is worth. What he's offering is great, but I'm thinking you can offer me something greater."

"What did you have in mind?"

"I want three million deposited into an account by the end of this week."

"Three million dollars!" Sade yelled louder than she planned to. She had that at one point because of her parents, but not anymore. "I don't have that much money saved, Imani. Unlike you, I've worked legally over the years. My books and paintings provide well, but not *that* damn well, and you know it cost me half of that to get my house and land set up the way I wanted."

"Well, you're with Dante now and he has that and then some. Get his ass to pay it for you. Either way, you have until the end of the week to put that money in my account. Otherwise, I'm going to let him get the DNA sample."

Sade laughed as her head shook. "Bullshit. What is this really about?"

Confusion covered Imani's face. "What do you mean? I just told you what this is about."

"Nah." Sade massaged her chin as she thought everything over. "If you were going to help him, you would have done so without calling me, *especially* if he was offering you a reduced sentence. You're money hungry, but no amount of money would have kept you in here. Either you're lying about Jones to get money out of me or you're up to something else. Which one is it?"

Licking her lips, Imani looked at her hands before rubbing them together. "You think you know me so well."

"I do, so spill it."

With a huff, Imani agreed with, "Fine." Her fingers slipped over her eyebrow as she pulled in a deep breath. "When I came to visit you, I told you I lived without thought of anyone else. I did what I wanted and said what I wanted, no matter who cared. Living like that is the reason I'm in here. I figured... It was time for me to change. That way of thinking and living has caused me to lose literally everything. My husband and my lover, my kids, my money, my freedom, my family... everything." Imani's eyes watered, and Sade momentarily looked away. "Yes, I considered giving him my DNA and telling him about our past so I could have a reduced sentence, but I... I decided for once to put you first. So, I'm not saying you're not going to go to jail for this, but I'm not going to be the one to make his case easier."

Sade wiped the tears that fell from her eyes. This was the first time Imani had ever done something for her. Hell, it was the first time Imani had put someone above herself. It had caught Sade completely by surprise. With all the scenarios that had been swarming around in her mind, she never would have considered this. Sniffling, Sade looked away.

"Thank you, sis. I don't know what else to say."

"Say you'll have my money in the bank by the end of the week, and we're even."

Nodding, Sade wiped her face. "I will." She smiled as she looked at her sister. "Thank you."

"If you want to thank me, look after my girls. They're about to go through a lot of monumental stages in life, and I won't be there. Make sure they stay close, okay?"

Imani's request only made Sade's tears stream more rapidly.

"Of course. I got them, and I got you, no matter how much you say you don't need me."

Imani's mouth twisted to the side as she suppressed her smile and stood. "End of the week, Day. End of the week." She tossed her sister a wink before telling the nearest guard she was ready to go back to her cell.

For a while, all Sade could do was sit there. She'd been as careful as she could, but murdering people was new territory for her. She had to get out of Vanzette ASAP before Jones made good on his threats of putting her in jail. She'd never forget this moment or the act of loyalty, protection, and kindness her sister had just given her. And now, Sade was wondering how she could return the favor.

DANTE

One Month Later

"WELL... THIS IS it," Sade said, looking around her empty home one last time.

When Imani was sentenced, and they returned to Vanzette, they made plans to leave. Since Sade owned her home, she decided to rent it out. Dante had purchased them a beach condo in San Diego, a home in Decatur, and a penthouse apartment in New York. New York would be their first stop so he could open his new financial firm there, then Decatur for his lounge, and San Diego to relax and enjoy themselves.

"Are you sure you're okay with leaving Vanzette behind?" Dante confirmed as they headed over to the front door.

"Positive. I'm ready for my next phase of life with you."

He couldn't imagine how she truly felt, but she said she was okay leaving this place behind. The night before, Lathan and Veronica had hosted a goodbye dinner for them, and the gesture was bittersweet. Dante wasn't sure what had transpired between Sade and Veronica to draw them closer, but he was glad she'd appeared to have made a new friend.

"Good." Dante placed a quick kiss to her lips before saying, "Why don't you go ahead to the airport? I'll do one final walkthrough and put the key in the lockbox for your tenant, then meet you there."

"Um... there's actually one last thing that I need to take care of. I can do the walkthrough and meet you at the airport."

Dante's head tilted in confusion. "What is it? I can take care of it for you."

Her head lowered and shook. "You really can't, Dante. It's best you know nothing about this."

"Okay... Now you're scaring me." Dante palmed her arms and stared down at her. "What is it, Smiley?"

"I said I would never share this with you." Her voice shook and lips trembled as her eyes watered. "You're going to be disgusted with me."

Dante's laugh was light as he cupped her chin. "Baby, there's absolutely nothing you could do that would ever make me disgusted with you. I love you and accept you unconditionally. Now, what is it?"

"I'll um..." Sade released a shaky breath. "I'll show you. Let's just do the final walkthrough."

Hesitantly, Dante agreed.

He walked around and made sure both HVAC units were off and all lights were off. He went down to the basement and made sure it was cleaned out, then to the shed. While he stayed there, Sade made him promise not to enter it. She told him she was working on a special project for him that she didn't want him to see. He made his way outside, and Sade was already standing in front of the shed.

Sade took a deep breath, and when she opened it and he saw Willow tied up, he rushed to her aid.

"The fuck are you doing here?" he asked, pulling the rag down from her mouth.

She'd lost a significant amount of weight and some color, but other than that, she looked okay.

"You don't even know what I did to make sure you didn't find out," she almost whispered, her leg shaking. *"And you already knew? The things I had to do."* Sade's head shook as she rubbed her hands up and down her thighs. She pulled in a deep breath before chuckling. *"I want to be mad at you, but I can't. We both lied, so I guess we're even."*

The sound of Sade's sniffles drew his attention to her. "She knew too much. She was working with Patrice, and they were going to ruin everything. I-I had no other choice."

"She's been here all this time? Since her folks did the wellness check for her?"

Sade nodded, wiping her eyes. "Yes. I was able to convince her family that she was on vacation, and I sent texts from her phone after paying her bill so they wouldn't get too suspicious, but Detective Jones never believed it. He always thought she was a missing person. He's been trying to pin her, Patrice, and Trina on me for a while now. That's why I really need to go."

"Wait." Dante stood fully, making his way over to Sade. "You killed Patrice?"

Avoiding his eyes, Sade nodded. "I wasn't going to let anyone take you away from me, Dante. If that changes the way you view me, I understand, but please don't tell the police. Imani not giving Jones a DNA sample hindered his case, but it's still open. Just let me leave, and you'll never hear from me again."

Willow's groggy groan forced Dante to look at her.

"D-Dante," she muttered. Clearing her throat, she looked from him to Sade. "H-help."

Dante didn't have much time to think. Now was the time to act. And after everything Sade had done for him, he knew exactly what he had to do. "I'm sorry, but I can't let you go." Dante looked around the shed. "You know too much."

"Dante, please—"

"Sade and I are finally getting our chance at forever. I'm not going to let you ruin that." He walked over to the wall that held several different tools and looked them over. "She's proven her loyalty. Now... It's my turn to prove I'm loyal to her."

Briefly, Dante looked back at Sade, who was so surprised her body swayed as she covered her mouth.

As he walked over to Willow with a chainsaw in his hands, Willow's eyes widened. Her head shook adamantly as she cried and released a low, hoarse scream. It didn't matter. No one would hear her. And even if they did, Dante intended to make this quick.

Sade left shortly after the deed was done. She was so surprised by Dante's display of loyalty she cried. It felt like he was living in some kind of twilight zone. Dante never thought he and Sade would take a person's life, but at that point, he was willing to do just about anything to keep their relationship going. For the first time in his life, he felt truly loved and accepted, and Dante wouldn't dare rob Sade of receiving the same thing.

After dumping Willow's body into the lake, all of the contents of his stomach came out through his mouth. Once he was composed and his nerves were calm, he pushed the image of her body out of his mind and went inside. Dante took a quick shower, then headed to the airport. When he made it to their gate and noticed Sade wasn't there, he called her. She didn't answer, setting off alarm bells in Dante's head. They'd gotten too close to forever for something to stop them now. He called her again, and again, Sade didn't answer. She did, however, send him a text that said, Listen to your latest voice memo.

"What?" he asked vocally, going to his voice memos. When he pressed play, Dante heard Sade's voice.

"Don't be mad. I can't have forever with you, Dante. You didn't choose me. In all these years, you didn't choose me. It took you almost dying and losing your memory to have the courage to love me, and I deserve better than that. Truth—I was willing to do just about anything to make my sister pay for her sins. Truth—I do love you and want what's best for you. That's why I did everything I did to help you and to make sure she served that time, not you. Truth—I did want to see what life as your wife would be like, but I always knew it wouldn't last. The day you married my sister, any chance we had to be together was over. I can honestly say I've enjoyed every day that I've spent with you, but it's over, Dante. You're free now. Live your life and find a woman that will love you unconditionally. A woman you value enough to choose first. I love you, and I'm sorry. Goodbye."

Dante replayed the message again, refusing to believe what he heard. When he finally accepted what Sade had said and done, all he could do was laugh. She was supposed to be his forever. His loyal wife. It seemed she'd chosen to be loyal to herself.

"Well played, Sade, well played," he mumbled, opening their text thread to shoot her a message that said, I heard your message. It was real cute. You're out your fucking mind if you think you're getting rid of me that easily, though. You loved me better than your sister ever could. We caught bodies for each other, Sade. I don't care how long it takes to find you, I will, and when I do, you ain't going no fucking where.

As Dante's flight information spilled out of the speaker, he grabbed his carry-on bag and prepared to board. He'd take this trip to New York and get his business up and running, but Sade was his... and he was going to get her back...

The End

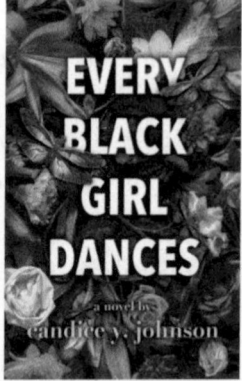

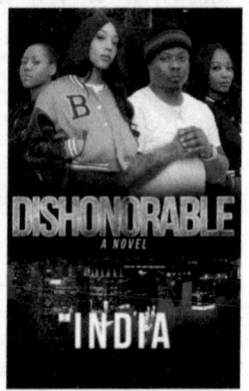